THE
BROTHERHOOD

Book Three of The Hayle Coven Destinies

PATTI LARSEN

ALSO BY
PATTI LARSEN

The Hayle Coven Universe

The Hunted Series
Fiona Fleming Cozy Mysteries
The Nightshade Cases
The Clone Chronicles
The Diamond City Trilogy
Didi and the Gunslinger

and much, much more.
Find your new favorite author at
pattilarsen.com
Sign up for new releases
bit.ly/pattilarsenemail

ONE

Normally the cushion of my favorite chair in my sunny living room felt soft, inviting me to curl up in it, flop to one side with my legs hooked over the arm while one or both of my children piled into my lap with a fluffy silver Persian perched on top for good measure.

As I sipped my coffee that tasted vaguely of ashes thanks to the burning in my veins, for the first time ever the seat felt more like a plank of concrete. Probably because my muscles were so tensed they vibrated.

The reason for my tension—both of them—sat delicately on the edge of the sofa across from me. Sonja O'Dane's smile screamed falsehood, as fake as the dyed-blonde of her hair and puff of her overly-plumped lips. My darling Liam's mother disappeared from my life shortly after Gabriel was born. And honestly, I hadn't thought anything of her since. She'd done enough to

1

betray her son and husband in my books, pairing with the exiled Sidhe Lord Venner to use the Gate Liam guarded to gain access to the Sidhe realm. Almost dooming me and all of Wilding Springs in the process. I would never forgive her for the bullet that laid Liam's grandfather, Fergus, low, forcing him to retreat to the realm to save his life. Or for thrusting Liam into the position of Gatekeeper way before his time. I still wondered if perhaps things would have been different if Liam hadn't died at Ameline's hand.

I simply couldn't allow myself to think that way.

Considering the fact my son's first reaction to his grandmother had been uncharacteristic unhappiness, I had been more than willing to watch her walk away and never come back. So much for that dose of wishful thinking.

"Warm September we've been having." Sonja's voice shook ever so slightly as she glanced with wide eyes sideways toward her companion. I ignored the statement, not interested in small talk. At least the woman next to Sonja had the good grace not to try to pretend she was happy to see me. Hortense Spaft hadn't changed a bit since I first met her all those years ago. I had no idea my former vice-principal was part Sidhe and an Unseelie servant, or that she had it in for me, not until the night Fergus almost died and Liam was forced to take over as Gatekeeper. Since then, she'd been an occasional pain in my backside, though not much since Venner got what he wanted and was allowed to return to the realm.

"The boy is well, I take it?" Spaft's black eyes held mine behind her horn rim glasses, beady and vaguely rodent-like.

The boy.

I wondered how much effort it would take to throttle her. Normally, Sashenka Hensley, my second, would be here to relieve the pressure, to give me the space I needed to rein in my temper. I'd gotten good at it over the years, but mostly, I was now realizing, thanks to her steady presence. But Shenka had left me, gone back to her sister, Tallah, only a few days ago, leaving me alone and unsure what to do.

Well, not entirely. Before I could decide on rude or ruder for my return comment, a busty redhead hurried into the room. Her entire being glowed with charisma, shining curls bouncing around her shoulders. Green eyes sparkling, Tippy Meeks flounced to the coffee table with a beaming smile and an almost physical wave of enthusiasm and set a plate of warm cookies on the surface.

"I hope you're hungry, ladies." She smiled all around, though when her gaze settled on mine, I caught the spark of emotion in her that had nothing to do with good nature. She perched next to me on the arm rest of my seat and I instantly relaxed.

PATTI LARSEN

Was I really that incapable of handling people on a normal level? Clearly. As Sonja helped herself to the chocolate chip wonders, I breathed an inward sigh of relief. About two days after Shenka left me in a panic over what to do, my old college buddies showed up at my door and hugged me into submission. All former Hensley witches, Tippy, Nicci Mortimer, Josie Ambrose and Donalda Pierce all expressed their distinct unhappiness with Shenka's decision to abandon me and bailed en masse from the vastly shrunken numbers of the Hensley coven.

To come help me.

So many tears that day. More than I was willing to admit to. Shenka's loss hit me hard, though I understood—or told myself I did—why she left. Since the Brotherhood attacks decimated over one third of the North American witch compliment, many covens were struggling. Tallah's had been hit especially hard. I thought I was doing the right thing, sending Shenka home to help her sister temporarily. I didn't intend for her to poach my second and best friend in the process.

But family was family, right? Except Shenka was supposed to be my family now.

I cleared my throat, surreptitiously squeezing Tippy's hand in thanks. She and the girls saved me from the daily tedium of the coven and I would be forever grateful to them. And guilty I had failed to check and see originally if they survived the attacks.

Bad friend, Syd.

Sonja helped herself to her third cookie until Spaft stared at her like doing so meant a death sentence. Not that I wasn't aware of the power dynamic, but it appeared the chilly stick woman hadn't lost her commanding presence.

"You didn't answer my question." Her thin lips pinched into a line, lipstick oozing into the cracks around her mouth. Her prim, black wool suit made me itch just looking at it, tight bun pulling her pale skin taut, collar tied tight around her neck in a precise bow of fabric that bobbed when she swallowed. As usual, she reminded me of a spider, all spindly and spooky, ready to attack at a moment's notice.

My temper rose at her tone, but I held it in, even managed a smile that might have passed for polite. Maybe. "Gabriel is doing very well," I said. No need to tell either of them about his power as a Gateway. I had no idea how much they knew about his early childhood, his capture by Ameline Benoit, his forced aging, the fact he almost destroyed our Universe by allowing through Creator's Dark Brother. Or his ties to the pieces of Creator herself. All because there had to be a reason for their appearance. No way Sonja showed up out of the blue after eight years looking to reconnect with her grandson.

I was just too cynical to believe it.

Say the word, boss lady, Tippy sent while continuing to radiate cheer and good nature. *And these two are out on their asses.*

As much as I would have enjoyed their exodus, my demon growling her agreement with Tippy's suggestion, my curiosity won out. Neither woman was a threat to me, and both had kept themselves out of trouble and under the radar for a long time now. At least, I hadn't heard of them stirring up anything. I'd be checking as soon as they left, mind you. But, for now, I was more interested in finding out what they really wanted.

Especially if Gabriel's safety and wellbeing were involved.

"Good to hear it." Spaft turned her head slowly toward Sonja. I could almost hear the creak of rusting metal as she did, picturing a hideous robot frame beneath the icy shell of her exterior. "Isn't it, Sonja." Not a question.

Sonja nodded quickly, nervously, swallowing her last bite of cookie. "That is, of course, why we're here, Sydlynn."

Of course. "You remember the last time you saw Gabriel," I said as coldly as I could. Maybe it was wrong of me to jab her as hard as I did with the memory, but my son's protection was all that mattered. No way I was letting her anywhere near him if she had an agenda.

Sonja actually flinched, triggering my empathy at last. Maybe she hadn't earned it with her past actions, but she was his grandmother. And family meant everything to me. It was possible she really was here just to see him.

Scratch that. She'd have come alone if she just wanted to see him. Spaft's presence changed everything.

The flush on Sonja's cheeks spread to a large blotch on her neck as she cleared her throat.

"I realize we didn't part under the best of circumstances," she said, fluttering her hands in her lap, white napkin rustling in her grip. "That cruel things were said on both sides." Um, yeah, whatever, lady. She smiled briefly before barging on. "I know I'm not welcome here. But Gabriel is Liam's son. And I deserve the right to get to know him."

Spaft didn't move or speak, simply watching me. I hated her silence and stillness. It made her hard to read, as did the shell she held over herself, the thick layer of Sidhe shielding. I could penetrate it and find her secrets no problem, but without provocation? Not a great idea.

Speak for yourself, my demon snarled.

I'm happy to do it for you, Shaylee sent, my Sidhe princess ego sniffing in royal arrogance in Spaft's direction.

Now, now, ladies, my vampire sent. *If Syd can keep her temper, you two should have no problem.*

Thanks for that. I shut them all down. Maybe there was

a time we could have bent the rules. But with the creation of the new World Paranormal Council, I had to tread lightly. The last thing I wanted was to add to the pressure on Femke Svennson's shoulders. Bad enough she and I had almost lost our friendship over my suggestion she take the job as leader. She had a whole pile of stress to deal with thanks to the vampires and werewolves. Me purposely incurring Sidhe issues wasn't something I wanted to lay at her feet just now.

Though hasty, your alter egos have a point. A soft but heavy bundle landed in my lap, silver fur ruffling as Sassafras, my demon cat, finally made an appearance. He smelled of fresh air and grass, so I could only assume he'd been outside doing the elements knew what cat things he did to keep himself occupied. Relief he was here with me took me by surprise, though it shouldn't have. He'd been my rock my entire life, even when I didn't want to admit it. *I take it you're allowing these two to remain out of a need to understand their ultimate motives?*

Smartass. I almost hugged him.

"Perhaps," Sassafras said out loud, amber eyes narrowed as he curled his thick, fluffy tail around his paws, "it would be best to allow Gabriel to decide if he would like to see you, Sonja."

I hadn't thought of that. *He'll say yes,* I sent, knowing my son. His heart was Liam's heart, huge and kind.

He may, Sass sent. *But it will give us time to prepare him, rather than thrusting him into a meeting he might not be emotionally ready for.*

Sonja's lower lip trembled. "How do I know you'll ask him?" She seemed truly distraught. Compassion bloomed beside empathy, held hands and sang kumbaya. A large tear trickled from the corner of her eye and down her heavily made up cheek. She dabbed at it with her wrinkled napkin, a second drop landing on the curve of her chest, spreading a dark spot of moisture on the pocket of her green silk blouse.

Tricksy, Sass sent. *Spaft is probably thralling her.*

Maybe. She'd done so before, controlling those around her to do her bidding with the glamor of Sidhe magic. But Sonja's pain felt genuine to me. "I promise," I said, standing with Sass in my arms, ending the visit with that simple act. The pair on the sofa reluctantly stood to join me. "I'll ask him tonight and let you know what he says."

Spaft nodded stiffly to me, while Sonja came toward me, grasping my wrist, kissing my cheek. She smelled of perfume and desperation, her high heels digging holes in the thick carpet.

"Thank you," she whispered against my skin before leaning back and stepping away.

Okay then.

"We're staying at the Hilltop Hotel." Spaft handed me a card, which Tippy swiftly intercepted.

"Wonderful!" She gestured toward the hall and the formal front door, still beaming. "We'll be in touch."

She guided our two guests out, leaving me to flop into my chair again, Sass hissing at me as he landed hard on my stomach.

"Am I really going to let him near her?" I shook my head at my oldest friend.

"Not without supervision," Sass said. "Or his permission. With both?" He sighed, leaned in and licked the tip of my nose. "We'll see."

The front door slammed firmly about a heartbeat before Tippy stormed into the room. Her happy-go-lucky charisma bubbled with irritation.

"Tell me," she said, "the next time that woman," I knew she was talking about Spaft, "shows up at this door," Tippy jabbed at the exit so hard her generous breasts bounced up and down like enthusiastic melons in a sack, "I get to tell her where she can take her freaking attitude."

I grinned at her. "You can," I said. "The minute one of you agrees to be my second."

Tippy grinned back, though with sadness. She sat down beside me one more time, touching my hair.

"Syd," she said. "The girls and I are here for you. But none of us are taking the damned job permanently." She snorted as she transferred her attention to Sassafras who rewarded her enthusiastic scratches with his deep, rumbling purr. "We love you, but none of us are that stupid."

I rolled my eyes at her, but smiled back. "I'm that hard to get along with, am I?"

Tippy kissed the top of Sass's head. "Should I be straight with her, my handsome prince?" He loved it when she called him that. His purr grew in volume. "Or kind?"

"Hit her with it." His amber eyes sparked before he settled into the scratching once again. Long, red nails dug into his mane as Tippy laughed.

"We love you," she said, going serious at last. "And the four of us are happy to take turns keeping you going. But Syd, Shenka is your second. And she'll come to her senses. I know it. You just have to have a little patience."

They'd all come from the very coven Shenka left me for and all of them said the same thing. I allowed hope to win.

"Thank you," I said. "For taking care of me."

Tippy winked, leaning forward so far I feared her ample bosom would burst out of the top of her low-cut t-shirt. "Someone has to," she said.

I didn't get a chance to comment. A surge of familiar magic pushed me to my feet, Sass dumped into Tippy's arms as I hurried to the kitchen to find out what kind of mood my husband was in now that he was finally home.

TWO

There was a time the feeling of Quaid's power made me shiver and run to him, pulling me toward him like iron to a magnet. When I would throw every thought out of my head for the chance to see him during one of our late night meetings in the backyard.

And while my heart still loved him as much as ever, it was with trepidation and worry I entered the kitchen, feeling around for the mood in the room before I said a word. Things had been touchy between us since he accepted the position of Enforcer Leader for the new World Paranormal Council. Who was I kidding? They'd been rather awful since the Brotherhood attacked. He'd made it clear he didn't appreciate being left behind while I did all the work. Personally, I would have loved to let someone else shoulder some of the burden that seemed to land on me on a regular basis. But the family had to come first for him when I wasn't in a position to think in those terms. He said he understood. I thought we'd patched up that particular rift. Only to have him turn around and make an arbitrary decision without consulting his wife. A giant decision that could impact our future and definitely left the family in a lurch.

I didn't begrudge him his new role. In fact, I was proud of him for everything he did. Had pushed Mom to rewrite the old law forbidding Enforcers to wed coven leaders so we could not only be together—something I thought he wanted as much as I did—but to reclaim the position I knew he loved and gave up to be with me. A huge sacrifice that never sat right with me. He was on the fast track to replace Varity Rhodes as the new North American Enforcer Leader until Femke swooped in and scooped him up. Mom wasn't impressed. I don't think she'd said two words to him since the day she found out. I didn't blame him at all for making the choice he did. I just wished he'd taken the time and trusted me enough to talk to me about it before he accepted.

I'd always thought marriage was about partnership. Was I fooling myself? I knew I could be a bit bossy. I think I'd earned some slack after everything I'd gone through. And his respect, thank you very much. I wanted nothing more than for Quaid to be happy, I really did. And this job gave him the status he had to be craving. I wasn't the easiest wife in the world, after all. Being married to the most powerful person on the plane had to be a bit of a pressure cooker, if I thought about it in male ego terms. Having his own responsibilities and sense of purpose was a good thing, as far as I was concerned. But Quaid's decision to cut me out of the conversation put things over the edge between us.

All of these thoughts revolved through a glass door built of regret and simmering resentment as I paused at the entry to the kitchen. Quaid's broad back was to me, hands busy with the coffee maker, the scent of fresh brew drifting through the sunlit space toward me. I forced all spinning contemplation from my mind as I leaned against the wall and just watched him a minute. He looked relaxed at least, dark head down, shaggy curls winding behind one ear as he tucked the overgrown locks with one big hand. I loved the way his black t-shirt tugged tight between his shoulder blades, how his jeans cupped his well-shaped behind just so. The peeking deliciousness of his bare feet below the frayed hem. Even his toes were perma-tanned, the soft, almost coppery glow of his skin reminding me of sun and summer and happiness.

Quaid turned as if sensing me watching him, deep chocolate eyes meeting mine. A half smile curved his wide mouth, the sexiest smile I'd ever seen. My whole body released its tension at the sight of that smile, the way sparks fired in his gaze as his lips parted, chest expanding when he drew breath to speak.

"Quaid!" Tippy bounced into the room, brushing past me, her rounded assets leading the way. I watched his gaze flicker to her endowments before his smile faded to a tight, patient grin.

"Hi, Tippy." He turned from me, spoon chattering inside his mug as he stirred the honey he always poured into his java. My jaw jumped, a burst of fury at the interruption startling me so much I took a half step back, hands clenched together behind me.

Tippy's voice rattled on as she leaned against the counter beside him, but I didn't hear a word she said. Quaid's murmuring response reached me, too, even as I clenched up inside against the need to toss the redhead out the kitchen door on her well-rounded ass.

Do not let her muscle her way in. Sassafras's tone was icy, making me shiver, breaking through my anger I now realized was mostly fed by my demon. Though Shaylee and my vampire were both immensely miffed, if their stiff silence and dislike were any indication. *You and Quaid need to work this out, Syd.*

Thanks for the marriage advice, Dr. Cat, I sent, more sharply than I intended.

You're welcome, he snapped back. *Now get your behind in there and chase her off.*

Sass was right. This was ridiculous. After all, Tippy was a flirt with everyone, including attractive women. I watched my uncle's undead wife and former queen of the

Wilhelm vampire blood clan retreat in vague horror from the redhead only last night. It was funny then to see Sunny react that way, but not so much now.

Before I could stop myself, I squashed my anger and forced a smile on my face, crossing over from the hardwood of the hall to the tile in the kitchen. Both Quaid and Tippy looked over to me as I did, as though I'd rung a bell just by making that simple decision.

"Thank you so much for all your help this afternoon." I went to her and hugged her, turning her away from Quaid. He grinned at me over the rim of his coffee, the smartass. I couldn't help but grin back.

Tippy blushed and hugged me with great enthusiasm. "You're so welcome, Syd." She let me go, blinking moisture from her eyes. "We're all just so happy to be here. To help."

My anger vanished in a puff of smoke. Even my demon grumbled her guilt. Tippy was Tippy, and I'd never change her. She meant nothing by her flirting, I could feel it in her power now linked to mine. I really needed to get over myself.

I guided her to the door. "Go have some fun, would you?" Her hand squeezed back as I grasped hers.

Her eyes flickered to Quaid then back to me. The broad wink she shared was all Tippy.

"Have a nice afternoon, you two." She blew me a kiss, one for Sassafras, then left in a flurry of red curls and soft, sunny perfume.

I leaned my back against the door and let out a giant gust of air. Quaid's grin grew in size, though he didn't move toward me, sipping still from his mug. "World's Greatest Dad." I thought of our kids and smiled back.

"She's a handful," he said in his deep voice, without malice.

"And a huge help." I pushed off the door and crossed to him. Symbolic of my willingness to move past our division? "I don't know what I'd do without the girls." His mug was hot as I liberated it from him, sampled the sweetness and handed it back. He remained relaxed, an excellent sign. Maybe we were both over the mess. That would be awesome. I'd been sleeping alone these past few nights and I didn't like that state of affairs even a little bit.

"What did I miss?" He tilted his head to one side, brow furrowing a touch.

I quickly filled him in on Sonja's visit. Quaid's scowl deepened, shoulders tightening as he set down his mug.

"You should have told me," he said.

Oh boy. Here we went again. But I refused to let this happen, not when we'd finally found the old place we used to be.

"I tried," I said, as softly and gently as I could. "You were cut off from me."

His anger solidified, then flashed to guilt, though his temper didn't go away completely. "Training," he said, gruff, deep.

"It's okay," I said. "I dealt with it."

"It doesn't sound like you did." Quaid's attitude sent sparks up my spine. What the hell was his problem? I wanted him here to help and he was—

Deep breaths, Syd.

"You don't think Gabriel deserves to make the choice?" I forced myself to stand as still as I could, proud I held my temper while my husband's seemed to feed from his guilt.

Quaid didn't answer me, turning away, arms crossing over his chest, head down. I knew that look, that stance. He'd shut himself off from me, from listening. I hated it when he did that, but there was no way to reach him. Except yelling.

Why did he want to fight all of a sudden? My vampire's cool calm helped keep me grounded while my demon warred with her, wanting to beat some sense into him. Shaylee just turned away, her sadness the most troubling of all.

I reached out and touched his arm, barely brushing the bare skin with my fingertips. He jumped a fraction, arms releasing at least, if his demeanor remained shut down.

"How are things with the Council?" Maybe if I steered the conversation toward work...

Quaid sighed deeply, scowl easing. The storm cloud

of impeding battle began to break up. Will wonders never cease.

"Busy," he said, rubbing one large hand over his face. He still didn't meet my eyes, but he seemed less ready to turn everything into an argument. I caught sight of Sassafras perched on the kitchen table, watching us. I'd forgotten he was there. Part of me wanted to shoo him away, and part of me was grateful he stayed. Not that the demon cat would have been able to diffuse a fight if it started, but his presence just felt like support even if Sass had his own agenda.

"Any news about the werewolves?" It had been such a short time since the death of Queen Yana Moreau and the forced birth of her daughter. King Danilo, brother of my werefriend, Charlotte, and ruler of the werenation, had taken his wife's death hard, not that I blamed him a bit. But his unreasonable resurgence of hatred for vampires was troubling. The disappearance of the Wilhelm Blood Clan, along with their leader, Piotr, bothered me in two ways. I wanted Piotr to stand trial for his role in Yana's death. When his family vanished, that chance went with him.

But worse, their loss just reminded me of the damage to the spirit magic on our plane. And, for all I knew, on all planes, thanks to the disappearance of Creator's heart from the statue of her physical form still hidden under the Stronghold. My dear friend and DeWinter vampire king, Sebastain, and my former bestie turned undead ghost something, Alison, were the first to go missing. The Empress of vampires, Moa, gave me the impression more had vanished than just the two blood clans I knew of. Which just added to the weight of pressure I carried to find and replace the missing pieces of Creator before it was too late.

Quaid shrugged, hands digging into his jean pockets. "Femke has her eye on Danilo," he said. And stopped. I waited for more, but when he didn't go on I sighed, temper finally winning through. He turned to meet my eyes, his own hooded and dark. The need to fight it out still bubbled in his gaze.

"Thanks for keeping me posted, Enforcer Leader." Syd. Oh, Syd. Really? You're going to give in to your temper now?

Quaid almost seemed relieved as he turned toward me, anger snapping around him in visible sparks. "If it was any of your business, Coven Leader," he snapped, "Femke would keep you posted."

Oh no, he did *not*. "That's not fair," I said. "Not even a little. You know how important it is, Quaid."

He rolled his shoulders in a shrug. "Then go fix it," he said, pushing off and turning from me, heading for the hall and the interior of the house. "That's what you're good at, isn't it?"

I stood there and watched him go, anger dribbling

away, leaving sadness behind. I hitched a breath, refusing to cry over that bastard. He knew how to hurt me, sure did. Funny how the ones we loved were the best equipped to do the most damage with the least amount of effort.

"Syd." Sass's amber eyes flared, tail thrashing. "I'll talk to him."

I shook my head, spinning to look out the kitchen window, tears burning though I refused to let them out. "He's right," I said finally, voice shaky despite my massive effort to the contrary. "I'll go ask Femke."

Sass's sigh was so heavy I turned back, managed a smile.

"What am I going to do with you two?" He hopped down from the table and sashayed his silver butt out of the kitchen, going after Quaid no matter what I said.

Let him. I sagged against the counter, lower lip aching between my teeth as I bit hard enough to hurt. We just needed a little more time, that was all. For Quaid to get used to his new role. For me to figure out how to let go of hurt and not let it bother me so very much.

We'd work it out. I just hoped it happened sooner rather than later. I'd spent too many years longing for him, thinking at last I had my happy ending, for it to fall apart now.

THREE

The smell of coffee finally lured me out of my sadness, the distraction welcome from my worries about Quaid and me. I had only just turned to pour myself a cup, deliberately looking away from his half empty mug so I wouldn't be reminded of the last few minutes, when Mom's magic gently touched mine.

Sweetheart, she sent.

Hey, Mom. I had to clench against the need to gush everything at her. Funny, no matter how old I grew I think I'd always have this kind of reaction. She was my mother, after all. The one I could turn to when I needed emotional support the most. I could be an all-powerful, immortal and near invincible being all I wanted. But, in the end, I was still Miriam Hayle's little girl.

She went on before I could make a total fool of myself and start sobbing about Quaid, thank the elements. *Are you all right?* Leave it to her to sense something was wrong. But her question helped, oddly. I deflected my concerns over my marriage to other issues weighing me down.

The usual, I sent, letting some sarcasm through my magic as I leaned against the counter with my hot coffee in one hand. *The pieces of Creator are still missing or in the control of our enemies, my son can't seem to open Gates anymore, my second ran off to her sister without notice and, to top it off, the creature attacks in the veil seem to have started up again.* Poor Max and the drach were busy cleaning up messes left behind by the critters who made it through the barrier between Universes. We'd spent years picking off groups of invading species during what I now privately called Pre-Massacre. But the attacks had vanished after the Brotherhood assault and Creator's heart went missing. The moment Max and I lost the hand of Creator to my former friend and betrayer, Trill Zornov, all crap broke loose and the insurgence of unfriendly species from the Dark Universe had begun all over again.

I needed to be with Max and his people, helping them. That was the biggest frustration on my plate. But Shenka's ill-timed departure left me with an uncertain coven. Yes, my college friends were fabulous about filling in, but the family needed reassurance, especially after everything we'd been through with the decimation of the witch population. I couldn't just leave them, not until I had a coven approved second in command I trusted to take care of everything.

Mom's concern came through loud and clear, the newly born Council power humming with sympathy. How different it felt from the ancient, weighty magic the North American Council used to possess. Though the theft of the power by the Brotherhood was a huge loss, I rather liked this fresh, enthusiastic young magic now representing all North American witches.

Silver linings.

Gabriel is doing his best. Mom's tone didn't chide me, but as his grandmother I knew she wanted to protect him. Still, she was a Hayle witch and a Council Leader and knew the stakes as well as I did.

I know, Mom, I sent, staring down into my mug as I thought of my darling boy, only seven years old, and how much pressure he carried on his slim shoulders for one so young and sweet natured. *I'm not blaming him. He had a big scare. We all did.* I shivered slightly at the memory of the Order, the massive, armored force that was Dark Brother's army, marching toward the Gate Gabriel created to the other Universe. Fortunately, we'd been able to shut it down.

Okay, who was I kidding? Gabriel shut it down. Max and I had been useless. But the understanding of what waited for us—a gigantic, powerful force even the drach leader was afraid of, ready, willing and able to conquer our Universe—still gave me nightmares. So I could only imagine what Gabriel was feeling. He and his sister, Ethie, had been living almost full time at Harvard with Mom and Dad the last few days. I felt safer knowing they were surrounded by Enforcers, and that Mom was there to watch over them both. Guilt at being a terrible mother warred with the need to keep them out of harm's way but there was no one I trusted more to protect my children than my mom.

Are you and Max still working on other options? Now the Council Leader showed in her crisp tone, her professional manner.

Absolutely, I sent, embracing my own role like an old teddy bear. *If we're correct that we're being tracked when we hunt the pieces, we should be able to lay a false trail and lure the others into a trap we're ready to snap shut*. It was the only explanation I had for how both the Brotherhood leader, Liander Belaisle, and Trill had figured out where Max and I went to recover the hand of Creator. They had to be tracking us somehow. And I was determined to use that against them before looking again in earnest. So it was probably a good thing Gabriel couldn't use his power at the moment. According to the dark maji, Trinol, having access to my son meant our side had the upper hand in finding Creator's lost parts and reassembling her.

I only hoped we could finish in time. With the damage done to the spirit magic of our Universe, we'd already lost several vampire blood clans. Who knew what other harm was happening around the veil? I'd been witness personally to the sudden and complete loss of an entire plane's population, watched as that plane collapsed and was absorbed into the veil. The thought of such a thing happening here, on my plane, wasn't something I wanted to contemplate.

I have faith the two of you will figure it out, Mom sent, though there was curiosity in her voice, and the barest hint of worry.

I'll be over later to see you and the kids, I sent. I missed them suddenly, with an almost raving hunger. So hard to balance the coven leader with the maji and the mother and wife… there were times I still craved a normal life, if only for the freedom to focus completely on my family.

Actually, Mom sent, slightly hesitant and with the same worry I realized had nothing to do with the bigger picture, *I was hoping you'd be busy for the day.*

Doing what? I hated that I tensed in anticipation of the answer. Though if Mom was asking for help with something, could I say no?

The kitchen door opened, four women filing through with grins on their faces. Tippy bounced in last, helping herself to a seat while Nicci tossed her dirty blonde bangs from her forehead and made a beeline for the coffee pot. I had a sneaking suspicion Mom was in on their sudden and grinning arrival, but gave her the benefit of the doubt.

I want to do a full tour of the covens, Mom sent. I caught a flash of her in her office, hands sliding over the pages in front of her, the dark wood making the scene gloomy, though sunlight shone on her from the window to her right. *Like a courtesy call, of sorts.*

Giving you the chance to check in and make sure everyone is doing okay. I caught myself nodding, shoved aside with a hip bump as Nicci began pouring coffee into four mugs. She wrinkled her nose at me, freckles dancing, eyes shining with mischief.

Definitely in on it.

Exactly. Mom's image vanished as she closed up a little. *I've already contacted a few of the covens, but I'm realizing just how worried they still are, Syd.* I caught myself nodding to her, though she wasn't in the room. *The Shadow Council makes more sense to me now that I've been in personal contact with some of the coven leaders.* Shortly after the Brotherhood fled with the Council's power, disappearing like rats in a sewer, I'd been approached by the collective leaders of the North American covens and asked to represent them in an alternate Council, as a watchdog for the powers that be. Considering the rough and rocky track record we'd had over the last decade and a half, I hardly blamed them. Mom hadn't been happy at first, especially when I failed to tell her personally, but she'd come around. Not much had come from the Shadow Council as of yet save for assistance to the covens from Steam Union sorcerers to teach them to use their sorcery for protection against the Brotherhood. Still, I was glad Mom understood how important the confidence and focus of the coven leaders really was.

We'd spent so many centuries in self-satisfied complacency as a race, pretending to protect ourselves by burying our heads in the sand. It had taken tragedy after mishap after disaster to finally change the system. And though I still mourned my own losses, at least there was positive forward motion on all fronts.

More silver linings. I'd take them.

I set down my coffee, arms crossing over my chest as the girls chattered over their own mugs, ignoring me while they filled my kitchen with happy talk and giggling. *Let me guess*, I sent to Mom as I grinned at them. *You want me to come with you.*

I do. Mom sighed, another flash of her location an odd contrast. The quiet, dusty dimness of her office at Harvard versus the cheery, chattery brilliance of the fall day in my kitchen. Not for the first time I felt like I was living in two places at once. *I realize you have a lot on your plate, sweetheart.*

I hate to leave the coven unprotected, I sent. *Especially with Shenka gone.*

I know, Mom sent. *As would I, in your place.*

That's why you've asked the girls to take over, am I right?

The four turned to look at me all at the same instant and I realized Mom had tied them into the conversation. Of course she had.

"We might not be your official seconds," Josie said, dark hair curling under her chin, pale skin almost glowing in the bright light of the sunbeam she sat in, "but we're perfectly capable of putting out fires for an afternoon."

Tippy nodded with enthusiasm, red curls bouncing as much as her jutting breasts. I really wished she'd stop wearing such low cut tops. I was always worried she'd have a wardrobe malfunction, though the idea didn't seem to bother her one bit. "And you're a call away," she said, flicking her ruby painted nails at me. "If we have an ounce of trouble, you can be here in a flash."

"Shenka might not get it," Donalda said, gray eyes sparking with anger, "but we do." Her tall, pole-thin body hunched over her coffee mug, narrow hands grasping it tightly. "You're not an ordinary coven leader, Syd. And you never will be. We can handle it."

"Your mom needs you." Nicci's voice was soft, low. I felt her block her words from my mother. "As powerful as she is, there are times we all have to ask for help. Even you, Syd."

They didn't have to convince me, not really. Though it made me a little teary they thought a tag team would be necessary. I'd begun to worry my outside activities as a maji and savior of the Universe was wearing thin my first responsibility. But, clearly, the girls didn't see it that way. If they were fighting this hard to make me step away from the coven for a bit, I had to be doing my job right.

Of course I'll come, Mom, I sent, smiling at the girls.

Thank you, sweetheart. Her love engulfed me, as familiar as the faint scent of lilacs that somehow made it over the distance and through her magic. *I'll see you in an hour?*

I let Mom go while I shook my head at the group of women sitting at the table. "You guys," I said.

"We didn't mean to gang up on you." Nicci bit her lower lip, suddenly worried.

"Yes, we did," Tippy snorted, saluting me with her mug.

"Syd can take it." Josie nudged Nicci gently.

"Don't be mad, Syd," Donalda said. "We're here for you and the coven."

I laughed and embraced them with my magic, the family power humming happily. "I was about to say," I told them as they opened themselves to me, "before I was interrupted," Tippy rolled her eyes at me, "that I think you four are awesome. Thank you for being here." Okay, now I really was teary, damn it. "It means a lot to me, considering everything. You could have stayed in California with Tallah. The elements know she needs you."

Donalda shook her head, long, narrow face pinched. "Tallah doesn't need anyone," she said, sharp and bitter.

"Not now that she has Shenka."

The others looked down, away. So there was a lot more going on in the Hensley coven than I knew, was there? "Anything Mom should be worried about?"

The four exchanged glances before Tippy shrugged, cleavage deepening a moment.

"Not sure," she said. "I guess Miriam will find out, though, won't she?"

On her own. I decided then and there that was one coven visit Mom would be taking without me.

FOUR

I had one errand to run before I left with Mom, something I'd been meaning to do since last night. A quick walk down the block helped clear my head a little, the still beautiful weather of late September making Wilding Springs feel surreal. None of the leaves had turned yet on the massive maples lining the street, the soft call of songbirds mixing with the sigh of the breeze as summer clung to the town as though unwilling to let go. My sneakers skipped stray stones into the clipped grass of neighboring yards, the coven's houses neat and tidy as usual. One great thing about living here now was the lack of worry we'd be uncovered by normals. Most of the neighborhood was now owned by the family. And while the loss of the Sidhe Gate years ago and the return of the Wild Hunt to the realm when we were forced to flee to safety might have left Wilding Springs without the influence of magic for the first time in over a century, the moment the family power settled back into my house the entire town seemed to sigh with relief. From the very rocks and grass and trees to the remaining normal residents, Wilding Springs returned to its happy, almost eerie calm and comfort after a brief stint where everything seemed dark, pale, hopeless.

While most covens were forced to move from time to time to protect them from discovery by normals—ours had done so often when I was a child, sometimes because of me—I truly believed Wilding Springs would be my home, and that of the family, for many years to come.

Enough power had seeped into its borders I didn't think this place would survive normal.

A small, white bungalow at the end of the block beckoned. I strode up the driveway to the front door, eyes flickering over the rusted, dented trailer parked on the grass past the pavement. It had a definite lean to it, well used and loved over the years. I'd been rescued in that trailer, saved from an eternity of bloodless mummification by Trill and her Nona. And though my former friend had betrayed me in the worst possible way, stealing the hand of Creator from me when she should have been on my side, I was glad Nona had stopped her wandering ways. The old human blood maji matriarch spent decades living her gypsy life, much as her people had for centuries. But with all the unrest and Trill's turncoat activities it was safer for Nona here in Wilding Springs.

Not to mention the fact her two beloved grandsons had taken up residence in this very house. I raised my hand to knock on the door, the glass vibrating as I did. Owen and Apollo Zornov were both sorcerers but I trusted them completely, despite their sister's betrayal. They'd proven their loyalty many times over the years and were more than happy to help teach the coven how to use their devouring power, to pitch in as part of the family.

The inside door swung open in answer to my knock, the glass storm door creaking as Owen pushed it toward me. I stepped around it, catching it on my hip as I let myself in past him. He'd grown a great deal since we'd first met, from a young boy with dark hair and impossibly blue eyes to a tall, lean young man with an easy grin barely hiding his constant worry for his sister. Owen hugged me when I crossed the threshold, now slighter taller than I was.

"Hey, Syd." He let me go, stepping back and gesturing for me to enter. "Si's been waiting for you." His slight, worried frown meant I was in trouble. That made me want to laugh. All the power of creation at my fingertips and I should worry about a computer hacker living in Owen's basement.

Then again…

I nodded, smiling as kindly as I could. I knew how hard it was on Owen to live with Trill's traitorous acts. The two of them had been on their own for so long before they found Apollo, before they met me even, it had to be tearing him apart she'd left him high and dry. "And you," I said. "How are you, Owen?"

He shrugged, looked away, hands cramming into the pockets of his jeans. The gray t-shirt he wore washed out his tanned skin, giving it a similar tone as his smile faded.

"Hanging in there," he said, shaking it off visibly. "The coven is making great progress." I let him keep the subject change, partly because I really didn't know how to make him feel better. Way to be a good leader and all that crap, Syd. "Your family learns fast."

"Good to hear it." I don't know why I hadn't thought of it before. Waking the sorcery in my coven was a brilliant stroke of genius. Maybe if I'd enacted that plan earlier the night the Brotherhood attacked might have turned out differently. Then again, I'd managed to save every single one of the coven. Who knew if that would have been true if it had come to a fight instead of flight? But at least now they would have the means to defend themselves if something happened again. "Thank you for all your help."

Owen bobbed a nod, grin returning, eyes haunted. "Si's in the basement."

As usual. I followed the young Zornov down the

center hall to the far end of the house, just past the kitchen. The boy's grandmother, Nona, waved at me from the sofa, the TV blaring a show I vaguely recognized as a soap opera. I waved back, trotting down the stairs behind Owen to the dim darkness of the underground, feeling guilty I didn't stop to talk to her. Especially considering the tension between us since Trill's betrayal.

Coward? You betcha.

This house's unfinished basement, empty and cool, had been transformed utterly when Simon moved in. My old friend from my high school days might have had his emotions damaged and his focus shifted when a cruel witch and a vampire clan recruited him at Harvard, but Simon hadn't lost any of his brilliance. I'd only recently reconnected with him, another boy turned into a tall and handsome young man. At least his old animosity was gone, his memories of what really happened at the Star Club returned thanks to a recent kidnapping by the Brotherhood. He'd blamed me for years, partial memories poisoning him, turning him from his dreams of becoming a scientist into darker pursuits. Now one of the best hackers in the country, or the world if he was to be believed, BitsandBytes was again one of my closest—if most cynical—friends.

I shook my head at the banks of computers and circled to the center of the wide open room, catching sight of Simon sitting in a swivel chair, hands flying over a keyboard while four massive monitors flashed different things at him. It would have given me a headache, started to just from the initial viewing, but he seemed to thrive on it.

"Syd." How he was aware of me at all during the chaotic frenzy of his focus I had no idea. "Where have you been?"

"You have news?" I purposely ignored his irritation. No way he was getting used to me running to his beck and call. Though, I had to admit unhealthy eagerness tainted with the need to hurt Liander Belaisle in various ways pushed me closer to Simon's sacred space. He had stopped typing, looked up at me through his black rimmed glasses, a glare holding me back. I might have been coven leader and maji, but to Simon I was just Syd.

"I've found a few pockets of the Brotherhood here and there, hiding in the shadows." He looked back to his monitors, colors and images reflecting from his lenses. "I've sent Apollo and Owen out a few times to investigate, but so far nothing concrete. You don't want the small fish."

We'd run into the same problem we always did when tracking the Brotherhood. Belaisle seemed to have this uncanny knack of vanishing and keeping himself hidden. Sorcery, as the first magic, was impervious to all other powers, but even my own devouring energy didn't seem able to locate him or his people. So, we'd turned to more mundane means. In the past, Belaisle had shown no compunction about using normals and their ordinary world to his advantage. He seemed to love technology and the power that gave him over those without magic, oblivious to the paranormal species around them. I'd been part of the collapse of his corporation, Coterie Industries, though he continued to operate it in small capacities as though unwilling to let it go completely.

I now knew the reason he always seemed to be three steps ahead of me was his access to the Helios family and their Oracle power. My friend, Zoe Helios, had saved me and my coven from Belaisle by warning me just in the nick of time he was coming to attack. She had lost her ability to see the future, as had the two Fates who were the hands and voices of Creator, when the heart was stolen from under the Stronghold. Which meant Belaisle no longer had access to the future, at least as far as I knew. With the playing field leveled, I hoped we'd discover he wasn't half as clever as I'd thought he was.

Of course, he was now the tool of Dark Brother. Which took all of my speculation on Belaisle's brain power and shook it until my own head ached.

"Agreed," I said, refusing to let my enemy's association with Creator's sibling in the other Universe get me down. "We need to take down Belaisle and his top lieutenants if we want to end the threat of the

参

Brotherhood."

Simon spun toward me. "I'm still looking," he said. "There's tons of false trail, and I've thought I was close a few times only to realize I was being hacked." He shook his head with a scowl, as though such a thing should be impossible. "But I'll get him. I promise." Simon pushed his glasses up his nose with one finger, looking more like the boy he'd been instead of the young man he was.

"So, if you don't have news," I said, "why did you want to talk to me?"

Simon jabbed a finger at his screen while Owen handed me a file. "There's something you need to see. Your werewolf friend is making ripples in the normal world and they aren't the kind that I'm thinking are good for business."

I flipped open the cover of the report and down into the face of Danilo Moreau. The wereking's scowl was a permanent fixture these days, since the death of his queen, Yana. He blamed the vampires—Piotr Wilhelm in particular—for her loss, and since I was there when she was rescued, I agreed with him. Trouble was, Piotr and his blood clan vanished, victims of the damaged spirit magic on our plane. At least, that was my assumption. Since there was no trace of them or some other vampires I held dear to my heart, I had to believe my theory was correct.

Seeing Danilo in Simon's file made my blood boil.

"What's he done this time?" Danilo knew how to hold a grudge. If he couldn't have Piotr to punish, he wanted each and every vampire dead. Femke had ordered him to stand down, but I knew the wereking better than that. The man I'd once called my friend had lost his mind over this, and though I sympathized I couldn't help but feel like this was my fault. I should have been able to save Yana. Should have seen the warning signs when the Empress of vampires handed control of the Wilhelms over to Piotr after deposing my aunt, Sunny.

What a mess. And, as I flipped the page to the first police report, I realized it wasn't contained to the paranormal world any longer. My head whipped up when I finally understood what I was reading, a record from Scotland Yard. "Arrested?"

Not Danilo himself. But the wereguard pictured I recognized as one of his elite.

Simon nodded while I flipped through the other pages, some in Russian, Ukrainian, French. All for drug trafficking, some for human trafficking, a fact that turned my stomach. Three for assassinations. What the hell was going on?

"I make it a point to track stuff like this," Simon said, turning back to his keyboard. "Now I know who is who and what they are, I like to keep an eye on who's making waves. For the most part, I might stumble on the odd witch family having to move base, blaming it on a natural disaster or something. But over the last week I've uncovered a lot of activity involving werewolves and the normal police." His glasses flashed the reflection of one of his screens as he turned toward me again. "Thought you'd want to know."

I sure as hell did. "Thanks." I snapped the report shut.

"Maybe next time," Simon said, ignoring me again, "you'll actually come to see me when I send for you."

Oh, he did *not*.

Apollo's arrival saved Simon from a life as a slimy, green amphibian.

"There was one more thing. We're working on a plan." I half turned as Apollo approached from around the computer rack, though he didn't look happy about it. "But we still haven't hammered out all the details."

Simon took the heavy hint, which only made me nervous. "We'll be in touch." He spun back, waving me off, and ignored me.

I turned to Apollo with an arched eyebrow. "Spill it." Not that I didn't trust the older Zornov, but he was known for his wild ideas and I wanted to be sure he wasn't planning something I'd regret later.

There was a time his arrogant sauciness made me grin despite the slight creep factor to his flirting. I'd liked Apollo from the moment I met him, casual boyishness barely hiding the huge heart that ruled him. But he was serious today, focused, more than I'd ever seen him. So when he shook his head, I just sighed.

"Please," I said, "at least tell me you'll read me in before you run off and get yourself killed."

Apollo grinned at last. "Oh, Syd," he said. "I knew you cared. Don't worry, princess. Your knight in shining armor will make it all better."

I laughed out loud and punched his arm. He winced, rubbing the spot.

"I mean it." I jabbed a finger at Owen. "You, too. I'm counting on you to keep Mr. Mysterious here from making a mess."

Owen saluted. "Aye, aye, captain."

Boys.

I left them to it, actually feeling a bit brighter as I started for home. Even though I really wasn't looking forward to this little tour with Mom, the boys had at least lifted the gloom from my heart that had been plaguing me lately. And though the trip hadn't been very fruitful information wise, it was well worth the two-block break just to get out of the house for a bit.

Time to return to duty. I just hoped Mom didn't expect me to wear a skirt.

FIVE

I stopped in the driveway, report still clutched in my hand. I had to tell Femke but, damn it, Danilo deserved the chance to explain things to me first. I reached for the wereking through the veil though I stayed put, feeling his resistance to my touch as I connected. He was getting good at blocking me. I couldn't see a glimmer of his location, though he felt stationary.

Just checking in, I sent. *Hear your people have been running into trouble.*

Not sure what you mean, he sent back, short and crisp.

My jaw jumped, temper snapping. *Don't play this game, Danilo. I know about the arrests.* The edge of the report crumpled in my hand as I squeezed. *If the normal authorities find out your people are paranormal—*

When this becomes your business, a new voice interrupted,

we'll let you know. Charlotte's mother, Olena, cut me off herself, slamming the connection shut.

The bitch. I hadn't trusted her, not from day one. But she was Charlotte's mom. Danilo's. I stood there in the sunlight, fuming a long moment before I was calm enough to reach for Femke.

No contact. She was clearly in a meeting or busy. Fine, then. I'd drop this report on her desk at some point in the next little while. She might already be aware, but I didn't want to leave this to maybes.

I knew the moment I walked through the door the girls were gone and, when I climbed the stairs to my room with a tentative touch, I realized Quaid was, too. I entered my bedroom with slowly sagging shoulders to an unhappy silver Persian. Sass stood at the end of the bed, tail thrashing on the quilt, eyes narrowed, ears back. Though for a moment I worried his animosity was aimed at me, he cleared up that concern with the first word out of his mouth.

"Quaid," he snarled, "is a hard-headed idiot."

I laughed, though with little humor, tossing the report on the table by the door before crossing to scoop Sass into my arms. "You're finally figuring that out, are you?"

He batted one paw at my lips, sparks dancing in his eyes. "I thought you were bad," he said. "Seriously."

I sank to the edge of the bed and sighed. "Please tell me you didn't fight with him?" The last thing I needed was for Sass to add to the tension between Quaid and me.

"I tried to discuss his present position and how it was affecting the family." Sass quivered with anger. "He actually told me to mind my own business." Those indignant words would have made me snort if it wasn't so sad. Broke my heart, actually, to see Sass's distress. "Syd," he said, anger sizzling out, ears going sideways as his whiskers drooped. "This family *is* my business."

I hugged him close. "Quaid's just trying to figure out his new boundaries," I said, feeling like I was quoting some self-help guru. And while I'd admit to perusing a few relationship books online just in case they might help, I certainly didn't want to turn into a pushover either. "But you're right, Sass. As much as he might not like it, you were here first. And the safety of this family has been in your capable paws for so long I'm sure we wouldn't have made it this far without you."

Sass laid his head on my shoulder, tail quieting. "I know your marriage is your responsibility," he said, voice low and soft. "But this discord is bad for the coven, Syd."

I let him go, stroking his fur as he settled on the covers in soft misery.

"We've been through rough patches before," I said. "And it all worked out. I have faith." I really did. The magic binding Quaid and me together was as strong as ever, no matter the pressures we were both under right now. "It's only been eight weeks since the Brotherhood attack, less than two since Quaid took over as the WPC Enforcer Leader. There's bound to be upset for a bit."

"With Shenka leaving, the coven is nervous." I'd felt it, seen it in the faces of those I cared about when I met them on the street. But the family magic was as powerful as my ties to Quaid and always would be.

"Everyone is nervous." I stood and headed for the closet. "If the family has learned anything from past events, Sass, it's that we will always endure." I had to believe that. And would give my life to make sure it remained the truth. I pulled out a dark suit from the closet and turned to show it to him. "Want to get out of the house for a few hours?"

He nodded, sitting up. "Where are we going?"

As I dressed behind the mostly closed door of my walk in, I filled him in on Mom's plan.

"About time," he grumbled. "I'm surprised Miriam waited this long."

"Don't be such a grouch." I fastened the last button on my sleeveless cream blouse and opened the door, jacket in one hand, heels in the other. "We're all doing the best we can, remember?"

Sass sighed, nodded. "I'm just in a bad mood," he said. "Thanks for asking me to come with you."

I bent over him, kissed the top of his head. "I figure I have to keep you happy," I said. "You and I are the only two in this family who are going to live forever."

His amber eyes blinked slowly. "Do you think that's part of Quaid's problem?"

He had to bring that up, didn't he? I turned away with a sharp frown, draping my jacket over the back of my dressing table chair. I loved the old wood of the heavy piece Quaid gave me as a wedding present. The Brotherhood shattered it when they invaded, but my husband managed to put it back together again. I ran one hand over the surface. Just like our troubles now, we'd patch things up. We always did.

But Sass's reminder my love would grow old and I would have to watch that happen wasn't helping me improve my mood or increase my optimism. And gave voice to the worry I carried with me about Quaid's true reasons for stepping back from us, from diving into work. Was he afraid of the very thing I knew was inevitable for us?

I really needed to talk to him. As soon as this tour was over, I'd make time.

Mom's magic tied to the power of the Council gently prodded the wards around the house. I wondered at her politeness as I invited her to pass, only to feel the touch of others with her as she entered the kitchen below. With a heavy sigh held tight in my chest and a need to roll my eyes continually barely grasped in check, I followed Sassafras as he sauntered out my door and down the stairs, a prince in his domain. At least his casual arrogance triggered my humor and took the edge off as I walked from the warm hardwood in the hall to the cool tile of the kitchen.

Not that I was unhappy to see my mother. It was just all the formalities that made my left eye twitch in irritation. The sight of two other Council members standing behind Mom, flanked by Enforcer Leader Varity Rhodes and a younger woman also in a black and blue trimmed robe made my teeth clench.

Sorry, sweetheart, Mom sent. *Official business.*

You could have warned me, I sent back, temper already coiling around my fight with Quaid.

I thought I did. Her calm never cracked as she smiled her best Council Leader smile at me. "Coven Leader Hayle," she said, warmth in her voice, magic formally greeting mine. "Thank you for welcoming us into your territory."

I nodded, not feeling all that gracious but willing to play the game for Mom's sake. "Council Leader Hayle," I said, sweet and sticky, "how lovely to see you."

Mom laughed in my head. *A little thick, don't you think?*

You asked for it. I crossed my arms over my chest, the firm hug of my suit feeling odd after the familiar comfort of my t-shirt and jeans. If only I could have gotten away with my usual casual attire.

"The Council wishes to call on your services today," Mom went on, gesturing kindly to the two women beside her. Both bobbed nods at me and I nodded back. I still wasn't used to the youth of the new Council, so accustomed to years of dealing with ancient witches stuck in their frustrating ways. Mary Parker of the Santos family and Sylvia Rhodes from the Rhodes coven were both in their late twenties, like me and, from what I knew of them, were at least moderately progressive. The looks of awe on their faces made me frown a bit, though. The Council needed strong voices, not witches who couldn't hold their own against the hard times to come.

"The Council is welcome to do so." Oh, Syd. I smiled to soften the quip as Mom's nostrils flared ever so slightly in response.

"We've begun a tour of covens," she said in her same glowing tone, though from the tightness around her eyes she'd begun to lose her own sense of humor about the whole situation. "And would ask your participation in visiting with coven leaders to ensure the continuing safety of our territory."

"I'm delighted to assist," I said, reaching for genuine. The smiles that answered my words from the two Council members told me I'd hit the mark, though Mom's pert poke of power was enough assurance she knew me better than that. "May I ask why I've been recruited?"

Mom shrugged. "We are rotating all large coven leaders into the visits," she said, like asking me was no big deal. Way to hit my ego, Mom. But her reasoning was solid and I nodded, actually feeling better about the whole thing, to be honest. At least, once my whiny side stopped complaining about not being the only special one.

Seriously. So childish sometimes.

"I'm ready and available," I said. "Whenever you are."

Thank you, sweetheart. Mom's mental voice was soft. *As foolish as this seems, appearances must be maintained, now more than ever.*

I don't know, Mom, I sent back as she gestured toward the front door, Mary and Sylvia preceding her. *We've lived with formality and stilted laws for long enough. Look where that got us.*

Mom's troubled mental touch wavered. *Perhaps*, she sent. *I hadn't thought of it that way.* She sighed in my head as we crossed the threshold and into the driveway, past the family wards. I felt Nicci's power softly touch mine, confirmation she was on the job, before Varity bowed to Mom and blue fire lit beneath me. *Maybe I'm the wrong leader, after all. New blood might be a good thing right now.*

I don't believe that for a minute, I sent, bending to scoop Sassafras into my arms as the flames engulfed us and carried us away. How different it felt to travel on the fire of the Enforcers and not through the veil. And to be out of control of said travel. I focused on Mom to keep my mind off the fact. *Your experience and willingness to be flexible are exactly what the Council needs, Mom. The day you tell me you think you're the perfect witch for the job is the day I'll worry.*

We touched down on well-manicured grass into a sunny afternoon. Tall, ancient maples cast shade over us, the scent of fresh air mixed with the tang of the ocean lifting my spirits immensely.

Mom's power hugged me. *I love you, sweetheart*, she sent.

Why did that suddenly choke me up? *I love you, too. Now, let's get this over with so I can go back to being a grumpy hermit.*

Mom laughed in my head and led the way toward the large, plantation-style house at the end of the long, gravel drive.

SIX

The library smelled faintly of fire, the whole back of the plantation house still in renovations. I sipped my tea past the crushing horror in the eyes of the witches sitting in a semicircle before me. The empty, hollow feeling of the place, the worn and weary touch of the Santos family magic reminded me in sharp pangs just how far most covens still had to go to recover from what happened only eight weeks ago.

It felt like a lifetime and looked like one on the face of their leader, Paula Santos. But the lines around her eyes deepened by pain and loss had lessened somewhat, and the optimism in her voice helped my guilt over abandoning her family for the sake of my own.

There was nothing you could have done, Sass sent in a tight touch of power as I choked on a tiny bite of sugar cookie, just to keep from having to talk to anyone. *We've been over this. Even you, with all the power you have at your disposal, could barely protect our coven, let alone all of North America. You saved them in the end, Syd. You did everything you could. The rest is up to them.*

Intellectually I knew he was right. But sitting here, listening to Paula talk about rebuilding her devastated coven, made my stomach churn acid around the sweet tea and cookies.

Paula's olive skin glowed with fresh pink, dark eyes clear and unguarded. When I finally met her gaze, she smiled at me. "We're grateful for the assistance of the Steam Union in teaching us to utilize our sorcery." She had a soft, Southern drawl to her voice, subtle but audible enough I caught myself mimicking her accent in my head. "Knowing we can defend ourselves is the most valuable tool we've gained." *That*, she sent directly to me, *and the return of our family fortune.* Her power hugged me gently. *For its safe recovery I will be eternally grateful, Sydlynn Hayle. The Santos coven is in your debt forever.*

Don't thank me, I sent back, biting down on the need to leave before I started to cry over just how badly I felt. She was grateful? Indebted? I let this happen, I screwed up, ran off to help Max when I should have been focused on Belaisle. *You owe me nothing. I'm just happy it worked out.*

I shrank from her further attempts to speak privately to me, soul quivering and shivering in my gut as Mom wrapped up the visit. I stood abruptly and spun to leave when she said her goodbyes, almost running square into Varity. The old Enforcer leader's careful gaze cut through me, though not unkindly. One thin fingered hand settled firmly around my upper arm as she guided me out the door and onto the lawn. I stammered my own formal farewell to Paula and her people just before Varity carried us away on blue fire.

Enough, she sent as we traveled. *I know where your head is, girl.* She sounded so much like her best friend, my grandmother, Ethpeal, I actually startled. *Don't be an idiot.*

The fire released us, but Varity held her grip. I met her eyes again for a moment.

"Sydlynn Hayle," she whispered in her hoarse voice. "The past is the past. What the future brings, none can say. But here, in the present, you can make a difference." She nodded curtly, steel gray hair shining in the sunlight as she let me go. "Stop punishing yourself for things no one can change."

I had no idea how deeply I carried my guilt, not until that moment. Her power held me kindly but with immense force as I shuddered and struggled with tears. Sassafras's magic wound around me, held me as tightly as Varity's. Blame and shame rippled through mine, bouncing back from their combined energy, forcing me to look at it, really see what I'd buried since the day I discovered Liander Belaisle defeated me again.

So hard to pull apart and examine. But, after a

moment, with the comforting support of the old Enforcer leader and my demon cat tied to the love and grief of my alter egos, I sighed out a deep breath and chose to let it go.

Varity's magic released me a moment later, Sass's lingering, linked to me no matter what. I looked up to find Mom distracting the others, though when she glanced our way I saw the troubled sadness in her eyes.

I'm okay, I sent to my mother, letting Varity and Sass in at the same time. *I guess I didn't realize how much this affected me.*

We've been wanting you to deal with it, Sass sent with soft sparks of amber power.

So this was a setup, I sent, not sure if I should be amused or angry.

In a way, Mom sent. *Two birds with one stone, as they say.*

I nodded slightly and stepped away from Varity, still holding Sass in my arms.

Thank you, I sent, feeling lighter than I had in weeks. *Let's keep going.*

We spent the rest of the afternoon and into the early evening visiting covens. It was still hard, don't get me wrong. New pangs of guilt emerged as I greeted each coven leader and met their wide eyed and, at times, grief stricken family members. Some covens had recovered faster than others, at least emotionally. It was nice to see Leader Dagney Rhodes in her natural environment, to greet her, not in the Shadow Council, but under the full supervision of my mother and Varity. The Rhodes family had shriveled to tiny numbers, but thanks to Dagney's persistence and patience they had grown already by at least a dozen new members, all refugees from fallen families.

The saddest visit was the least expected. Though I wasn't exactly besties with the Bradford coven, finding out the entire family had been wiped from the earth by Belaisle and the Brotherhood hit me like a battering ram. A new family resided in their old home, the Picallo coven. And though Amanda Picallo seemed like a lovely person and a strong witch, knowing the Bradfords were lost completely weighed on me like no other loss.

To distract myself, I prodded Mom about the replacement as she and the Council members chatted with Amanda and her people.

It's happening everywhere, Mom sent. *Belaisle and his people targeted the largest covens to weaken us all. Those who were once the leaders of our territory are now the least powerful and new, up and coming covens are taking their place.* She sounded sad but optimistic. *I would imagine there will be Council seat challenges soon to reflect the changes in dynamic.*

Why doesn't every coven have a rep on the Council? That would make the most sense, wouldn't it? Lack of input was what got us in trouble in the first place.

Too many voices, Mom sent, though her response

sounded like rote, not conviction.

Mom, I sent. *That's crap and you know it. We're here, right now, because too few decided for the whole. Why do you think the Shadow Council was formed?* Mom's power twitched in response. *They feel helpless. You know that already. Maybe it's time to give them a voice so they don't need to work behind your back.*

Mom hesitated before standing and offering her power to Amanda. I liked the young woman, barely twenty-five, who led the Picallo family, and warmly shook her hand when we exchanged magic. Her pale green eyes smiled at me as she guided us out.

It wasn't until we were on our way again, the blue fire carrying us to our next destination, Mom reached out to me.

Perhaps you're right, she sent in a rush of words. *Syd, this is massive, you understand that?*

If anyone can handle it, you can. I grinned at her with power so she'd see and feel my amusement. *Have fun with that, won't you?*

She grumbled at me but with good nature. I was still smiling when we materialized at our next location, a smile that dropped from my face the moment I recognized the grand front steps and castle like exterior of the massive, stone mansion before me.

Mom, I growled in her head.

She cast me a glance that said "payback".

With a sigh and gritted teeth, I followed her in stomping steps up to the front door of Dumont House.

SEVEN

The place hadn't changed much. Memories flooded in, of finding Mia here, my old friend now long burned at the stake, once leader of this coven. She'd been attacked by the Brotherhood, stripped of her family magic. That act completed her destruction. After a lifetime spent with her power shut down, losing to Andre cracked her so badly she shattered. Poor Mia, who I first knew as Pain, a fitting Goth name for a witch forever tormented by the choices of her parents. I often wondered what would have become of her had she the fighting chance Ameline Benoit and I both had. Mia was lost to me, her ghost simply the dying echo of her memory inside me, something I clung to those moments I needed an extra dose of guilt to make me feel worse than I already did.

The wide, sweeping staircase hadn't altered, dark wood panels and marble floor adding an ominous feel to the place that never seemed to go away. The Dumont family power felt sullen in the dry and dusty grand foyer, simmering with resentment. Aimed at us or the Brotherhood? Or at its leader, Andre, who seized power from Mia and claimed the family magic when she had fallen so low? I hardly cared these days. There was a time when Andre and his mother, the long-dead Odette, were thorns in my side, along with the two brothers, Jean Marc and Kristophe. But I had thought little of them in the last eight years, aside from the one run in Charlotte had with them. All the dislike and disgust I felt for the Dumont family was aimed at the leader and his children, with good reason. I knew only a fraction of what Andre subjected Charlotte to, and what little she had shared with me warmed my blood to boiling with plans to hurt him as much as possible.

The faint scent of decay carried in the air of the quiet house, reminding me my werefriend had her own plans for the Dumont family leader. She'd inflicted him with wounds she swore would never heal and I wondered if he suffered enough. If that was even possible.

With my jaw locked in a permanent frown of disapproval and unhappiness, I stopped beside my mother in the gapingly empty foyer and glared at nothing in particular, hoping this little visit would be over sooner rather than later. For a moment, I imagined Mia might appear, sweeping down the staircase in her tall, black boots, thick eyeliner making her ice blue eyes pop, shiny black bob swinging around her pale cheeks and shoulders. Instead, two familiar forms oozed from a doorway on the other side of the stairs and came to an arrogant halt ten feet from us.

Jean Marc hadn't changed much in the years I'd known him, still tall with buzzed short dark hair and cold eyes. He'd acquired a few lines around his mouth from scowling all the time, but he was as lean and broad shouldered as ever, a dark suit making him look more like his father despite their coloring difference. Kristophe, on the other hand, wasn't weathering age very well. Only twenty-nine, like me, he'd gained a fair bit of weight on his formerly model slim body, long, light brown hair now frayed and stringy, hairline receding and giving him a widow's peak. His pout appeared no longer European runway attractive but sullenly spiteful and far too young an expression for a man almost thirty. He hid his paunch behind a silk shirt but it was impossible to miss the roundness of his cheeks and the flares of red dots under the thin layer of makeup he wore to hide acne.

There was a time I almost feared them, the Dumont family. A time I saw them as my enemies and equals. But that time had long vanished. The diminished coven's loss of power showed clearly in both of them, though Jean Marc did his best to bluster as he crossed his arms over his chest and glared directly at Mom as though I weren't even there.

"What is the meaning of this intrusion?" He'd been selected as second when Andre took over the coven leadership, unprecedented as it was for two males to lead a witch family. Jean Marc's cramping bitterness showed through with every word out of his mouth and I wondered if all was congenial between him and his father.

"You received notice of this visit." Mom wasn't taking crap from anyone, least of all Jean Marc Dumont. Where she'd been calm and caring with the other coven leaders, she was short, abrupt and cold with him. "Run along and tell your coven leader duty calls him."

I almost grinned, only holding it back out of sheer will.

Nice, I sent to her.

I'm tired of this whole family, she sent in return, though there was sadness in her voice. *Perhaps it's time they were allowed to put themselves out of their misery.*

No argument from me.

Miriam. Sass's voice interrupted. *You know what you're suggesting?* He sounded shocked, appalled even.

We're talking about the Dumonts, Sass, I sent. *We do have the same memories of their interactions and betrayals, don't we?*

Syd, he sent, quiet, personal, *I know very well what the Dumonts have done. But consider.* He paused, his own sorrow soft but powerful. *How many witches we've lost. How many families. And that Miriam is advocating we let another family fall?*

Despite their leader's lack of good judgment, the Dumont family has been a powerful force in our territory for many years. The loss of their presence, even if it might satisfy our need for vengeance, is a blow to the Council and all witches.

I guess I could see his point. *I understand your trepidation, Sassafras,* Mom sent as I mulled it over. *But they have created their own pain and suffering. And I'm tired of rescuing those who will not stand for others.*

Sass sighed in my arms. *As you wish,* he sent.

"Our leader," Jean Marc snapped after a moment, "is not at your beck and call, Hayle." The two Council members gasped at his rudeness, Varity tensing, her two Enforcers doing the same. Mom waved them down as the second went on. "Your message was received, which means ours was as well. You are not welcome here. Leave before I am forced to make you leave."

Bad bluffing, but enough to outrage the Council further.

"How dare you," Mary said, dark eyes snapping with blue fire. Sylvia's tight, thin lips told me she was about as impressed as her counterpart. They might have been young but both understood the insult.

Mom shrugged elegantly. "I will go," she said. "But only under the request of your leader."

Ha. So there, you pompous, arrogant asshat.

I was still celebrating Mom's zing when I felt the blossom of black power from the two men and understood we weren't the only ones working on waking our sorcery. I suppose I shouldn't have been surprised these two were preparing themselves. They might have been creepzillas but I never considered them stupid.

Considering the Brotherhood decimated their family as much as any other they were smart to take action. As long as they kept their dark magic to themselves we wouldn't have a problem. Was it wrong I hoped they'd overstep their bounds?

Like I needed more trouble. Still.

Jean Marc opened his ugly mouth to say something, only to be silenced by a crack of magic. I turned away from the two men to watch a shadow wheel forward. A tall, quiet man without expression gently pushed a wheelchair only as far as the base of the stairs. Still in darkness, his face hidden from us, Andre spoke.

"Miriam Hayle." His voice sounded wet, as though he were drinking some thick liquid while trying to speak. A deep, tearing cough followed his words, one hand rising to cup over his mouth. I caught a glimpse of him in the gloom as his face partially entered the light. His pale skin had a faint gray cast, marred by what looked like a tear to his flesh that wept clear liquid. I shuddered but didn't look away, though my demon's desire to see him with her vision more clearly I suppressed as he went on. "I had not heard of your pending visit." Even in the darkness of the shadows he hid himself in I could feel and see his animosity as he glared at his sons. Jean Marc glared back, though sullen and quiet, open rebellion not yet an option it seemed. "You would speak for me, boy? You think me that far gone?" Again Andre coughed, longer this time, his whole form shaking. Kristophe looked away, uncomfortable, hands trembling as he stuffed them in his pockets. But Jean Marc watched with a hunger that had nothing to do with kindness or compassion but only with the need for power.

He was waiting for his father to die. How kind of him.

Not for long, Sass sent.

Agreed, my vampire sent. *His death will come sooner rather than later.*

If Charlotte allows it, my demon snarled. *Which I hope she doesn't.*

Even I didn't hate him that much.

"We've come to speak about coven safety," Mom said, light, almost airy. "To offer support and a network of protection against further attacks."

Andre waved her off, one hand in the light, lined and thin. The glamour he used glittered around the edges, but even his magic couldn't hide the full extent of damage, no matter how hard he pushed. I could only imagine what he really looked like past the power disguising the worst of his affliction. He'd once been a tall, handsome, blond aristocrat despite his black heart. The man in the wheelchair hiding from the light appeared a withered, wasting old man.

"To hell with all of you," he said without anger or emotion of any kind. "I care nothing for your Council or your power or the fate of the Universe." Was he speaking directly to me? Impossible to tell. And yet, I had the feeling he knew about the pursuit of the pieces of Creator despite his apparent disregard for what happened around him. "You've failed me for the last time, Miriam. The Dumont family wants nothing to do with you."

Mom failed him? Even now, he was a self-centered asshat. Charlotte's affliction was clearly messing with his already scrambled mind. But instead of arguing as I might have done, Mom just nodded and shrugged again.

"Our assistance is always available," she said, empathy showing at last. How could she? But even Sass shook softly in my arms and I began to understand. The death of a coven wasn't something to take lightly. I could feel the agony of the Dumont family's magic and released my anger toward him and his abhorrent children. They had endured enough suffering. I didn't need to add my animosity in the moment.

"Your assistance is unwelcome." Andre sagged lower in his wheelchair. "Our family can take care of itself." He gestured and the tall servant turned, wheeling him away. I watched Andre leave, felt the family magic retreat with him and turned toward Jean Marc and Kristophe as their father disappeared.

Kristophe spun and left, head down. But Jean Marc stared right back at me, defiant and horrible, until Mom gently led me away.

EIGHT

Mom stopped at the bottom of the stairs and pulled me aside as the others continued on. *Sassafras*, she sent, eyes locked on mine. *You felt it?*

His pending death? Sass shuddered, fur tickling my hands.

No, she sent. *Something else.*

Sorcery, I sent, nodding. *Both sons have woken their power.*

Sass grumbled softly in my head. *We'll have to keep an eye on them, Miriam*, he sent. *Jean Marc especially.*

There's no question he's just waiting for Andre to die, Mom sent, eyebrows pulling together. *But I think the elder son is in for a shock when his father passes.*

You don't think the family magic will accept Jean Marc? That would be a kick in the teeth. It happened, in fact was the reason Andre was leader and Mia was dead. It rejected her for not being strong enough. If Jean Marc couldn't keep control of it the days of the Dumonts leading this family were over.

No, Mom sent, sad all over again. *I fear something worse.*

The coven's magic will simply die, Sass sent, looking up at me with his amber eyes. *The family power won't survive Andre's death.* He fixed his gaze on Mom again. *You're certain this is what you want?*

Mom wrung her hands ever so slightly, her only outward show of stress. *Not what I want,* she sent. *But what must come to pass. It's time this tainted magic line was allowed to perish.*

Sass nodded. *Agreed,* he sent. *After what I felt in there... but you realize that leaves Jean Marc and Kristophe as sorcerers. And vulnerable to recruitment by Belaisle.*

He can have them, I snapped at the pair. *Right after I smother them both in their sleep.*

Mom didn't get a chance to respond to my burst of anger. Not when the front door opened and an anxious, attractive woman hurried out and toward us. She stopped in her tracks when she saw me, but only froze a moment before coming to curtsy to my mother. I stared in open mouthed shock as the former Enforcer, Payten, rose from her gesture of respect and smiled faintly.

"Council Leader," she said, hasty, words tumbling over themselves. Payten had grown up, time only making her more beautiful. Her tawny hair hung loose over her shoulders, expansive chest reminding me I used to hate her for stealing Quaid from me. Such a long time ago, but still fresh enough to make my temper snap and crackle with jealousy. There was a time I despised her for allowing Ameline Benoit to manipulate and use her, thought unkindly of her. Turned out that time wasn't past.

"Payten." Mom seemed as surprised as I did. "I had no idea you were a Dumont now."

Hold on. She was a what? I felt her family affiliation with surprise. She'd been part of another coven when I knew her. What brought her here?

"My family was almost destroyed in the Brotherhood attacks." Payten's old bravado and extroverted nature seemed to have reversed. Her voice was soft, hesitant, chin tipped down as she spoke directly to Mom. "The Dumont family absorbed us after the fact."

Not rescued or helped. Absorbed. "I'm sorry to hear that." Mom reached out, squeezed her hand and I had to look away. "How have you been, dear?"

Okay, yes, so Payten hadn't acted entirely on her own free will when she did everything she could to keep Quaid and me apart. She'd been partially under Ameline's control. Made things worse, in my opinion.

Grrr.

"I can't stand it here." Payten's tears rang in her voice, even as hushed as it was. She finally turned and met my eyes for the first time, hers full of pain. "I know you would never offer me a place in your family," she said, "but I hoped there might be a coven that would take me." Her hands dropped to her sides, desperate unhappiness digging holes in even my animosity. "Can you help me?"

Mom nodded immediately. "Of course," she said, firm and confident, arm around Payten's shoulders as she guided her toward Varity and the others. "There are countless covens desperate for witches to swell their ranks. You have your choice of families, my dear."

Just. Not. Mine.

"Unless." Mom stopped, turned to face the former Enforcer. She'd been stripped of her position and sent home when Pender found out about her association with Ameline. I knew that gleam in my mother's eyes, though, and clenched my teeth against what might come out of her mouth next. "I have a position available, am in need of an assistant. If you'd like to apprentice for the role, I would be happy to have you."

Payten's eyes lit up even as my stomach rolled over in a slow simmer of fury.

WHAT THE HELL, MOM. I hit her with a sharp poke of power as I yelled in her head.

My mother didn't even flinch. *Get over it, Syd,* she sent as the blue fire of Varity's power engulfed us. *Bygones are over, sweetheart. You're even friends with Ameline's soul, if I recall correctly.* I flinched at that. Because, damn her, Mom was right. *And Payten has always been an excellent witch. With time and training, she can be a valuable member of my staff.*

At least Quaid wasn't around. That made accepting Payten a little easier. For the first time I was happy he'd taken the job with Femke. Nice and far from the tart.

Oh, Syd. Mom was right. Get over it already.

We've lost so many good people, Mom sent. *It's a waste for her to be used up by the Dumonts.* Her mind swelled. *Varity, please have one of your Enforcers escort Payten to Harvard. We have one last stop to make.*

I felt two powers leave the flames even as I prodded Mom's mind. She was suddenly closed and, as we appeared on a familiar stretch of beach, I understood her newfound quiet.

Bile churned in my gut, threatened to rise while I turned slowly on my heel in the sand, the white stuff grinding under my shoe, and I looked up at the open patio doors leading into Hensley House.

Oh, *hell* no.

The Dumont visit might have made me feel irritated and off color, but looking up at the sprawling California home of the Hensley family set me on fire. I was about a half a heartbeat from tearing open the veil and going home when Mom's mind embraced mine.

Sweetheart, she sent, remorse at war with need, *please. Just listen.*

You're in so much trouble. I sent that to both her and

Sassafras who didn't seem at all surprised by our location or my reaction. Which meant she'd warned him ahead of time. Sneaky buggers, the pair of them.

Syd, Sass sent, no nonsense crackling with amber fire, *this is important. Listen up*.

Whatever. My demon hissed and snarled, Shaylee grumbling enough I was sure the ground would shift under my feet any second. Only my vampire remained silent. Shenka's defection burned like an open wound, Tallah's poaching made worse by the proximity. I could forget about it, at least a moment at a time, when I was home in Wilding Springs or anywhere that wasn't right here, in this spot. But looking at the mouth of the beast just fired up my sense of outrage that did little to mask the broken heart I did my best to hide behind my temper.

I can't do this alone, Mom sent. *I'm worried about Tallah, Syd. But I can't tell anyone else. You're the only one I trust*.

Donalda's comment about the Hensley leader made me pause despite my anger and hurt. She'd said something similar. That she and the girls left because Tallah was acting strangely. I held my breath as Mom went on.

This is business, Mom sent. *I need you*.

I finally nodded while the girls inside me calmed down, my vampire sighing at last.

We're all in pain over Shenka's loss, she sent, resigned and with weight to her words. *But there must be a reason she left,*

Sydlynn. Shenka would not simply abandon us lightly. Perhaps there is more here that needs exploring than even your mother is aware of.

Fine, I sent, directly to my mother and Sass, though I knew my vampire understood she was the tipping point. *I'll do my best to be civil.*

Mom's hand took mine, squeezed gently as she led me after the Council members and Varity toward the wide deck. The wood stairs thudded under me, the scent of the surf bringing back memories of vacationing here. Of liking Tallah once, seeing her as an ally. Of my best friend and former second and all we'd been through. The way we parted.

I paused at the open patio door into the open concept living room/kitchen. After all the horrible, terrible, wrenching things I'd endured over the years, I actually wondered in that moment if I was physically capable of crossing that threshold.

I'm with you, my vampire sent, Shaylee and my demon joining her encouragement. *We will never leave you.*

I exhaled the breath I was holding and took the final step.

It was almost as bright inside as outside, giant skylights letting in the dazzling afternoon sun. The time change always threw me for a loop, considering we'd just left early evening and the Dumonts behind. I stayed in Mom's shadow, out of the way, as Tallah rose from a stool at the kitchen island and approached. She didn't close the full distance, instead leaving a few feet between her and Mom. Her gaze flickered over me but I ignored her in favor of the short, muscular woman who joined her.

I knew her face, had met her once before. My mind fished for a name as a slim woman covered in tattoos, ears gaping with three giant holes, bowed to Mom with an almost professional manner.

"Miriam Hayle," Tallah said, silky, black hair swinging over one shoulder as she gestured to the woman my power identified as werewolf. I made the connection the moment she spoke her name. "Nina Dillon, leader of the California werepack."

Mom accepted the werewoman's small hand. Nina's eyes met mine and she smiled quickly.

"Sydlynn Hayle." She sounded more like a lawyer, crisp and professional, than the rough-around-the-edges biker chick she appeared to be on the surface. "How are Charlotte and Sage?"

"Very well," I said, warmth in my tone. Their old leader, Cicero Caine, might have been a jerkwad who deserved the fate Charlotte handed him—no pun intended. I could still see his pumping heart beat its last in her clawed fist. But the rest of the pack seemed to be rather decent. "I'll let them know you asked."

"Thank you." Such a dichotomy, excessively polite

for someone so tattooed and I kicked myself at last for judging her by her appearance.

"And you know my second, of course." I couldn't look as Tallah spun, gesturing behind her. I already knew Shenka was in the room, felt her familiar magic hiding from mine. A rustle of fabric and she moved forward, though I kept my eyes locked elsewhere. On Anna, as it turned out. Tallah's best friend and former Hensley second wasn't looking at me. She stared with anger at her leader and I wondered if it was jealousy at the fact she'd been replaced or something different.

Maybe I should pop by later and ask her personally.

"Council Leader." Even the sound of Shenka's voice cut me to ribbons. I held tight to Sassafras as Mom murmured a greeting. There was silence a moment before Shenka spoke again. "It's good to see you, Sassafras."

"I'm sure." He sniffed, turning his head away, startling me so much by his coldness I switched focus from Anna and met Shenka's eyes. Hers widened before she cast her gaze away, staring at the floor at her feet, hands clenched in front of her.

Mom's sympathetic magic wasn't helping. "We won't keep you," she said. "We're just checking in to make sure everything is going well."

"Thanks for the visit." Tallah sounded a little cold and I bristled, but held myself back from commenting. "We're doing just fine."

"The coven is growing," Shenka spoke up, kind and quiet. "And the assistance of the Steam Union in accessing our sorcery has been a boon. Thank you."

Mom nodded. "You can thank Syd," she said, a bit dry. Was that irony in her voice? "And Piers, of course." My friend, the leader of the Steam Union, had agreed to help witches and I couldn't have been more grateful. Especially considering Piers Southway had his own issues to deal with.

"We have our own ideas about what the future of our coven looks like." Tallah felt like she was ready for a fight, her magic bristling under a sullen layer of resentment. Against what? The Council generally or my mother specifically? She gestured again to Nina. "We've welcomed the werepack to join us as official family members."

Mom flinched slightly, though I'm sure I was the only one who saw it, knowing her as well as I did.

"A bold decision," Mom said, ever so carefully. "You do know such a choice goes against witch law?"

Did I know it. Her own brother and his vampire wife had been held apart from the family for as long as I remembered. Uncle Frank and Sunny had never been officially part of the coven, though Mom and I both made sure they were included in family activities and were welcomed, no matter the law.

Tallah had taken things to a whole new level.

"A law I intend to challenge," she said. "As outdated and short sighted as the rest of the rules keeping us small and controlled by a few who have led us to near disaster."

Mom, I sent before she could respond. *It's a great idea and you know it.* "I'll vote with you, given the chance," I said openly while my mother continued to hesitate. "All paranormals should be welcome. Diversity and cooperation will mean the survival of our races as a whole. I'm tired of standing alone."

Tallah looked startled at my agreement. Some of the bluster went out of her as she nodded.

But it was Nina who sealed the deal. "Council Leader," she said, her wolf rising to shine in her eyes, "we are a small pack, but loyal to the family who have adopted us." She smiled at Tallah, at Shenka. "And we will die to protect them, to a lychos, with our last breath."

I'd been hearing that term lately, from Charlotte and Sage, and now here. Not mere werewolves any longer, developed past their brutish creation and fully embracing their power. The lychos were an entirely new breed, it seemed. Evolved to the full potential of weres thanks to their unusual creation. Not controlled by sorcery, but able to use it to their advantage along with the power of elements tied to demons and witches alike.

It made me happy, oddly, Nina made such a distinction. They were free weres, though I wondered what that meant for their connection to the werenation.

Mom finally nodded. "We will broach this with the full Council," she said, "but I will support altering the law. The time for segregation is long past."

Tallah seemed relieved, Nina gently punching her in the arm with a satisfied grin before crossing her arms over her narrow chest.

I risked a glance at Shenka to catch her watching me again. Before she could look away, on impulse, I reached out to her with magic and hugged her.

"It's good to see you," I said, surprising myself with the level of emotion behind my words.

Instead of answering me, Shenka let out a low cry, eyes blurred with the sparkle of tears, and ran across the room, slamming her bedroom door behind her.

Kindness, Sassafras sent with more gentleness than I'd heard in a long time. *You might as well have hit her.*

When I turned back, Tallah's scowl did its best to make me feel guilty.

Not this time.

NINE

Mom sat next to me in the dark kitchen and sipped her tea with a slight frown between her eyebrows. I reflexively rubbed the line between my own in sympathy while Sassafras lapped at a cold bowl of cream, amber eyes flickering back and forth from my mother to me.

We'd wrapped up our little tour of North American witchdom with the Hensley family. Rather than go back to Harvard with Varity and the Council members, Mom opted to stay put and share a cup with me while the quiet house settled around us. The kids were still at Harvard with Dad, since it was a school night. I'd intended to visit but wasn't sure I wanted to burden them with the way I was feeling just now, not to mention I'd have to wake them at this late hour. Though I was more and more an absentee Mom than an actual parent these days, it did make sense for Gabriel and Ethie to stay with Mom and

Dad at the college where they were safe. Then again, was anywhere safe? There were times I wondered if they would be better off with me, and other times keeping them as far from me as possible seemed the best choice. Seeing Shenka, feeling Tallah's resentment and anger against me and my mother, made me think of my kids and wish they were here for me to hug.

Maybe it wasn't too late to see them, after all.

Mom hadn't said much since I filled her in on Sonja's request to see Gabriel. That little talk wasn't making things any easier for me either. The suspicious and angry part of me was prepared to march up to Hilltop and kick her ass halfway across the continent just to protect my baby from her influence. But every time I considered the option, Liam's gentle, smiling face bobbed into my head and I couldn't bring myself to do it. As much as I disliked and mistrusted Spaft and Sonja, I owed it to my son to allow him to form his own opinions about his father's side of the family.

And to trust him enough to make the right choices.

Mom finally sighed and set her cup down on the table, the soft sound of ceramic on wood. "I'd like nothing more than to handle this for you," she said, grim, blue eyes dark. "I could, you know. Legally. One word from you and the Council could make her leave your territory."

That felt wrong, like she was asking me to be some

kind of tattletale whiner. "Thanks, Mom," I said. "But, no thanks."

She nodded, fingers tracing wet patterns through the ring of spilled tea that pooled on the table around her mug. "I knew you'd say that." Her lips twisted into a wry grin. "I taught you better."

I smiled back. "And I want to teach my kids the same lessons." I never thought I'd say such a thing. There was a time, really not so long ago, I swore when I had children things would be a lot different. Funny how maturity and time prove otherwise.

"Gabriel is a wonderful boy," Mom said, straightening in her chair. "Smart and compassionate. But he has enough of you in him I'm not worried she'll succeed in lying to him successfully." Thank the elements for that. Though my insides bristled against the comment. Everyone underestimated Liam, thought him too soft, too weak and kind. I knew better. My oak tree would have seen through his mother, and did in many ways. But he also understood and refused to judge her for her failings.

That was true strength, a far cry from the temperamental woman sitting in my seat who threw a fit and asked questions later. Who was the more powerful, then?

"He'll make the choice that's right for him," I said, standing. Mom joined me, hugging me, though with some hesitation. Whether because she sensed my irritation or out of worry I was angry about our trip to California, I didn't know. When she pulled away at last, I had my answer.

"You have more access to Tallah than I do," Mom said. "Through the Shadow Council. Please, watch over her. Something is going on that worries me." She bit her lower lip. "Her magic felt…"

Sassafras grunted, winning our focus. "Off," he said. "I assumed it was the inclusion of the weres, but that's not it, is it, Miriam?"

Mom shook her head. When she met my eyes again, hers brimmed with concern. "I have no idea what Tallah is planning, or what the loss of her family's strength has driven her to do. But I hesitate to bring the Council into it unless I have to, Syd." Because that would mean an official investigation which could end up in a very bad place.

"But," I said, "if she's up to no good, Mom, she can't be allowed to continue." We'd had enough sneaking around and secrecy in the past to prove inaction was far worse than waiting to see what might evolve.

"Agreed," she said, stepping away from me. Her hands squeezed her upper arms, the silk of her dark blue blouse bunching in wrinkles under the pressure of her grip. The pentagram around her neck sparkled as blue fire erupted at her feet. "I'll kiss the kids for you," she said.

"Just do your best and I'll do mine."

I waved to her as she left, sighing heavily before sinking back into my chair. My head ached from all the emotion and thoughts and speculation, the constant weight of the fate of the Universe in the backdrop of the minutia of my not-so-normal life. Sass's paw gently settled on my hand where it rested next to my mug and I looked up with a weary smile.

"Sorry," I said. "Just a little tired." Probably for the best the kids were at Harvard. I just didn't have the emotional energy for them right now.

"Don't be," he said, tingle of power passing between us. "I, of all others, understand."

I gathered him into my arms and rested my cheek between his ears. "I really should go kiss my kids goodnight." Waffle? Who, me? Actually, the more I thought about it, the better it sounded, tired or not. A little dose of Gabriel's sweetness and Ethie's enthusiasm would go a long way right about now. And I hated the thought of being one of those mothers who lost sight of the everyday in favor of the big picture.

Selfish to wake them. Selfish to stay away. How much did that suck?

But, as I stood to step through the veil, the wards shuddered, preceding a soft knock on the kitchen door. I held still as the door opened a heartbeat later and a blonde werewoman stepped through.

Charlotte's beautiful face pinched with distress, the mirrored worry from her mate, Sage, dashing my hopes of a kid visit. The pair of lychos almost vibrated as they stood just inside the door, Charlotte's wolf, now fully integrated and with her whole power at her disposal thanks to her evolution, surfacing a moment, proof of her agitation.

My heart pounded painfully once or twice before I could settle myself and grit my teeth. "What's wrong?"

"My brother," Charlotte snarled. "We have to do something about Danilo."

Sassafras hissed softly. "What's he done?"

Sage's hand settled on Charlotte's shoulder, fingers sliding through her thick, blonde hair. His own dark locks had grown out past his ears, sea green eyes flaring with power as he gently pulled her to his side and tucked one arm around her waist.

"Nothing we can prove," Sage said. The martial arts instructor turned lychos sounded calmer than his mate, as though he disagreed with this visit, but I knew him well enough to read the tension in his face and shoulders.

Charlotte looked like she wanted to shrug him off. "Yet," she said. "But I had to speak up."

I thought of Simon and the information he'd handed me earlier and nodded. "I have proof of illegal activity, for all that," I said. "What do you know?"

Charlotte hesitated. Damn it, she came to me. It

hadn't been long since, but the death of Yana Moreau, Danilo's wife and queen, had to be laid to rest.

"Charlotte," I said, grim as Sassafras hummed his own anger, "if you know something and you're not telling anyone, I'll kick your werewolf ass."

She shivered just a little, eyes flickering from angry to sad and back again. "He's my brother," she whispered. "But I'm here, aren't I?"

Darkness flooded the kitchen as I tried to find a way to respond, a tunnel of black forming, a tall, blond man with pale gray eyes and a long, gray coat stepping through. Piers Southway's grin of greeting disappeared as he looked first at me and Sass, then to Charlotte and Sage.

"My timing," he said in his crisp British accent, "appears to be as perfect as ever."

A hastily ordered pizza served as dinner while the five of us huddled around the kitchen table. Charlotte picked at her toppings, silent while I carefully chewed the crust of my second piece and did my best to be patient. She'd talk when she was ready. For now, I couldn't stand the silence.

"How's the Union?" I tried for chipper. Piers winked and swallowed a big drink of soda to chase his bite of pizza before answering.

"Progress is being made." I loved the sparkle in his eyes, something that had been missing for a long time. I just didn't notice until it came back. Though he'd been forced to depose his own mother, ever since Piers took over as leader of the Steam Union he'd been an entirely different person—the one I'd met years ago in Ukraine.

Simpler times. Straightforward enemies and, if I was willing to admit it to myself, a whole lot of fun, honestly. Kicking ass and taking names, letting the girls out to play. Cut and dried, black and white.

I missed those days.

"We've lots of new, young recruits," Piers went on, "though many were Brotherhood initiates." He grimaced at my frown. "Don't worry," he said. "I'm not the fool my mother was. We're housing them separately and training them away from those we've tied to Steam Union sorcery." Poor Piers. He'd watched Eva Southway almost destroy his beloved Steam Union by welcoming Brotherhood sorcerers into the fold out of her need to show everyone she was a power to be reckoned with. That led to the near destruction of not only the Steam Union, but left the door open for Liander Belaisle to keep his base of power ready, willing and able when he tried to take over our territory.

Tried? Succeeded. That still rankled.

"You're testing each of them, I take it?" Sassafras nibbled a piece of pepperoni I'd set before him.

"Of course," Piers said, bowing in his seat toward the demon cat. "We're mostly hunting new blood, those freshly wakening. Why should the Brotherhood have all the fun?" I hadn't thought of it before, not until Piers brought it up. But it made sense—where did new sorcerers come from? They woke, on their own, usually in their early teens. And the Brotherhood were usually there to scoop them up.

But no longer. At least I hoped that was the case.

"I know there are some still falling through the cracks," Piers said, frowning, his concern as real as mine. "And it will take time for us to organize and figure out how to track new wakers. But, once we do, we'll make sure the Brotherhood recruitment drive comes to an abrupt and painful halt." He grinned at me around another mouthful of pizza. "Can't wait."

Any word from Zoe? I sent that privately, gently, knowing how much he worried about the young Oracle. Zoe Helios may have lost her ability to see the future, but, as it turned out, my son's ability to open Gateways to anywhere in the Universe gave her and the Fates the chance to see the future again, if only for a little while. She'd left the last time Gabriel used his power, out of worry for her family. Piers's concern for the woman he loved showed in his gray eyes and in the way he slowed his chewing before putting on a false face of bravado and cheer just like always.

Not yet, he sent. *But you're right. I know she's fine. Doing what she needs to do.* He looked away. *Family first, Syd.*

How many times had I heard that? How many times had I said it?

Piers set aside his pizza before prodding Charlotte. They were old friends, too, though there were times I thought he got away with much more than I ever could with her. She glared at him, but he just leaned in and kissed her noisily on the temple.

"All righty, then, sweet cheeks," he said in his best arrogant accent. "Tired of all the bollocks. Spit it out or forever hold your little weregirl peace."

She grunted at him, but Sage's hand tightened on hers and she finally sighed. When she looked up, she met my eyes first.

"Femke ordered Danilo to stand down," she said.

I nodded. I knew that already. He was told in no uncertain terms to stay away from the vampire blood clans.

Her teeth gnawed at the inside of her cheek a moment before she shook her head.

"He didn't listen," she said.

Why was I not surprised?

TEN

I stared my werefriend down as she went on.

"I take it you haven't heard," she said, normally stoic nature stirring with anger. I opened my mouth to tell her I had, about the drug arrests and the trafficking. But Charlotte stopped my agreement in its tracks. "About the deaths in Europe?"

Deaths? What the hell was Danilo up to? And why hadn't Femke… "Femke knows?"

Charlotte nodded. "She's the one who told me," she said. "Vampires, Syd. Going missing."

I almost corrected her. Missing vampires wasn't necessarily the fault of her brother. But Charlotte went on as though unaware I was ready to reassure her.

I wished she hadn't.

"Bodies," she said. "Tortured and quartered." Charlotte looked away. "Drained of blood and left as husks. Some with souls still inside, but without enough left to resurrect." She rubbed her arms with both hands, the red leather crinkling under her touch. "Brought out to madness if they are revived at all."

Okay, so not the spirit magic issue, then. "You're sure it's Danilo?" Sage might have said they had no proof, but this was Charlotte. She wouldn't come to me, betray her brother, if she wasn't sure.

Charlotte's worry grew visibly, which meant this was serious trouble. "I think…" she choked on the words before going on. "I think he has help."

What kind of help could Danilo possibly need? He was king of the werenation. All the pieces clicked together in my head when Sage took his turn.

"The Russian mafia," Sage spoke up when Charlotte fell silent. "We fear he's renewed the associations the weres used to have with organized crime."

That was… unfortunate. And stupid, though it explained Simon's intel, didn't it? Only problem was, if Danilo had gone to the mafia, that meant it wasn't just werewolves at stake anymore. If he turned the mafia onto vampires…

Normals with more information than was good for them could lead to a war none of us were prepared to fight.

"The mafia knew all along about us," Charlotte said, defensive but angry enough I knew she wouldn't stand with her brother on the issue. "And about the Black Souls, though only a fraction of what they could do. And only the most senior of the organization understood the wereguards they employed were not just berserker warriors but actual werewolves."

There was a reason normals didn't know about us. Too many years of fear fed by the propaganda and dogma of the Brotherhood through organized religion and fairy tales. All meant to make paranormals seem like monsters and instill fear of other races. Normals might not have had access to the powers we did, but they had weapons that could kill us, more powerful weapons and more numbers than we could easily fight.

"I have no idea how much Danilo has told them," Charlotte said. "The Czar of the Black Souls kept the mafia leaders in check, under control. He refused to answer their questions and blocked their attempts to recreate our race by making revenants." Humans bitten by werewolves no longer went mad and turned savage or soulless, but that didn't mean it was legal. Aside from Sage and the California pack, making werewolves was still against the law. Even the insane former leader of the Black Souls knew better than to give too much to the mafia. What was Danilo thinking? "I worry my brother doesn't have the foresight to contain his need for vengeance and has given up too much already." She dropped her hands to her lap, anger gone, sadness brimming. "If the mafia leaders finally see just what paranormals there are, they will stop at nothing to acquire and use those powers for their own gains."

Exactly what we couldn't allow to happen.

"Damned idiot," I snapped before unclenching. "Sorry, Charlotte. I adore your brother. But he's going to get himself killed."

Because I could be sure Femke wouldn't allow the mafia to do anything of the sort. And if Danilo was involved in such a scheme as part of a plan to gain allies, his head would be on the chopping block.

I stood, chair legs making a scraping noise on the tile floor, the sound grating in the quiet of the house. "Let's go," I said. "Before Danilo does something we'll all regret. If he hasn't already."

Charlotte joined me, silent and still a moment before she hugged me tight. *I would have come to you sooner*, she sent. *But I honestly only found out just now.*

I hugged her back. *I believe you*, I sent. *And I love you, Charlotte. I'm sorry this is happening. I'm grateful you came to me.*

She blinked away the wolf in her eyes and nodded.

"Mind if I join you?" Piers was already scooping Sassafras into his arms. "Hear Ukraine is pretty this time of year."

"I have somewhere else to go first," Charlotte said, exchanging a look with Sage. "Someone who asked to see me." Sage nodded and stood, heading for the door, his power gathering.

"I'll keep an eye on Danilo," Sage said, waving to us as he left. "Just don't leave me hanging too long."

It would be the middle of the night in Ukraine. Hopefully Danilo could keep his nose clean a little while longer.

"Where are we going?" I offered my hand to Charlotte who took it firmly in hers.

"Maybe into a trap," she said. "Or, to help an old contact. I'll know more when we get there."

That sounded optimistic. I jabbed one finger at Sassafras.

"I need you to stay home." Really did, too. The coven was quiet, the power of the four girls running through it, watching over everything. But we could be a while, and every time I left I felt the stress on the family. Leaving Sass here, especially with me being gone at night when they felt the most vulnerable, would help. He was the backbone of the coven, after all, the one, steady constant.

Sass sighed and nodded as Piers set him down again.

"I knew you were going to say that," he grumbled. "Be safe. Don't break anyone."

I shrugged. "We'll see." Piers came to join Charlotte and me. "Haven't broken anyone in a while. Might be good practice."

My usual humor fell flat, even in my own ears. Sass huddled on the table, whiskers sagging. I hugged him with power. *It'll be okay*, I sent.

Danilo could ruin things for all of us, Sass sent. *Syd, this is terrible news.*

We'll take care of it, I sent. *I promise. I'll keep you posted.*

The best I could do. I took second seat as Charlotte's power swelled and she led Piers and me into the veil.

Again, so odd to be out of control, to allow someone else to take the lead. Especially here in the veil. Travelling on the Enforcer fire was weird enough, but at least it was unfamiliar to a point. The veil was my second home. It reached for me, asked for my attention, but this was Charlotte's show and I held back, as hard as that was.

Power freak.

Charlotte delivered us to a quiet street that smelled vaguely of gasoline and rotting food. I scanned the darkness past the streetlight at the end of the alley, following with firm steps as Charlotte strode out into the light and turned right without hesitation. Her confidence gave me confidence and I was glad I didn't have a chance to change from my power suit and heels. At least I looked the part of person of position.

We approached the front of what I guessed was a restaurant, a sign over head illegible to me, though the icon of a steaming bowl gave me that much info. Charlotte ignored the two giant bodyguards, while I purposely gave them the once over, letting them see my disdain. Maybe a bad idea but I was tired and cranky and no one glared at me like that, especially not some hulking dudebros in black jackets trying to look intimidating.

The interior of the restaurant was empty of patrons, save for a round faced man sitting alone at a central table. I followed Charlotte to the middle of the room where the rotund, balding man with a stringy dark comb over dressed in a pinstripe suit waited. His giant gold ring clanked against the side of his glass, smoke puffing nervously from his thick lips as he watched us approach. I could tell from the way he looked at me he knew exactly who I was.

Danilo had a lot to answer for.

"Iosif Greshnev," Charlotte said, "may I introduce Sydlynn Hayle and Piers Southway?"

The mafia man dropped his cigar with a soft curse before hurriedly fishing it off the table, too late to save the white cloth from scorch marks. The small pile of ashes left behind released a curl of smoke before going out as he clamped the cigar firmly between his trembling fingers. He was doing his best to put on a front, but I could feel right past him. Normals had no idea how to mask their emotions from us. His fear pulsed along with his overly active heartbeat.

"What took you so long, Sharlotta?" Iosif's voice shook, masked by a veneer of anger. As though we were late or something. I grinned at him and crossed my arms over my chest while Piers smirked and casually bumped me with one shoulder.

Scared witless, that one, he sent.

I'm going to kill Danilo, I sent back.

Might as well have some fun with it in the meantime. Piers's gray eyes sparkled and I almost laughed. Pushing normals around wasn't my usual fare. But if this Iosif could give us the information we needed… who was I kidding? He already had. His reaction alone told me Charlotte was right to worry.

That took the humor out of the moment.

"I came as soon as I could." The faintest trace of her Ukrainian accent broke through Charlotte's tone. She only ever slipped when she was upset. "Tell me what you know."

He fidgeted with his cigar, his glass, his napkin. Looked everywhere but at Charlotte. "I owe you nothing," he said, harsh with fear. "You owe me a boon. That is why I summoned you."

Charlotte leaned forward, both hands on the table. Iosif shrank back from her, finally meeting her eyes. I had no idea the typical dynamic between the two, but had the impression from the way he spoke to her the odds were usually in his favor. Did he sense the change in her? Or was my presence and that of Piers enough to tip the balance? Regardless, he seemed more amenable to talking with her simple gesture.

"I can't help you unless you p-promise to protect

me," he stammered, hands shaking openly now. He dabbed at beads of sweat on his upper lip as the door behind me opened and closed again. I felt the presence of his bodyguards, noted them and their crude weapons. Freed my demon to use her power to seize the working parts on their guns with her fire as I returned my focus to Iosif. "They will kill me if I tell you anything."

"Your leaders." I couldn't help but interrupt. He nodded to me, eyes huge.

"They say," he whispered, "you can do anything." Was that hunger behind his fear? He licked his lips quickly, gaze darting to Charlotte and back to me. "Perhaps we can work out our own arrangement. In exchange for protection."

I laughed out loud, dropping my arms to my sides, honestly amused. "You're not serious."

This is the only language he knows, Charlotte sent. *You help him, he helps you. For a price, always.*

Iosif sank back into his seat, suddenly pale. I wondered if he was going to upchuck the deep red soup he'd eaten, half a bowl still in front of him, and felt my own bile rise in reaction.

"I have had my eyes opened, Sharlotta," he said, voice so low I had to take a step closer to hear him. "I was shown what is truly out there, what creatures of the night, once thought myth." He shook his head, crossed himself. Like his belief would save him if a vampire decided to take his life. "My *babusya* knew better, warned me as a little boy of the undead and their blood thirst." Definitely vampires. Which made sense. Danilo was after revenge, after all. "I should have believed her." He looked up at me again, sagging, sinking in on himself as his fear stole his courage. "The world has gone mad and I wish I lived yet in the dark." He paused, set down his cigar, ran both pudgy hands over his thin hair. "Will you save me if I help you?"

Taking on the weight of the paranormal world was bad enough. No way I was shouldering the fate of all normals, too. I shook my head, feeling my temper heat up.

"No deal," I snapped. "You chose this life, Iosif Greshnev. Live with it."

Syd, Charlotte sent. *We need him.*

Screw that, I sent. *We have what we came for. Your brother crapped the bed and now we have to clean up the mess.*

She flinched from me as I did my best to rein in my temper.

The two bodyguards moved in closer, their fear as rank as Iosif's. He ignored them, as though they didn't exist, desperation growing by the moment. He struggled to his feet, came toward me. Piers tried to block him but I waved him away.

"Please," the round bellied man said, hands wringing before him. "I'm a simple mafia soldier. I never asked for any of this. Just a life of peace and quiet among a people I've learned to adore." Charlotte's subtle nod told me he was telling the truth. I felt no duplicity in him so I let him go on. "Ambition has led me to a place I can never return from. But I have information that can help you, I swear." He closed the last step between us, smile vibrating on his trembling lips. He barely reached my height, belly in my personal space. He stank of cigars and cabbage, a sweet taint over shading the deeper scents making me feel nauseated. "If you will only take me from here."

It might be worth hearing what he has to say, Piers sent.

Fine. Whatever. "Disclosure first," I said. "Then, we'll see."

Iosif shot a look at Charlotte who rolled her shoulders in a casual shrug, grinning at him like this was funny. "I trust her," was all she said.

The round mafia man sighed so deeply I thought he might collapse in on himself before he met my eyes once more. "I have been ordered to hunt two people. Of your kind." He winced as he said it. "And kill them both."

Interesting. "Targets?"

"The first is like the Black Souls of the old days," Iosif said. "A sorcerer?" He said the words like a question, unnatural from his lips. I nodded. "Liander Belaisle."

Well now, that was interesting. "What does the Russian mafia have against Belaisle?" Not that I cared if someone else was hunting him. Keep him busy. Only that if they managed to find him first, I'd be very, very disappointed.

Iosif and his masters wouldn't like to see me disappointed.

"His organization has been encroaching on our territory." He shivered and shrugged. "I'm to have all my resources dedicated to finding and killing him."

Good luck with that. They'd never catch him.

"And the second?" Piers's casual tone made me nervous. Did he know something I didn't? The stiff way his shoulders sat under his longcoat, the tightness of his hands as his forced smile didn't reach his snapping gray eyes.

Who was the second target?

"A woman," Iosif said, "also a sorcerer and a compatriot of Belaisle." The word came out easier this time.

Oh. Crap. On a crapstick.

Piers raised his eyebrow at Iosif, showing his teeth as he smiled. "Her name?"

I already knew her name. And so did Piers.

"Eva Southway," Iosif said.

ELEVEN

I'm sure he was expecting to hear his mother's name spoken, but that didn't keep Piers from lunging for Iosif. The rattle of guns being drawn didn't faze me. My demon had dealt with the bully boys already. And I had absolute faith Charlotte could handle them physically from that point on. In fact, I felt her move past me, the whisper of her wolf emerging at the same moment I reached out and grasped Piers by the shoulder of his longcoat and pulled him sharply back and to my side.

He snarled at me but caught himself, straightening up while Iosif cowered away from my friend like he expected to be killed. I kept a firm hold on Piers as I spoke to the quivering mafia man.

"Eva Southway isn't Brotherhood," I said, letting some outrage creep into my voice if only for Piers's benefit. He must have been thinking the same thing, because his whole body relaxed somewhat at the tone I used.

"If you say so," Iosif said in haste, pudgy hands up, diamond ring flashing. The squeak of a girl's voice caught my attention, a slender young woman in a rumpled uniform disappearing through the kitchen door just the merest flash of movement. Smart. Part of me wished I could go with her.

Liar, my demon sent, grinning.

Okay, yeah.

"All I know," Iosif went on when neither Piers nor I crushed him like a bug, "is my bosses want them both dead for instigating takeovers in our territories." He shrugged his round shoulders inside his pinstriped suit. "She's as busy as he is and they have been photographed together."

It has to be a trick, Piers sent, a faint tone of desperation reaching me through his power. But I wasn't so sure. I let him think what he wanted while I mulled it over.

When Eva was deposed she already had a plan, forming her own sorcerer's union, the Sorcerer Guild. And while I didn't expect her to run off to Belaisle, she'd already been in cahoots not only with the Empress of vampires—someone I struggled to respect and yet despised for her terrible choices—but also with Piotr Wilhelm. Eva had been present when Yana was kidnapped and stood next to the king of the Wilhelm blood clan that day. Not to mention the fact she'd imprisoned her own son after the near fatal mistake of trusting the former Brotherhood soldiers who came to the Steam Union after Belaisle's failure eight years ago.

But work with Belaisle? Maybe to gain his trust so she could betray him. Still, I wouldn't put it past her to use him to her own ends if she thought she could get away with it. Power seemed to be the only thing that mattered to Eva now.

And yet, none of this really made sense. "What does Belaisle want with guns and drugs?" I shook my head as Piers relaxed further, brow furrowed, but in thought. "He doesn't need either."

"Money?" Piers turned sideways, physically cutting Iosif out of the conversation, if only by body position. "Power?"

I chewed my left thumbnail as I dug around my aching brain for answers. I'd been here before, trying to suss out the reasons for Belaisle's actions, only to be left by the wayside and him three steps ahead. But he'd had access to the Helios Oracles, something I had no clue about at the time. So it was possible he wasn't actually as clever as he made out to be.

Which worried me, really. Because I didn't consider myself particularly sneaky. And if he could still outthink me… yikes.

I stepped away from Iosif. "I'll do my best to take care of Belaisle for you." My demon came through my smile, her amber fire burning in my vision. The pudgy mafia man stepped away, paler than ever.

Piers leaned in, grasping Iosif's lapel. I caught the sound of a scuffle, someone grunting, falling heavily. Charlotte was entertaining herself. "But if anything happens to my mother," he said in a deadly quiet voice that even worried me, to be honest, "I'll be coming for you personally. Understood?"

Iosif just stared. I pulled Piers away again as Charlotte joined us at last. She dusted her hands off, face rock hard and cold.

"I suggest you gather your things," she said. "We're leaving."

What are you doing? I caught her gaze out of the corner of my eye as Iosif spun and scrambled toward the back of the room, disappearing into the kitchen.

He gave us what we needed, she sent. *The least we can do is dump him somewhere his bosses won't find him for a while.*

Fine, I sent. *But he's your responsibility.*

Charlotte grinned at me, teeth glistening. *I didn't say I'd drop him anywhere nice,* she sent. And sighed in my head. *He's not a bad sort, really. Once you get to know him. He did help Sage and me, Syd. I owe him. And I always pay my debts.*

I thought of Andre and nodded.

Piers at my side, I spun and left, retreating to the dark

street and the fresher air. A quick sniff of my clothes told me I'd be carrying the stink of garlic and cabbage until I had a shower. Delightful. My friend stared off into the night, entire body stiff and silent until I prodded him with power.

"Talk to me." I took his hand, cold in mine, tugged gently.

"What is she doing, Syd?" The pain in his voice hurt me. I hated to see him so broken up over a woman who obviously didn't care about him at all anymore. And yet, I always had the feeling everything Eva did was for Piers. That she loved him far more than his sister, Clover, more even her husband, Felix. That Piers was her whole world, until he "betrayed" her by leaving the Steam Union out of frustration.

No way I was bringing that up with him. Knowing his clever brain, he was already thinking, and had been for quite some time, that all the horrible things his mother did had been his fault.

Birds of a feather, we two.

Charlotte emerged behind us, Iosif in tow, no sign of his two bodyguards. He'd donned a heavy leather jacket lined in fur and carried two large bags. Looked like he'd planned for this escape ahead of time.

"Pays to be prepared in my business," he said when he caught me looking.

Piers spun before I could comment. "I'm going after

her."

I could tell by the look on his face there was no stopping him. But I also knew if Eva was with Belaisle, Piers would never find her. Still, it would be good for my friend to run off some steam—no pun intended. I needed him thinking straight.

He hugged me abruptly, lips brushing my cheek before he did the same to Charlotte. A black tunnel appeared beside me, the sorcery channel waiting for him to step through. He was upset to create such in the wide open like this, but it was late enough I didn't worry so much some random normal might see it. More that Piers really wasn't thinking straight.

Maybe I should have stopped him. But, I was too late. With a wave more a salute than a goodbye, my sorcerer friend disappeared into the black just as it collapsed behind him with a whoosh of air.

I turned to Charlotte, jerking my thumb at Iosif. "Now what?"

She shrugged. "Home, first," she said. "We must talk to Danilo."

Which meant she was taking her responsibility for Iosif seriously. Her casual eyebrow raise told me not to worry my little head about the rotund and staring mafia man who gazed after where Piers had been with wonder befitting a child witnessing magic for the first time.

Okay then.

I took the lead this time, clasping Charlotte's hand, knowing she would have a firm grip on Iosif on the other end. The veil parted to me, welcomed me as I did the same as Piers and stepped into it in the open street. But my magic masked our passing, blending the edges of the tear so only one who possessed power would even notice we were there.

The front lawn of the werepalace was wet with rain, my feet quickly soaked as I stepped out into the grass, bits clinging to my heels and coating the tops of my bare feet. Lovely. The circumstance just added to my most excellent mood. I'd come a long way in smoothing out my temper, but seriously. There was only so much a girl could take before she turned cranky ass on a body.

I marched to the front doors, the wide stone steps ringing with my passage, and to the entry. Where four big wereguards barred my way.

Oh, hell *no* they did *not just do that*.

Oh, *hell* NO.

Before I could hurt someone, Charlotte snapped something in Ukrainian. Only then did I see the fear on their faces, the way they shifted uncomfortably in my presence. They didn't want to be here, would rather be anywhere else from their anxiety and the internal whining of their wolves.

Orders to keep me out, then.

Oh, Danilo.

Calmer now, anger diffusing away from the innocent guards and toward their troubled king, I gently inserted some power between the middle two, Shaylee assisting with solid earth magic, and pressed them apart. Unable to resist the strength of my suggestion, they finally relented, though without gaining wereform, a good sign they just wanted this to be over with.

"He will punish us," one whispered to me on the way by.

I stopped and faced the young wereguard. "He will not," I said, crisp and commanding. "This is on my head."

The four nodded, backed away, relief on their faces. Don't get me wrong. Werewolves aren't cowards. When they are given orders, they'll lay down their lives and honor and all that stupid duty *can* stuff just to prove they're werewolf enough. But it was a testament to the disarray of Danilo's rule their entire auras felt miserable, strained, pushed to the brink of disloyalty.

They don't know what to do, Charlotte sent, sadness in her mind and magic. *They love him, our family. And they hate the vampires who killed Yana. But they see the loss of Piotr as a loss of a target. They feel my brother spiraling down into vengeance they can't comprehend. It is the nature of a wolf to seek revenge only against the perpetrator, not an entire race. Our animosity toward vampires is long gone and they have enjoyed friendships with the spirit ones.* She strode beside me across the purple carpet bisecting the grandiose interior of the palace foyer, reminiscent of walking through the middle of a Faberge egg. *Danilo's insistence is hurting them as much as it hurts him.*

So they had some sense after all, did they? Wonders and never ceasing and such things.

Sage met us at the doors to the throne room, shoulders stiff, face set. We were in for a fight, were we?

I don't suppose suggesting you go lightly will do much good? My vampire's ironic tone just spurred me on.

He needs his ass firmly and roundly kicked for being such an idiot, my demon snapped at her. *Stay out of this. Let me handle it.*

If he's put us at risk, Shaylee said, thunder behind her mental voice, reminding me of the great black hound, Galleytrot, *I'll bring this whole palace down around his damned fool head.*

You ladies all chillaroonie, I sent. *I've got it.* Nice to know I had them on my side, though. Even my reluctant vampire who wiggled closer to me and whispered so the other two wouldn't hear.

Cautiously, she sent. *But firmly. This must end.*

The massive doors to the throne room were closed, another double set of wereguards standing in my way. I'd been here before, back when the Czar ruled the werenation, when Danilo was trapped in full wolf form and Charlotte and her grandfather, Oleksander, were still slaves along with the rest of their people. I'd done some damage during that visit. Brought down a few walls, a couple of floors. Destroyed these very doors in a fit of anger and enthusiasm.

This situation called for more subtlety.

Subtle? My demon snorted. *This should be good.*

Smartass.

King Danilo Moreau of the werenation. I sent the words at full volume, the whole palace seeming to echo with the sound of my mental voice. *Knock, knock.*

The four wereguards paled, one shifting sideways away from me. I pushed gently on the doors with witch power, but they remained sealed, Danilo's power holding them closed.

I said, I sent, *knock.* And hit the door. *Knock.* Again. This time with Shaylee's help. They shook on their hinges, a faint powder of crushed marble falling to dust the wereguards on their shoulders. Their eyes rolled with fear but they stood their ground. I wasn't interested in them.

Again, no response from Danilo. I sighed, turned to Charlotte, remembering only then Iosif stood with her, staring at me like I was some kind of horror come to life. Let him stare. He was about to get a thorough education in paranormal activity.

"I tried," I said, flicking some imaginary dirt from my sleeve.

She shrugged. "You really did," she said, almost

bright, before gesturing to the wereguards. "You lot might want to make a path."

I smiled. They quivered. "Before I make one through you."

They scrambled out of the way even as Shaylee laughed in pure glee and shattered the throne room doors. I caught all the bits and pieces with my elemental magic, pulling the mess tight together and set it gently aside in a pile of crushed wood.

"That's two pairs of doors I owe your people," I said to Charlotte as the pair of us strode into the throne room, Sage grinning behind one hand.

"I'm sure you're good for it," Charlotte said.

Iosif just gurgled, tripping over his feet as he struggled to keep up.

Danilo sat on his throne, glaring down at me, fury on his handsome face. His heavy, black beard made him look more bear than wolf, giant shoulders rippling under his robe. I was so not impressed.

I really don't want to do this here, I sent to him with a hammer blow. Damn him for making me turn this public at all.

He stood abruptly and spun on his heel, disappearing behind the throne through a door draped with a purple curtain. I followed into the small anteroom where, to my shock, I found an old, gray haired werewolf waiting for me.

Charlotte's grandfather watched in grim silence as I entered, head down, eyes tired and full of grief. Oleksander had been wereking before Danilo. He ruled fairly and led his people through one of the most difficult times in their history—their initial years of freedom. Charlotte had been meant to follow him, to be his heir. But with Danilo's recovery and her reticence to become queen it made more sense for the elder brother to take the throne. Still, I wondered if my werefriend had stepped up...

No. If the vampires killed Sage, Charlotte would have turned the world upside down to destroy them, no matter the cost. I truly believed that. And, as selfish as it sounded, I was glad I wasn't facing off with my friend instead of her brother. So, Danilo it was.

Oleksander acknowledged my presence with the barest nod of his head and it was only when Sage closed the door behind me I realized there was one more person in the room. Olena, Charlotte's mother, sat in a chair, looking as weary as her father, if less willing to bend. Charlotte's eyes looked back at me from her mother's lined face, the beautiful older woman appearing worn out by the revenge drive of her son. And though I knew she supported Danilo's need to avenge Yana, it seemed even Olena had grown tired of the fight.

Not so Danilo. Grief radiated from him still, feeding his rage, a burning, coiling monster in the core of his soul.

I reached for him with magic but he was too far gone. Sadly, wishing I could do more, that I'd been able to alter this outcome, I retreated.

"Your presence is no longer welcome here," he said, gruff and wolfish, his animal rising to elongate his jawline, to color his eyes.

"You need to get one thing straight," I snapped at him, poking him firmly in the chest with one finger. "I come and go as I please. Just try to stop me."

Even Charlotte winced at that. Okay, I really didn't think that way. Of course I honored other people's privacy. But this was huge and he was being an asshat.

Danilo didn't back down. "I've already informed Council Leader Svennson of your intrusion," he said. "Leave or face the consequences."

He reported me to Femke? Okay, this had gone way too far.

"What the hell are you thinking, telling normals about us?" I hit him with power this time, shoving him back into the small table. His mother scrambled out of the way, but I didn't care she was almost caught in the crossfire. She was part of the problem as far as I was concerned. "Do you realize what you've done? I could report you, Danilo. And me breaking down your throne room doors will be the least of your worries."

Guilt rose in his eyes, his face twisting with resentment, so much bitterness I was amazed he didn't choke on it. "It was their price," he grumbled.

Price? For what?

Charlotte moved before I could, slamming into her brother's chest with both fists, fury like I'd never seen on her face. Oleksander looked away, grief twisting his expression and even Olena looked ill.

What had Danilo done?

"I needed their cooperation," Danilo said, voice cracking and warbling in the face of his sister's fury. "Their network. To find the bastard who killed Yana." He sagged as Charlotte's face paled and drew tight.

"Dani," she snarled. "What did you do?"

"He indebted the werenation to the mafia once again," Oleksander said with defeat in his entire body. "All for the sake of vengeance."

TWELVE

I don't know what I was expecting, but that answer wasn't it. Sure, the arrests and charges of drug trafficking and human sales were damning, but I never considered Danilo might do something so reprehensible. Partnership, sure. Slavery? Never.

Guess I was wrong. Charlotte's reaction happened so fast, and I was so stunned by the revelation Oleksander shared, she was already beating her brother with her fists by the time I understood what happened.

"YOU BASTARD!" Charlotte's wolf emerged, her voice dropping from a shout to a gravelly cry, claws appearing, tearing through the velvet robe Danilo wore. I suppose I should have been shocked he didn't fight her, instead just stood there and let her attack him. Nor that his mother and Oleksander simply stared, mute, hurt as Charlotte's body twisted in the need to turn wolf.

But, she didn't. Instead, a moment after the beating began she stepped back, away from him, human face returning, panting air out past her flushed, red lips filled with color compared to the paleness of her face.

"Traitor," she said, all the anger rushing out of her. "You enslaved our people for what, Dani? For a dead woman who would hate you for doing it in her name."

He flinched as though that hurt more than the physical blows, but his anger didn't return. It was as though his grandfather's statement took all the fight out of Danilo.

"Think of your people," Charlotte said. "Of what we went through to free ourselves." She sobbed once, more out of frustration than the need to cry. "Think of your own children, Dani. What you've delivered them into!"

"I KNOW!" He roared at her, the pressure of his power shaking the room, though Charlotte stood her ground before him, unfazed, unafraid. "I know." Danilo's shoulders sagged, but the rage had returned to his face, the burning need for revenge now as much a part of him as his wolf. I feared he'd never be free of it now. "And yet, I'd do it again. I won't stop until Piotr Wilhelm is dead."

Charlotte shook her head, hands over her mouth, eyes staring, tearing up. She turned from her brother toward Sage who offered his open arms. I glared at the wereking, heart pounding, heavy with so many emotions I could barely tell what I was feeling.

"You've endangered all paranormals with your selfish actions," I said, jabbing a finger toward Iosif who cowered in the corner. He squeaked at the attention, jowls shaking as he tried to back up further against the immobile wall. "For a vampire that very well might have been destroyed by the Universe itself." I didn't know that, hoped it wasn't true. Because that would mean Sebastian and his family were also gone. But I needed ammunition, to break the stubborn and hurting wereking out of his dark pit of despair. "Was enslaving your people and exposing all of us for a futile search worth it, Danilo?" I really, really wanted to hit him.

"They will die for what they did." Spit flew from the corner of the wereking's mouth, splattering the front of my jacket as he lunged toward me. I stared him down while his muzzle grew, wet nose quivering within a hair's breadth of my skin. His hot, panting breath washed over my face, sharp teeth clacking shut as he licked his heavy jowls with his thick, pink tongue. Madness shone in the wolf staring through his eyes and I wondered, then, if I'd missed something. If Danilo was more damaged than we'd thought by his years as a full wolf, trapped inside the furred form and without his humanity to guide him. He hadn't heard a word I said.

"No," I said, softly and kindly, heart breaking for him and his family now, knowing what Femke would be forced to do. "You will, Danilo."

He snapped his teeth in my face. "You can't report me if you're dead."

I sighed heavily, the last of my compassion for him washing away as the three alter egos inside me rushed forward, ready to tear him apart. An empty threat, he must have known that. And told me his own claim to have called for Femke was a lie. If he'd turned me in for intruding on his territory, she'd be here by now. And he wouldn't be tossing around his plan to murder me.

"You're really threatening me?" I wrapped him in the power of the maji, rainbow magic glistening, sparkling. Danilo licked his chops again.

"You threatened first," he said.

I shrugged. "Just stating fact," I said. "I really wish you hadn't done this, Danilo. We had other options. If only you'd let me help you."

He backed away, then, shaking his wolf-like head, the beast retreating until he was just a man again.

"If you'd saved her," he said, gruff and full of blame. "But you didn't."

"Neither did you." No way I was taking the full brunt. He needed to accept this wasn't anyone's fault.

Danilo's shoulders twitched. "No one did," he whispered.

"And now your children will not only be motherless," I said, "but fatherless if the WPC decides this is an offense punishable by death. Surely you knew that."

He didn't respond. Not to me. Instead, he turned on his sister. "Sharlotta Moreau," he said, "I hereby banish you from the werenation and forbid you or the mongrel you mated with from encroaching on my territory." His voice sounded calm, almost level. What the hell was Danilo thinking? He'd truly gone mad. "For as long as I'm wereking, you are not welcome here."

Oh, dear, my vampire sighed, soft and sad. *He's protecting her.*

By pissing her off? I stuttered over the truth as Charlotte's face crumpled. She reached for her brother but he turned his back on her and she let her hand drop.

By sending her away, my vampire sent, *and cutting her off from him he leaves her free to take the throne when Femke comes for him.*

Damn. Damn, damn, damn.

Danilo looked up, a moment of sanity returning. "And you, Sydlynn Hayle," he said. "Get out."

There was no further conversation to be had, clearly. He'd made his bed. I could talk to Femke on his behalf, maybe find a way to keep him from the noose or stake or however they decided to cut his life short. But Danilo was well aware, from the steady stare he gave me, his time was limited.

And also told me he wasn't giving up his throne without a fight. I wanted to beg him to release his people, at least, so they wouldn't be caught in the crossfire. But he had work to do, I could see it in every line on his face, in the way his hands twitched at his sides. And he would not stop on his useless mission to find a vampire long gone until we made him stop.

I could have, right then and there. But this was a job for the World Paranormal Council. As impulsive as I was, even I knew better than to just deal with this without giving Femke and her Council members a chance to handle it. As hard as it was, I turned my back on Danilo and went to hug Oleksander.

Come with us, I sent to the old werewolf, knowing what he'd say before he answered.

I cannot, he sent, mental voice aching with sadness. *I must stand with him and protect our people, if I can.*

Why didn't you come to me? Now my anger was aimed at him, suddenly. This was a train wreck.

I am a werewolf, Oleksander sent as he held me at arm's length and looked down into my eyes. He hadn't changed since we'd met the first time, in a quiet house on the outskirts of the coven town, Yutsk. Except he seemed broken, at last.

Sage left first and I followed, jerking Iosif along behind me. I waited for Charlotte who lingered one long moment, looking around at her family. Olena finally turned her back, hands over her face. As though that motion triggered her release, Charlotte spun on her black booted heel and marched past me, her face impassive.

By the time we reached the front lawn of the werepalace, Charlotte's empty expression had settled into icy calm.

"He will destroy our people for his stupid revenge," she said, crisp and precise, not a trace of accent in her voice. "He must be stopped."

Not wanting to think about the kind of damage this was doing to my friend's soul, I pulled open the veil and stepped through, hoping Femke could find a way to make this all go away.

THIRTEEN

There was a time I wouldn't think twice about just popping into Femke's office without even a toodly-do. We just had that kind of open relationship. But the last little while had left us strained and uncomfortable around each other, so I erred on the side of polite and sent her a gentle nudge to let her know Charlotte, Sage and I were on the way.

She welcomed me instantly, though with a touch of distance that still made me sad. I wished there was a way to repair the damage we'd done to our friendship. And we might find one, yet. But neither of us, it seemed, were prepared to be the bigger person and let everything go. Until that happened, I feared we'd continue to have this awkwardness where once there'd been only support and confidence in each other.

I still thought she was the best choice for the job as

leader of the World Paranormal Council, no matter the cooling off between us. And though she'd poached my husband both from my mother and from me, I also admitted he was the perfect person to lead her Enforcers. Didn't make things any softer between us, though.

The veil parted before us in the hall outside Femke's office. I let my gaze settle on the harbor below the towering office building, the mix of cruise ships and old Chinese junkets giving Hong Kong's Victoria Harbor a flavor of new and modern mixed with culture as old as organized mankind. I loved this city, the vibrancy and busyness of it, though I rarely had time to explore. Maybe one of these days I'd bring the kids and we'd wander the markets, the streets among the bustling and hurried people who lived here.

Right. Because my life allowed for relaxation and fun. Yup.

The large, smoked glass door swept open, a slim young Asian woman in a prim, gray suit bowing to me. Xue's slick, black bob barely moved as she gestured for me to enter the office past her tiny form, the faint scent of lotus so exotic I inhaled it and caught Charlotte's nostrils flaring, too. She spun toward the cowering form of the Russian mafia man we'd somehow dragged along with us despite the mess we'd left behind—yes, I admit, I forgot Iosif was even there. One jab of her finger in his face and a second at the floor and he nodded, rooted in the spot. I was quite certain if Charlotte never came back for him Iosif would remain there until he could no longer stand.

Femke's office ceilings soared overhead, a far cry from her old world paneled wood retreat at Oxford in London. This skyscraper was the epitome of ultramodern with ergonomic white furniture and a low, ebony desk stretching an impossible width along the long end of the space. Femke rose from her matching black chair behind it, back lit by the skyscape behind her through the wall of tinted glass that did nothing to block out the rising sun. I shook my head at the time zone shift messing with my mind and went to greet her.

I paused a half a step at the sight of Quaid rising from another chair, only then realizing he was there. Why hadn't I felt him in the room? He was so rigidly blocked from me, even the thread holding us together hummed in sympathy. My husband was getting good at hiding from his wife. And that made me nervous.

My lips wanted to smile, but his face seemed grim, brows furrowed, those delicious chocolate eyes dark with something they'd been discussing so I chose to go for professional. I nodded to him instead, though I did go to his side and gently squeeze his hand before greeting Femke who circled her desk to offer me a quick embrace.

At least she thought we were back on hugging terms, as stiff as it felt. I'd take it.

"Sorry to interrupt," I said as Femke smiled at Sage and Charlotte in greeting. "Early morning for you two."

"Not at all." The tall, stunning blonde Leader's blue eyes seemed as troubled as my husband's, but she was as gracious as ever, gesturing for us to sit. "Late at night for you." Charlotte remained standing, though Sage, ever practical, sank into one of the white chairs. I waved Quaid down into his own seat, spinning to pace a little, my favorite pastime when I was troubled.

"This can't be good." There was no humor in Femke's voice as she sat on the edge of her desk, her deep blue pencil skirt hugging her slim knees, long hands folding over her arms when she crossed them on the soft silk of her white blouse.

"When do I ever bring good to you?" I meant that as a joke, but choked on it. Because it was true, damn it. Femke's full lips parted, a protest, maybe? But I shook my head at her and sighed.

"I think this is Charlotte's story to tell." Quaid arched an eyebrow at me as my werefriend grimly launched into her stoic telling of what her brother had done. Amazing how collected she managed to be, honestly. I'd have been throwing things and yelling if it was my sibling who screwed over my entire race.

Thank goodness my sister, Meira, had her priorities straight and her own people to manage.

Femke didn't comment until Charlotte finished her

few, succinct sentences. The sadness on her face tightened into resolve as her hands dropped to her sides, bracing on the top of her desk as she spoke.

"Charlotte," she said. "I'm so sorry." Simple, clean. But authentic, touching. Piercing, really. Reassuring me yet again Femke was the perfect leader to protect us all.

My werefriend's lower lip trembled ever so slightly, enough to tell me Femke got to her. But when Charlotte spoke again, her voice was steel. "I need your help," she said. "We must save the werenation."

Femke nodded, jaw jumping before she offered a small, sad smile. "You know what I'm going to ask you," she said.

Charlotte's head jerked from side to side. "Don't do it, Femke."

My heart crushed slowly in my chest as the WPC Leader stood and crossed to my werefriend. Both hands settled on the blonde werewolf's shoulders, the slightly taller Femke looking down with her icy blue eyes into Charlotte's own deeper shade. The rest of us might as well have not been in the room, a soft cocoon of emotion wrapping up the pair and keeping them bound to each other, early morning sunbeams shining on them like a spotlight. I held my breath as Femke sadly spoke.

"Charlotte Girard," she said, "you have a second identity, one you hoped to avoid. But you are also Princess Sharlotta Moreau. The World Paranormal

Council would ask you to step up and do your duty. To take the throne of the werenation and save your people."

Irrational, this sudden burst of hate for Femke. It wasn't her fault and I certainly wasn't expecting to feel so passionately about the issue. Charlotte was a grown werewoman, after all. She made her own choices and didn't need me to protect her. But the girl in me that still railed against being bullied, being told what to do, being pushed into a corner despised Femke for hurting my dear, dear friend and forcing her to make a choice about the people I knew she adored.

Hypocrite. I'd been as big a bully to Femke.

Charlotte remained rigid, unbending, and I knew her answer long before the burst of fury toward the WPC leader faded.

"I decline," she said in a voice that rang with conviction.

Femke sighed, dropped her hands, but didn't frown. She just offered that same, sad smile. "You have another plan, then? Because, I will tell you, for his actions Danilo must be held accountable to the WPC. He's put not only the werenation at risk, Charlotte, but every single paranormal race. And our mandate is to protect those races, especially from normals." Charlotte nodded, though she seemed suddenly unsure.

"I can't." Her strength seemed to run out of her, desperation surfacing, horrible fear. I unconsciously reached for her, but her wolf blocked me. Sage surged to his feet as Charlotte spun and ran from the room. He waved me off and followed his mate, leaving a heavy, horrible silence behind.

"You had to ask." Quaid's deep voice finally broke the quiet. I wanted to snap at him, to shut him up. But he was right and my reaction was as irrational as my fury toward Femke.

"I suppose." Femke's eyes met mine. "Though I'm sure there are those who would disagree."

Gulp. Did she feel my anger toward her in that instant of rage? I truly hoped not.

"Charlotte understands the stakes," I said. "She'll either change her mind or come up with an alternative. I trust her."

Femke nodded. "As do I," she said. She turned to Quaid who stared at me like he didn't believe a word I said. I refused to meet his eyes as she addressed him. "We must act, and as quickly as possible, if carefully." She rubbed at her eyes with stiff fingers, shoulders sagging, though only for a moment. She had to be carrying a ton of weight with her and my heart went out to her with empathy, dispelling the last of my temper. Like me, Femke could only do her best with what she had. "Please begin preparing our forces and contact the territory and race leaders."

Quaid nodded and left, brushing past me with the

barest touch to my hand. A gesture of warmth or a mistake? I had no idea and I was suddenly too tired to care. I sank into a chair beside Femke as she did the same, one foot bobbing in a shining black high heel over her crossed knee.

"We can never seem to catch a break or our breath, can we?" She stared out the glass over the waking city, though from the pensive look on her face she wasn't seeing a thing.

"Breathing is for wussies," I said.

Femke laughed, though it really wasn't that funny, a deep, throaty sound. Her eyes sparkled with it as she turned to smile at me, the first genuine smile I'd seen on her face in a long time. When her hand lifted and reached for mine, I took it, squeezed her fingers with a lump in my throat.

"I'm sorry," I whispered.

"Me, too," she said.

Was that really all it took? Felt like it. The bubble of tension between us burst, our power connecting, stronger than ever. The healing we'd begun on the steps of the werepalace not even a week ago finally completed, leaving not even a scar behind.

Amazing what genuine regret could do between true friends.

Femke kept her grip on me as she spoke. "Damn him, Syd." My mind drifted to Quaid on impulse before realizing she wasn't talking about my husband. Okay, so I still had issues to work out with a certain stubborn ass. Me. Femke's manicured nails bit into my skin just a little as her grip tightened. "He's forcing us to take him out. He knows this is the only result to his actions. The whole thing is bollocks." I loved her English accent melded with Scandinavian flair. Her pale, blonde hair shimmered as she shook her head, ivory skin white against the spots of pink anger on her high cheekbones. "This is a massive step, a huge test for such a young organization." The WPC was barely months old. "Acting against a sovereign ruler of a paranormal race could make or break this Council."

"But what other choice is there?" We couldn't just let Danilo continue to instigate a war with the vampires while informing normals about other races. Especially normals as hungry for power as the Russian mafia. Not to mention lacking in anything resembling morals.

"I had no idea he'd gone so far." She sat forward, both feet landing on the floor, hand slipping free from mine as she clenched them, elbows resting on her knees. The light coming through the tinted glass made her pale eyes transparent.

"You've been watching him." Of course she had.

"Maksym." Charlotte's friend was paired with Isabelle Wilhelm, a vampire sympathizer.

"You realize Danilo would have cut Maks out of the

know." I didn't have to tell her that, chewing my lower lip against my harsh words.

Femke shrugged. "I figured he'd at least be able to give me some advanced warning. But I should have known better. He's been lost since Isabelle disappeared with the rest of her blood clan." Damn it, of course. I forgot she would have been part of the mass exodus to who knew where of the Wilhelms. In fact, I was sure the only reason Sunny and Uncle Frank were still with us was the fact the Empress severed their ties to the Wilhelm family.

We might not see eye to eye on much and had a bit of a love/hate relationship, but I would always thank the Empress for her inadvertent protection of my family. I just wished I knew how to keep them safe.

An issue for another time. My brain simply couldn't keep all the balls of stress in the air at once and not shut down.

"You've done everything you can," I said. "More than most would have managed. But, it's time to act." I paused, guilt rising. "I really am sorry, Femke. This is my fault." Not Danilo, no. But the position she was in.

Femke turned and smiled at me, a girlish smile with a gleam of joy in her eyes. "I was so angry with you at first," she said. "Until I finally admitted you were right. I love this job, Syd." She stood, stretched, and I joined her as she went on. "It took me a while to embrace it. But I can't imagine not being here." She gestured around her. "With all of this in my head." Her long fingers tapped her temples. "As stressful and maddening and sometimes horrible as it is, it's also exciting, full of passion and people I adore." She reached out and touched my cheek with her fingertips. "And I see so much progress. I'm part of something I never imagined I would ever be witness to. So, please, stop saying you're sorry." She closed the distance, looking down into my eyes, hands on my shoulders as she'd done with Charlotte. "Because I want you to know I'm not."

I hugged her, so hard I heard her ribs creak. Femke didn't protest, just clung on as firmly. It took me a long moment to swallow back the tears threatening but I finally won. As I pulled away at last, I realized she was as emotional, eyes glistening, voice thick as she spoke.

"Quaid," she said.

I shook my head. "He's going to kick ass," I said.

She laughed, coughed through her mix of emotion and joy. "He already is." Her gaze lifted over my shoulder and I half turned before she strode past me while I stared into chocolate brown eyes. "Excuse me a moment." The glass doors swished shut behind her, leaving me alone with my silent, watchful husband.

He observed me from the open space just inside the doors, body tall and stiff under his black robe. What was wrong with me? I wanted to run to him, to hug him as hard as I'd just hugged Femke. To heal this breach between us. But something held me rooted in place, struggling with fear and love and the magic binding us together.

Quaid finally moved first, taking long strides until he was at my side. I did hug him then, though I felt his continuing tension.

"Guess I'll make the first move," he said. And kissed me.

Normally his warm lips and hot breath and the feeling of his body against me made me melt. But all I could think of, standing there in his arms with his mouth on mine, was the words he'd just said.

When we parted, he was frowning. "What's wrong?"

I shook my head, a small core of hurt awake and aching in my chest. "Is that how you think of me? Unbending? That you always have to be the one to break the ice?"

Quaid didn't answer, jaw flexing. What was going on in that handsome head of his? The longer he stayed silent, the more the hurt grew.

"Syd," he said at last, a groan more than a word. "We don't have time for this right now."

While I knew he was right, that we had more important things to think about, my heart asked me how could anything be more important than me and Quaid?

I let him go as he turned and headed for the doors,

just as they swept open and Femke returned. Her open, almost hopeful expression faded and I could only imagine the look on my face—and her need to make sure everything was all right between my husband and me— wasn't what she'd been aiming for. Regardless, as Quaid nodded to her, all business, she took the hint.

"It's going to take some time to assemble the full Council." I could tell from the frustration in her voice there were those who were dragging their feet. And I hardly blamed them. Who wanted to be in on a decision to take away the power of one of their fellow leaders? Especially witches, who were notorious for waffling. I'd run into their reticence enough times over the years it was hard not to sigh and roll my eyes at Femke.

"Are you sure it's a good idea to wait?" I didn't want to challenge her on this, but time was of the essence, in my opinion. "You know he's got to be fortifying against us right now."

"She knows that, Syd." Did Quaid really just chastise me in front of Femke?

Oh, *hell* no.

The Council Leader waved him off. "We have to do this by the book," she said. "As much as I'd love to send you in there to mop up this mess for me—and I would, if I thought I could get away with it—if the WPC is going to stand as an organization for paranormals, by paranormals, we have to make sure we do it together."

I was all for mutual culpability, but damn.

Just damn.

I didn't envy Femke one bit, yet I put her here. Time to trust my choice completely.

FOURTEEN

My kitchen groaned with an overabundance of testosterone when I crossed the threshold from the back hall and onto the tile. Stomach clenching ever so slightly in response to the three grinning faces of the Zornov brothers and the sly sarcasm of Simon, I crossed immediately to an empty seat and sank into it. Sassafras watched from his perch in the middle of the table, amber eyes swirling with magic, though he didn't seem agitated.

I had to take that as a good sign.

Apollo, on the other hand, almost bounced in his seat while I rubbed with tired vigor at my burning eyes. When had I slept last? The sky was just beginning to brighten, though I knew it would be full morning soon. I'd only just left the midday sunlight of the other side of the world, disoriented by the lack of the same here in Wilding Springs. Just as well. Full daylight would have made me cranky with its happy cheer.

Stupid sunny morning.

Not to mention the fact any time Apollo was excited about something, I got nervous.

"We found him." The words blurted from his lips, handsome face childlike in his glee. Owen grinned in turn, Simon's foot tapping on the edge of the table from where it crossed over his knee.

"How awesome for you," I said in my driest tone. "And I'm sure whoever he is, he's thrilled by this state of affairs."

Apollo rolled his eyes, but his smile didn't falter. "No biggie," he said. "Sorry to bother you. We'll go." He started to stand, gaze sparkling with good humor.

Owen sighed at his brother, waved him back down into his seat. "Long day?"

What part of me showing up at dawn had they missed? I shrugged and tried to focus. They wouldn't be here on a whim. "Just tell me the deets," I said.

"She wants deets." Simon's tone cut, thin and brittle, but without true animosity.

"How about this for details." Apollo sat forward, teeth flashing as his smile turned feral. "We know where to find Liander Belaisle."

I gaped in shock. They what? A surge of adrenaline washed through me, driving me to my feet. We had to go. This was awesome. We'd catch the bastard leader of the

Brotherhood flat footed for once, pin him to the ground, tear him into tiny little demon-bite-sized pieces—

Owen burst my rapidly expanding bubble of excitement with a cautionary glance at his overenthusiastic brother. "Well," he said, drawing out the word. I sank back to my chair, hope dashed, irrational anger for getting me wound up aimed at Apollo. "That's not entirely accurate."

The elder Zornov sat back, arms crossing over his chest with a snort. "Close enough," he said.

I took a long moment to gather myself, to shove down the swirling mix of emotions threatening to take over. I felt Sass's magic slip around me, supporting me. My demon snarled and spun in fury, Shaylee deep breathing past her need to smack Apollo silly while my vampire just hummed in displeasure.

I have no idea if he caught on to my struggle or not, but Owen certainly did. He leaned forward and squeezed my wrist, anxiety in his eyes.

"We have a plan to find him," he said.

"Not." I snarled. "Close. Enough."

Got Apollo's attention that time. His arms dropped, hands landing on the table top, smile failing. Only Simon's smirk remained.

Hear them out, Sassafras sent.

My nostrils flared, I just couldn't help it. *Sass.*

Trust me, even if you don't trust them. His eyes flared with magic.

Fine. Whatfreakingever.

Blackness surged behind me. It was a testament to my irritation I didn't even turn around to find out who emerged from the dark tunnel. Okay, so I had a good idea it was one of three people, all of whom I cared about very much. When Piers collapsed the pathway and folded his tall, thin body into the chair next to me, I barely grunted in greeting.

"Idiot," he said, shaking his head. "You knew I'd run off and try to find Mother and fail miserably." The faint glint of annoyance in his gray eyes barely survived his good humor. "Thanks for letting me make a fool of myself yet again."

"If only you needed help," I said.

Piers laughed, looked around. His face went from amused to curious in a flash. "Walked in on a bit of a mess, have I?"

I shook my head, sitting back in my chair, Owen's hand falling free of my wrist. "Trying to decide if these three are jerking my chain or have a point to their story."

Syd. Seriously. When had I lost all sense of adventure? I really needed sleep. Crankass.

"Thing is," Apollo said, more subdued this time, though he leaned forward again as though unable to contain all of his enthusiasm for their plan, "we're almost one hundred percent sure we know where."

"Well, ninety-nine percent," Owen said.

"Seventy-five, minimum," Simon added with a grin.

Great.

"But there's a better way to track Belaisle and make sure we don't lose him this time than just plowing our way into the place and trying to catch him by surprise." Apollo blanched before shaking his head. "Not that... I didn't mean..."

Piers laughed, prodded me with one finger. "Bull in a china shop syndrome I believe it's called," he said.

"You'd know," I shot back before returning my attention to Apollo. "Agreed," I said. "Just spit it out, would you?"

"Easiest way to get under Belaisle's skin," the older Zornov said, "is to become Brotherhood."

Become...

I blinked as my mind spun sideways, my alter egos all holding their breath.

"That." I stopped. "That's brilliant."

Apollo beamed at me as I broke the stunned moment holding me in place.

Why hadn't I thought of that?

But the weight of Piers's disapproval was so strong it turned me around to face him. His face, now dark and shadowed by worry, old anger, told me it wasn't such a great plan after all, at least in his estimation.

"You'll be killed," he said, the bluntest I'd ever heard

him. "Within moments of contact. And I won't condone throwing your life away."

The snappish, cranky feeling holding me in thrall broke as empathy won yet again. "You've tried this before?" Of course, the Steam Union must have. Now who was the idiot?

Piers looked away. "We used to attempt infiltration on a regular basis," he said, big, thin hands clamped on his thighs, shoulders tight under his gray longcoat. He turned and met my gaze, his full of hurt. "You're well aware of one of the many failures, Syd. Demetrius Strong was lost to us for years because he thought he could succeed where so many were laid low."

Apollo drew a breath, lips parting, but I didn't give him a chance to interrupt. Instead, I held up one hand, cutting him off, magic reaching out to the other familiar souls who carried the darkness with them.

Gram. I felt her first. Of course. Though the loss of her witch magic had meant the severance of the connection between us, I think my grandmother and I would always be able to find each other somehow, some way, no matter what happened. Her magic felt cold to me now, the devouring darkness of sorcery a far cry from her old power, but her heart was the same heart, her soul the same soul.

Girl. She sounded a little sleepy. *Trouble?*

Question for Demetrius. I sent an apologetic burst of

magic with my words.

Here. I caught an embarrassing glimpse of the two of them in bed. Thank goodness for sheets. I clamped down on the vision, blocking it out as Gram laughed in my head.

Need a favor, I sent. *Can you come over?*

Be right there. Demetrius's magic left me. The man I'd first known as the leader of the Chosen of the Light had been insane, driven by, it turned out, the control of Liander Belaisle and the Brotherhood. I knew he'd been tortured and thralled by them, but I had no idea he'd been captured trying to become one of them.

"You've seen the best case scenario result of an attempt," Piers said as I returned my attention to the kitchen. "Most young Steam Union sorcerers who try it are captured immediately and either killed or turned into damaged souls driven to work for the Brotherhood."

If he called what happened to Demetrius best case, I disagreed. Had things gone badly for me and Belaisle won on the Stronghold plane, if Demetrius had remained lost, broken, he would have preferred death.

Good thing we won, I guess.

The kitchen door opened only a moment later, Gram and Demetrius stepping through. I waved them over to the last empty seat. His white curls mussed, Demetrius took it, Gram perching in his lap with casual ease, not a speck of self-consciousness showing on her face.

"You got us before breakfast," she grumbled. "Better be coffee."

Mmm. Coffee.

Piers stood, heading for the counter, face still dark. "Allow me," he said. Probably wanted the distraction. I wasn't arguing with him. Coffee was a good thing.

"The guys think it's a good idea for Apollo to pretend to be Brotherhood and join Belaisle's crew as a way to track him down." As serious as the topic was, it was fun to drop bombs like this every now and then. It was so hard to shock my grandmother, ye old pretender of knowing everything. The look in her wide, blue eyes was almost worth it.

"You young fool." She leaned over the table and gently slapped Apollo's cheek. "Where did the damned death wish come from?"

His lips flapped, fish like, as he tried to speak, but Demetrius wasn't allowing it. For the first time in a very long time, I saw anger on his cherub face. And deep hurt, still unhealed.

"I beg you," Demetrius said, voice shaking. "Abandon this plan before you suffer for it."

"You don't get it," Apollo began.

A coffee mug slammed down on the counter behind me, spinning me around and cutting off the Zornov brother. "No," Piers spit out through clenched teeth. "You don't get it." He jabbed the air in Apollo's direction with a spoon. "Do you have any idea how many people we've lost to the Brotherhood? My own uncle..." Piers looked away, shoulders bowed. "He was the last of our order to try it. He and Mum had this grand plan, guaranteed to work." Piers's laugh was hollow, angry. "When he turned up dead, Mum blamed herself and made it illegal for anyone to try again." His gray eyes laced through with black a moment as his sorcery struggled against his old hurt. "It broke her, Syd." He wasn't seeing anyone else anymore, despite addressing me directly. Piers was talking directly to his own pain. "It was the beginning of the end of my mother."

At last I understood Eva Southway's spiral into darkness. Guilt and regret were old friends of mine. I could see if I caused the death of my sister, Meira, I might be in a similar place as Eva. But if that was true, why was she working with the very organization that killed her brother?

"If you would just listen." I turned back at the anger in Apollo's voice. Simon's grin was a smirk, eyes narrowed behind his glasses, Owen looking almost apologetic.

"Indeed," Sassafras said, tail swishing. "If you're quite through you may want to hear what the boy has to say."

"Thanks, Sass-man." Apollo's anger disappeared as fast as it showed up, his mercurial nature always baffling to me. But when he met my eyes again, his were serious, calm. Almost mature. So, I kept my lip zipped and nodded. Apollo's flashing smile nearly changed my mind. Would he ever grow up?

Would I ever want him to?

"You're all worried about me, I get it." He bobbed nods around the room. "I really do. But, I have an in none of those Steam Union dudes had." Apollo winced slightly as Owen jabbed him with a worried look on his face and a glance at Demetrius. "No offense, D."

"None taken." Demetrius's mild voice soothed even me. "Though, I'm curious to know why you think you have a better chance than countless others?"

"Simple." Apollo sat back in his chair, all triumphant. "I've done it before."

This time, the mug shattered on the tile behind me. I heard it break, ignored it, locked on Apollo and his grinning face.

"You *what?*" Demetrius's words breathed out of him in shock and awe.

Apollo smirked at all of us before going on, taking his time to put on his little show. "What you don't know," he said, "is that when Trill and Owen found me, I wasn't on my own." He shrugged, casual, cocky. "I was a Brotherhood initiate. And if I decide to go back to them, I'd just be reenlisting."

FIFTEEN

Demetrius's power was already on the move before I could react to Apollo's revelation. I followed, tied closely to Gram who did the same, pursued by Piers whose incredulity colored all our magic.

But, the moment I dug into the Zornov's power I saw it, felt it, really for the first time ever. I guess I never really looked that closely or it would have been obvious to me. Guilty of underestimating Apollo, I understood as the faint taint of the Brotherhood waved in gallant response to our probing, sinking into my seat with a grin growing on my face.

"Well, I'll be damned," I said.

Someone loomed behind me but I didn't turn around as Piers leaned forward, fists on the table, intense gaze locked on Apollo. The Zornov brother's cocky attitude faded a little at the fierce focus of the Steam Union leader's attention.

"Why," Piers snarled, "am I only hearing about this now?"

"Because," Simon said, cold, precise. He'd changed so much from the sweet and innocent boy I'd once known, the trials and pain he'd been through turning him into a sharp edged weapon of words and intelligence. "You never asked." He flared with sudden anger, aura shifting visibly into red, making me wonder if the boys had been tampering with him, waking his sorcery, though I felt nothing of the sort from him. "Instead, you chose to ignore the value of one who's given so much to your little cause." My lips pursed in my own temper at the wording, and because Simon was right. But was he talking about Apollo or himself?

I waved off Piers's angry retort before he could give it voice. "Enough," I said, a little surprised my sorcerer friend actually listened. He straightened his tall body, glaring down at the table while I turned to Gram and Demetrius. Let Piers brood. I wanted to take advantage of this sudden opportunity if we could.

"What do you think?" Gram didn't meet my eyes, her own gaze on her husband while the sweet faced sorcerer mused with a mix of surprise and fiery joy growing on his face. His cherub smile beamed at me as his mind finally settled.

"I think," he said, turning that thousand watt grin to

Apollo, "this boy is a genius and we have a way to bring down Liander Belaisle once and for all." He shifted in his seat, Gram with him. "Apollo already carries the power of the Brotherhood with him, a power that has never been broken before."

"Ever?" I found that hard to believe, no matter what Demetrius had been through. When he turned his blue eyes to me, I shivered inside at his angry intensity. But it wasn't aimed at me, more within himself. How tortured was he still by what he'd gone through?

"The power that claims your sorcery when it's first woken is the power that owns you the rest of your life." Demetrius swallowed visibly, hands shaking as he clasped them around Gram's waist. "That's why turning Brotherhood sorcerers never works. Once your power is claimed, it's done."

I had no idea, though it made some kind of odd sense. And reminded me of something Piers mentioned in passing the day we rescued Simon from his Brotherhood captors. Being the first magic, the connection would be far stronger than the elemental magicks. Almost like blood clan allegiance, only unbreakable. "But Apollo." I turned to the grinning Zornov.

"That might be true under normal circumstances," he said. "But I don't think any Brotherhood initiate—or Steam Union, for that matter—has a sister and brother combination like mine." He rattled the tips of his fingers on the table top in clear excitement. "I can feel them, still. The pull of the Brotherhood. That's why I knew I was still hooked up to them. But it's faint, distant. The connection to Trill and Owen is stronger." He flinched from mentioning his sister, but barreled on. "They claimed me a long time ago. And now they think they own me."

"What if they do?" I wasn't taking chances. No way could I allow first Trill, then Apollo, to betray me, especially in his case when such betrayal could be prevented. Who was to say he wouldn't go to the dark side if Belaisle got his claws into Apollo again?

But the older Zornov was shaking his head already. "That's the beauty," he said. "Trill, Owen and me, what we have, cancels out everything. It's the only way I was able to leave in the first place." He was making sense, at least. "Otherwise I never would have been able to desert those that claimed me." Okay then. "I know I can do this, Syd."

Demetrius was nodding his agreement. "It will work," he said, the most optimistic I'd ever seen him. And he'd know, wouldn't he?

Maybe, Gram sent to me just as I was about to grasp at hope. *My darling husband might be right. Or, he might be diving headfirst into wishful thinking.* Her worry tempered my excitement. *He's never fully recovered emotionally, though he has magically and mentally.*

Understood, I sent.

And yet, Sassafras interrupted, *we would be foolish to ignore such an excellent opportunity.*

I raised an eyebrow at the silver Persian. *Since when are you all for risking the lives of others on a maybe?*

Since we have no other options, he snapped. *And despite your lack of interest in Apollo, I've been watching both Zornovs carefully. He's equal to the task, Syd. You give him less credit than he deserves.*

Consider me chastised, I sent, meeting Apollo's eyes. "We can't just send you in there willy nilly and hope things work out," I said, good sense rising to the fore, for once.

"No one has ever turned a Brotherhood sorcerer before," Demetrius said. "Not completely, thanks to the initial bond. The same with a Steam Union sorcerer. Only torture and brainwashing techniques work, and only the Brotherhood are willing to resort to such methods. Considering the results are less than reliable and typically lead to madness, the subject is rarely of much use." Was he thinking of himself just then? Because he had turned out to be of great use to Belaisle along the way. Still, his devolution to insanity before his mind was restored was proof enough. "Apollo's bond to his siblings makes the chances of this working much higher than we could hope for. But, Syd is correct. You need some kind of safety net."

Apollo shrugged, gestured at Piers. "You're working with some young recruits," he said.

Gram and Demetrius both turned to look up at the Steam Union leader. My grandmother's grim expression told me she wasn't a happy camper and when she spoke I understood why.

"You said you'd expelled them," she growled, blue eyes simmering with darkness.

Piers shifted his shoulders under his longcoat. "I'm being careful," he said. "They are allowed nowhere near the rest of the Steam Union."

Demetrius shook his head, face sad and troubled. "You risk repeating the mistakes of your predecessors," he said. "You know better, Piers. They can't be turned, not now."

"I'm not my mother," Piers snapped, far too defensive for my liking.

"Not just her," Gram shot back. "Don't be an idiot, Piers."

Something I should worry about? I sent the message directly to Gram, shielding it from everyone else.

We'll handle it, she sent, short and cold.

Okie dokie.

"Let's say we do this," I said, changing the topic back to the plan at hand. "I see one giant obstacle to your success."

Apollo nodded. "You're worried Belaisle will kill me

on sight because he knows my family and yours are aligned." I really had underestimated him. Shame on me. There was more weight and seriousness in his expression than I'd ever seen before. "I've thought this through for weeks, Syd. Ever since Belaisle attacked the covens. Even before then." He shifted in his seat, face falling ever so slightly. "I should have brought it to you sooner," he said. "I could have saved a lot of lives."

"Not your fault." I reached across the table and took his hand, Sassafras between us, purr rising softly from his furry body and linking me to Apollo with the cat's sympathetic, supporting power. "Don't ever blame yourself for that, please."

He nodded, swallowed hard. "I know I can do it, Syd." His fingers squeezed back. "Belaisle knows by now Trill betrayed you. He was there when she stole the hand of Creator out from under both your noses." He had to remind me. "I can use that to my advantage. And we have more ideas on how to keep me safe while I'm under cover." He glanced at Simon who nodded slowly. "Hear us out?"

I let go of his hand, sitting back again as Sass's purr rose in volume before falling away.

"I'm all yours," I said. For the first time, but not the last. No more prejudging the people I cared about.

That's the Sydlynn Hayle I raised, Sass sent.

"Our plan is twofold," Simon said. "With magic and

PATTI LARSEN

with technology." He gestured to Owen who pulled out his smartphone. The screen moved, wobbled as he set it on the table. I looked down into it and pulled hastily back as the top of my head appeared in the image. A look up had my eyes following Apollo's finger to one of the buttons on his shirt. "Button cam," Simon said. "Has a built in unidirectional microphone to cut out surround sound and will only pick up on Apollo's voice and someone standing close to him." I returned my attention to Simon whose smug smile almost triggered my anger again. "We can track him using GPS with the same device, though I'll be implanting a number of chips on him—in clothing, one under his skin—to ensure we don't lose him if one is discovered or destroyed."

Piers sank back into his seat, coffee obviously forgotten. "The Brotherhood is notorious for using technology to their advantage," he said. "What makes you think they won't suspect Apollo is bugged?"

"Because," Apollo said, "they might use tech themselves, but they would never think we were smart enough to do the same." He shrugged, hands spread wide on the table, eyes locked on mine. "We can do this, Syd. I just need you to trust me."

I looked away from him a moment, gathering my thoughts. This would mean sending Apollo into the Brotherhood fold on his own with only a flimsy electronic tie to safety. "There are no promises we can get

154

you out if you're in trouble," I said.

"You'll know where I am at all times," he said. "I know you'll have my back. But I won't need it, I swear. It's time we had the inside track on the Brotherhood for once."

Amen to that. I turned to Simon. "You trust this tech?"

He shrugged. "Best your money could buy."

I scowled, though it amused me. "You have your own fortune. One I gave you, if I recall correctly."

Simon's expression didn't change. "More fun spending yours," he said.

Sigh.

"Even if Apollo's power is blocked," Owen said, pointing to the phone, "we can still find him and pull him out on a moment's notice."

"And what if the Brotherhood blocks the tech?" Piers reached for the phone, wiggling his fingers at the camera on Apollo's chest.

"Doesn't work that way," Simon said. "They'd have to find them and destroy them."

Wait a second. "Are you saying technology is stronger than magic?" Whoa. What?

Simon shook his head, brow furrowing. "Not stronger," he said. "Just different. I'm surprised you didn't realize that already."

I'd honestly never explored it before. Never thought

to. From the odd, almost shaken looks on Gram, Demetrius and Piers's faces, they hadn't either. But very good to know.

"I've been experimenting with Owen," Simon said. "Attempting to augment tech with magic. So far, we've run into glitches. The two don't seem to understand each other. But we're working on it."

"As for the equipment," Owen said, "we've already done extensive testing." He'd always been the most serious of the three despite his younger age. "But you're welcome to do your own."

"That would be wise," Demetrius said. "I would be happy to do so since I have the most experience with the Brotherhood." His blue eyes met mine, clear and hopeful. "But I am optimistic. This could work."

I had to tell Femke. But I wanted to make sure Apollo's infiltration succeeded first. She had enough on her plate to worry about. Or did she? This was important. And the last thing I wanted was to piss her off by acting autonomously on such a huge issue.

Decisions, decisions. I finally nodded to Apollo whose grin flared with triumph.

"Demetrius is the lead on this," I said, as the three young men high fived each other. "If he approves the tech route, you're good to go." I really had to tell Femke. Didn't I? I wanted to bring her a victory. Damn it, Syd…

"Agreed." Apollo stood abruptly. "Let's get to work."

I held up one hand, to rein him in a moment. "Before you run off half-cocked," I said, "let me talk to Max." Knowing Belaisle had a way to track me when we sought out the pieces of Creator still rankled. The thought he might be using ordinary, normal tech to do it hadn't crossed my mind, not really. But now it seemed a real possibility.

"Simon, I need a favor." And damned quick. Anxiety woke up and knocked on the inside of my temples. "Check my house, Mom's office, see if you can find any bugs planted." Was that where Belaisle was getting his info from? Was I really that far detached from the normal world, despite my former desires to the contrary, I'd missed the obvious?

Damn it, was Belaisle listening to us right now?

But Simon was shaking his head. "Already scanned your place for devices," he said. "I'm happy to do the same for Miriam at Harvard. And Femke, too. But, from what I can tell, you're clean."

I wasn't sure if I should be pissed he was in my house doing tests without telling me or grateful he thought of things I failed to.

Settled on happy and left it alone.

That meant, though, we still didn't know how Belaisle was tracking me. My drach friend and I had been planning to set a trap and see if we could make our enemy's life an unhappy place to be. If Apollo succeeded, it might make more sense to use him to help set up the trap rather than going after Belaisle directly. That way, we wouldn't be walking into a situation of the Brotherhood leader's making, but one of our own. And minimizing the risk I put Apollo in made me more comfortable with the whole thing.

The more I thought about it the more excited I grew until I stood as well.

"Let me know the moment you're ready to go," I said. "We'll be ready to back you up."

Apollo nodded, the others rising to join him. Need compelled me to reach out to the Zornov brother.

I swear, I sent, not meaning to be so intense but unable to stop myself. *If anything happens, I'll come for you.*

His eyes met mine, confidence rippling down his power to me. *I know*, he sent. *Why do you think I'm so sure this will work? Sydlynn Hayle has my back.*

I let him go, shivering on the inside, hoping his faith in me wouldn't be proven false.

SIXTEEN

I let the boys leave, waiting until the door closed behind them before turning to Gram and Piers. Sassafras shifted from his perch on the table and into my lap, paws resting on my forearm as he faced off with the two remaining sorcerers. I was glad Demetrius left with the Zornovs and Simon, not only because that meant the three would have some supervision, but I wanted to ask Gram more about how far she believed Demetrius would go for revenge and if it might be an issue we had to add to the mix.

But she was already on to me before I could ask. "He'll be fine," she said, flicking her fingers at me. "Sorry to worry you."

I tapped my own fingertips on the tabletop in answer to her dismissal. "You know I love Demetrius," I said. "But if there's potential for a problem here, Gram, I need to know about it."

"He won't put the boy in danger," she said, heat and barbs in her words.

"I never said he would," I said. "You're the one who suggested it."

She drew a hot breath but Sass beat her to it.

"One step at a time," he said. He turned his glowing gaze to me. "Femke?"

So I wasn't the only one thinking she needed to be notified. "I'll tell her," I said, sighing inwardly at adding to her stress. But it was the right thing to do.

"If it makes you feel better," Gram said, "Demetrius and I will take shifts with Simon watching over Apollo."

That did make me feel better. "Thanks," I said, sending her a burst of love. Her anger dissipated and she answered in kind.

Sorry, girl, she sent. *Touchy times.*

You never have to apologize to me, I sent.

Piers shifted beside me, drawing me away from Gram's mental grunt of disagreement.

"I can't believe it, Syd," he said, eyes downcast, voice deep but soft. "Mum would never join the Brotherhood."

Of course his head was still there. Gram raised an eyebrow at me while I reached out and took his hand. Sassafras's purr rose, amber magic touching him as the cat had done with Apollo only a few minutes before. I never fully appreciated Sass's ability to soothe until I understood what his purr really meant. And though there were times when I was younger I wished he'd mind his own business, it was moments like this I believed Sassafras was truly the heart and soul of our family, the mesh of love and commitment that held us all together.

"Piers," I said, leaving the way open for Sass to do his thing, "we don't have solid proof of that yet." I sent the conversation we'd had with Iosif to Gram in a tight burst of power. Her only acknowledgment of receipt was a subtle tightening of her jaw. "Until we do, no conclusion jumping, agreed?"

He looked up slowly, gray eyes troubled. "It's hard not to," he said.

"It's fully possible your mother is working with Belaisle," Gram said, tone harsh. I scowled at her but she ignored me. "For her own reasons. You really think Eva would ever bow down to Liander or the Brotherhood?" Piers's shoulders lifted a little, expression turning thoughtful. "If anything, she's playing him. And has her own agenda." *Which worries me more than collusion,* Gram sent privately. *We have no idea what she's up to.*

Agreed, Sass sent. Leave it to him to poke his nose into a conversation meant only for the two of us.

Piers's attitude slowly changed until he finally shook his head, pale, blond hair rippling over one shoulder as the silken stuff cascaded across his lap and to his knees. "You're right, of course, Ethpeal," he said. "Mum must have plans of her own." He smiled, weak but present. "And no matter the situation, Apollo will uncover the truth. If this plan of his works."

But even Piers sounded slightly optimistic.

"Tell me we're not sending him into a death trap." My heart clenched in time with the sudden roiling of my stomach.

Piers sighed. "I don't know," he said. "But if anyone has a chance it's a former initiate. And Apollo is clever enough, streetwise enough, to take care of himself."

Even Piers seemed to know the Zornov brother better than I did.

"Now," Gram sent, "tell us what's happening with Femke."

I grimaced. "Yeah," I said. "That." And filled her in on what went down with Danilo. Piers remained quiet while Gram's expression darkened, blue eyes black as sorcery crawled through the irises.

"She's playing a dangerous game," Gram said.

"No game," I said. "She has to act."

Gram nodded, brusque and abrupt. "I realize that," she said. "But if even one of the paranormal races—if even one of their leaders, sub leaders, anyone of authority—speaks up against Danilo's removal, the WPC could have a war on its hands."

I hadn't thought of that. "We'll just have to make sure that doesn't happen," I said.

Gram's grim expression didn't help much. "You're planning to beat submission into the opposition, are you, girl?"

That was uncalled for. "I just meant Femke has to have her ducks in a row," I said.

"And you as her bully on the side." Gram shook her head, waving me off as I protested. "Don't think I miss seeing where this could go," she said. "And how easy it would be for Femke to use you to her own ends. Just, be careful, girl. Promise me." Her blue eyes stilled.

Like that was going to happen. To this point, Femke had basically told me to stay the hell out of things. So Gram's fears were unfounded and more than a little paranoid. Still, I nodded and looked away, unwilling to argue with her.

Gram stood and came to my side, kissed my cheek before doing the same to Sass, then Piers. "I'm going to go check on Demetrius," she said. "You two look like crap. Get some sleep." I watched her go, not sure if I should be offended or amused, while Piers grinned at her with a weary expression.

"Always a delight, Ethpeal," he said as she closed the door firmly behind her. When he turned his tired smile to me, I smiled back.

"Ain't that the truth," I said.

We chuckled together while Sassafras kneaded my arm with both paws and purred.

"There's a spare bed upstairs if you want to crash," I said, barely able to speak past the sudden, jaw cracking yawn that seized me.

Piers yawned in turn before laughing. "Might take you up on that," he said.

I was halfway to my feet, picturing a hot shower and a collapse into bed, when magic grasped for me and Femke's voice broke through my weariness.

Syd, she sent, firm but worried, the massive power of the WPC washing over me. *I'm sorry to trouble you, but I need some backup.*

I'm there, I sent, all tiredness vanishing. Piers surged to his feet beside me, his own face dark with worry as I let him into the conversation. *Just tell me what you need.*

The image she shared made me gasp. Werewolves fought vampires on a mountain peak, Enforcers attempting to come between them. It wasn't until I jerked open the veil, Piers at my side and Sassafras held firmly in my grip, I realized Gram's warning might have merit after all. But I couldn't say no, not when so much was at stake.

SEVENTEEN

The air tasted purer, if thin, as I lurched out of the veil and onto a narrow dirt path edged in scrub brush. Sunlight poured down from the crystal blue sky over the towering, square edged castle carved into the side of the mountain. For a moment I felt the disorientation of confusion as I looked past the struggle before me and around at the barren peak, the surrounding mountain range of gray stone. But no, this wasn't the Empress's palace in Nepal, but another of a different shape and bulk. Its design felt Aztec to me, though the knowledge vampires seemed to enjoy hiding away on mountain peaks was reinforced by the sight.

The surge of Enforcer magic, encasing the entire mountain top in power, pushed me forward and into the fray. I formed my own magic into a wedge shaped shield, shoving with sheer force toward the center of the strife.

Werewolves spun from their focused attempt to break through the front line of vampire defense, leaping toward me, only to rebound from my wards. High pitched yelps of pain echoed from the rock as they crashed into stone and bounced away. The small human contingent—vampire protectors, clearly—had formed a small knot near the temple-like structure's entrance. Black haired and muscular under their brown skin, the tiny human army seemed even more fearful as I approached the dozen or so Enforcers who circled Femke and formed a seal against the attacking werewolves who threw themselves—and their focused magic—at the barrier between them and entry into the castle.

From the torn and bloody bodies scattered before her, Femke had arrived too late to save all of the human servants, though her magic now refused the werewolves further entry.

I have this, she sent. *But there are too many and most of my Enforcers are elsewhere collecting the Council Leaders*. Her mental voice was grim, if wound up with adrenaline. *A little help with the werewolves would be excellent right about now.*

You got it. I could have played nice, asked them to stop. There were over a hundred of them, all in full wolf form, snarling and pacing around me, looking for an opening. I loved Charlotte and Sage and a few other weres I knew and respected. But this crew seemed bent on making my life miserable. Not exactly fearless, but unrelenting and unwilling to back down.

Screw it. Diplomacy was never my strong suit anyway. With a frustrated scowl, I called up my maji power and smothered their magic like a candle being snuffed out.

As a group they collapsed, writhing, bodies shifting from wolf shape to human. Most appeared of the same nationality as the human servants, but a handful were of definite European descent, even a few familiar faces.

Damn it, Danilo. As if I didn't already know he was behind this, he had to supply me proof by sending his own personal wereguards as backup.

Femke dropped her shielding, the human servants near collapse as she did. I crossed to her, stepping over a fallen werewolf who groaned as he rolled over onto his back. I blushed, averting my eyes from his nakedness, and focused on Femke. Her Enforcers surged forward, their power containing the fallen weres as I joined my friend, silent Piers at my side, Sass perched in my hands.

I'd almost forgotten they were there but only until my sorcerer friend joined the ranks of Femke's Enforcers, his magic draining the last of the fight from the werewolves while her forces mopped up the mess.

"Thank you for the assistance," she said formally while her mind touched mine. *Syd, this is a disaster.*

I didn't get to respond, not when a large woman in a tight, blue pantsuit joined us. She felt human, if augmented slightly, her dark eyes almost black, hair falling in straight, shining silk to her knees.

"Our thanks," she said, voice gruff, full lips pursed as she glared at the werewolves being gathered up into a large group of mostly unconscious, naked bodies. "Our queen will deal with these when she wakes." Her accent told me she was educated in the States, though from her dark skin and Hispanic features she was likely a native of wherever we'd found ourselves. Somewhere in South America I was guessing from the height of the sun in the sky.

"They are our responsibility now," Femke said, smooth but insistent. "Your queen can bring her grievance directly to the World Paranormal Council." The Enforcers began to vanish one at a time while the woman glared, taking werewolves with them. When the human servant tried to protest, Femke stepped between her and the disappearing attackers. "We deeply regret any loss you have endured and would like you to reassure your queen this matter will be dealt with the utmost care and severity to the guilty parties. I can assume this attack was unprovoked?"

Of course she was going to agree. Silly question, even if it wasn't true. But the woman surprised me with her answer.

"There have been tensions growing between our people for many days," she said. "And atrocities on both sides. But this attack was unexpected." Owning up to it?

Good for her. My respect leaped about a million times as she went on. "We are most grateful you answered our call personally, Leader Svennson."

"It is my responsibility to ensure the safety and preservation of all paranormals," Femke said, with so much poise and self-deprecation I was again reassured I'd pushed the right person into the job. "You must trust me now to continue to do so."

The woman bowed at last, though from the unhappy look on her face she was thinking ahead to how she would explain her actions to her vampire master. "The moment she wakes, my queen will contact you," she said, before spinning to return to the rest of her people.

Femke exhaled, though her face remained composed. "That was close," she said. "We can't afford a challenge right now."

True that.

I'm going with the Enforcers to contain these weres. Piers waved at me and Femke from where he stood with one of the last groups. We watched him go as my husband made an appearance out of a flash of blue fire. He settled on the ground next to Femke before speaking.

"All rounded up," he said, brown eyes meeting mine. Shining with something that looked like... what? Joy? Was he having fun, the jerk? Then again, I felt my fair share of adrenaline and excitement at the most inopportune of times so I could hardly blame him. We were made for this kind of work, weren't we? Or we wouldn't have survived this long.

"Excellently done, Leader Hayle," she said. "Efficient as always."

Quaid's tiny smile was all the response she got. But I knew that look, how self-satisfied he felt just from that simple expression. And had a thought.

"I'm borrowing your Enforcer Leader," I said, offering him my free hand, Sass still curled against my side. I passed the furious cat off to Femke with a soft touch to his mind. He relented, eyes sparking as he glared at me. Quaid took my fingers in his after a quick glance at Femke who nodded. He really needed her permission, did he?

Knock it off, Syd. Jealousy doesn't become you.

"You have a plan?" Femke's pale blue eyes held a question.

"Just figured one of us should head to Nepal and put out fires," I said. "And considering you get all the boring paperwork stuff and I'm the action hero," I flashed her a grin to show her I was kidding, "I figure I'd borrow your boytoy and trot off to make sure the Empress doesn't get her knickers in a knot."

Femke's snort made it through her attempt to remain serious, blue eyes sparkling as Quaid scowled at my irreverence. "Permission granted," she said. "Proceed."

I saluted with fake enthusiasm before taking Quaid's

hand again. "Keep a line open," I said as I tore at the veil. "Just in case we need a rescue."

Femke laughed. "You mean just in case you start a war and I have to save you from yourself?"

My grin was wicked. "More like mop up the mess I leave behind. You might want to be on standby, just in case." I arched my eyebrow at my husband who sighed and rolled his eyes. "Ready for a train wreck?"

Quaid didn't comment.

Smart man.

EIGHTEEN

Maybe I should have gone the diplomatic route and appeared out of the veil on the mountain side of the gates to the Empress's palace. Perhaps it would have been prudent to knock, to ask for an invite inside, or, at the very least, to make my presence known in some way before barging in on the most powerful vampire on our plane.

But that just wouldn't have been me, now would it?

And, in all honesty, part of me worried if I did try to be nice and apologetic and crap she'd make me fight my way in. Considering the fact I was already tired and more than a little cranky all over again, thinking of doing a werepalace on her ass wasn't an idea I was willing to entertain. Instead, to cut to the meat of the matter, I tore open the veil in the Empress's personal bedchamber and dropped Quaid and myself into the thick of things.

Shielded, naturally, while his power prodded mine in irritation.

One of these days, he sent in a tight and angry burst as all eyes in the dark chamber fixed on us, *you are going to get someone killed. Since you're immortal, it won't be you.*

Whatever, I sent. *I have your back.*

Quaid's blue Enforcer fire licked out beneath us, feeding my shields. His magic usually felt all warm and bubbly, with the same chocolaty overtones as the heat in his eyes. But even my demon—his most staunch ally— seemed put off by the harshness of his contact.

You were right not to take the leadership role of one of the Councils, he said before cutting off my thoughts in return and speaking.

"Empress," he said, bowing at the waist while I fumed in his general direction. "I am Enforcer Leader Quaid Tinder of the World Paranormal Council." He was *who?* Last I knew he was a Hayle witch. Since when did he start using his parent's old surname?

Empress Moa didn't seem to give a crap who he was or that my anger toward him was suddenly more important than Danilo and the near disaster I'd left behind in South America. Quaid had barely finished speaking when the scrawny, ancient vampire threw herself at us. With supernatural speed and motion, she stopped just shy of my shielding, landing at a crouch, wasted body dressed in a simple, white shift, leaving her yellowed skin exposed at knees and elbows. When she snarled it was aimed at me, teeth elongating, beaded black eyes flaring with pinpoints of white fire, back hunching as the spirit power inside her pushed her seemingly frail body into a primeval shape.

"Sydlynn Hayle." Her normally youthful voice hissed my name. "You have one heartbeat before you die."

My vampire essence reacted before I could, even with my temper burning hot. She lashed out through the shield, slamming Moa into the stone floor of her chamber. I spotted her slim, black clad servant, Jiao, circling and watching with a dark, blank expression, and knew she was likely as dangerous as the Empress. But Quaid would have to deal with her if it came to a physical attack. My vampire was far too focused on Moa to allow me to do anything else but hold the writhing old undead woman still.

"Moa," my vampire said in her cold voice, through my lips, "you will be still. Or I will retrieve the heart of spirit I gave you, the power that sustains your life, and I will let you die at long last."

She stopped moving, though her eyes glared with hate. "Release me." Calm, the edge gone from her tone, the oddly young sound of her voice more level than the fury in her face.

"You have brought this on yourself," my vampire said. "Your duplicity and plotting has created a monster in Danilo Moreau. And you alone are responsible for what happens next."

I wasn't sure that was exactly true—blaming Moa for everything felt off. But when the Empress didn't argue, I sighed inwardly.

She plays a dangerous game, my vampire sent, sadness whirling with anger and a hint of pride. In a way, I understood. Moa was sort of like a daughter to the essence living inside me, the first vampire. Would I feel the same about Ethie if my daughter's soul became twisted? Probably. *She has been powerful and unchallenged for far too long. And though I don't wish to humiliate her, or create an enemy of her, Moa must understand her actions cannot be allowed to alter the fate of this plane.*

"You're behind Piotr Wilhelm's attack on the werewolves," my vampire went on. Damn her. Moa didn't answer, though she did stand as my vampire released her. She waved off her minions who hovered behind her, their fear clear on their faces to a vampire, to a human servant. They might be afraid of their mistress, but it was likely they'd never seen anyone subdue her before.

She'll never forgive me for that, my vampire whispered.

A problem for later. I prodded Moa with power as Jiao joined her Empress, standing just behind her, dark eyes locked on me. She was the only one of Moa's people who showed zero fear of me. I caught a whiff of magic from the young woman as I dropped my shields completely.

Are you out of your mind? Quaid tried to rebuild, but I squashed him.

They have to see we're not afraid of them, I shot back. *And this is how I do things. If you don't like it… be still or go back to Femke.*

"You have no proof," the Empress said, snapping her fingers, not meeting my eyes. One of her servants hurried forward, a slim boy holding out a thick, black furred robe. When it engulfed her, it just made Moa look all the more miniscule, though her massive power was in clear evidence as she probed and pushed against me.

I shrugged, letting her feel my irritation through my magic. "Femke and the Council need proof, Moa," I said. Leaned on her with power until she flinched ever so slightly. "I don't."

Quaid sighed in my head. *You're a disaster*, he snapped.

I was seriously regretting bringing him along.

"The werewolf king has attacked my people for the last time." Moa's beady eyes watched Quaid for a moment and I realized she sensed our division. Clever old creature. "No matter the source of his insanity, he must be stopped." Her magic stroked Quaid's flames, spirit power enticing. "We will deal with this matter ourselves."

"No," he said, shoving her aside, shocking me with his strength. I almost cheered, so surprised by his ability to avoid her thrall I grudgingly let go of my anger toward him. "You will wait for the WPC to deliberate and then announce their decision on the matter." He crossed his muscular arms over his chest, black robe rippling, blue fire flashing around him. "Until then, you are forbidden from approaching Danilo Moreau and any of your vampires caught engaging in battle with werewolves will be arrested."

She writhed in place, fury flaring, sparks of white cascading from her as her temper flashed. "YOU DARE!" Her power hit him full in the chest and, for a moment, I stood rock still, heart pounding, too slow as the spirit magic began to devour him.

Only to be burned away by blue flames. Quaid's magic grew, pushed outward, pulsing with the combined force of all paranormal races, fed by the Council itself. I had never truly understood the vast reserves of Enforcer power, why it was so different from ordinary witch magic. But I caught a glimpse in that moment that made me wonder if there was an end to the energy of it.

"I dare." He didn't raise his voice. Quaid didn't have to. Moa backed off, sullen, fury still burning visibly inside her. "Danilo Moreau will meet justice, Empress. But justice must be allowed its evolution. For the sake of all paranormals."

This isn't over, she sent directly to me before turning her back. I let my jaw unclench as the tension in the room eased somewhat, though my teeth ground together a moment later as she spoke over her shoulder.

"Jiao." The young woman in black bowed abruptly. "You will go with these," she gestured at us as though we were unimportant, a side note to her anger. "And you will be my voice with the Council."

Jiao's face twisted briefly, as though she were about to protest. I caught the subtle push of magic the Empress forced on the girl before Jiao bowed again and strode toward me. Her dark eyes were empty of emotion, face a plain, uninterested mask. But her magic churned a moment, the oddness of it reminding me strangely of Max before she shut herself down.

"We will keep you apprised," Quaid said. "The Council thanks you for your patience and assures you we are treating this issue with the utmost concern and speed to avoid further conflict."

The Empress didn't bother responding. I should have stayed, talked to her further, maybe tried to diffuse the situation with her. But Quaid was already lighting his blue fire and dragged me—the staring Jiao still facing me—along with him.

NINETEEN

Femke was waiting for us outside the Council meeting room when Quaid and I arrived in Hong Kong. From the grim expression on her face he'd either filled her in on what happened or things weren't going well on her end. She greeted me warmly and personally, so I could only assume the latter and was actually bummed. At least if she was mad at me that meant there might be progress made.

"Welcome," she said to Jiao after Quaid introduced the young woman in black. Jiao simply nodded her head and left us as Femke instructed her secretary to lead the Empress's envoy inside. Femke faked a little shiver when she turned back to me, voice low. "Is it just me or is there something... off about that girl?"

"Max gave me the impression he knows more than he's saying," I said. "So, yeah."

Quaid's scowl told me he was about to give me

trouble, but I saved him the effort.

"You're probably not going to like how I handled the Empress," I said.

Femke just waved me off. "What I don't know won't hurt me," she said, before gesturing for Quaid to leave us alone. That surprised me and, from the shock and faint irritation on his face, him, too.

Quaid left us with his back straight, shoulders stiff, entering the Council meeting room alone. It took everything I had not to go after him and shake him, just to see if sense fell out. Then again, I wasn't exactly the poster child for manners these days so I guess we were perfect for each other after all.

"Tell me." Femke lowered her head, blonde hair falling across her cheeks, blue eyes sharp and intent. I sighed and filled her in while she listened with her usual focus.

The WPC Leader finally sighed when I finished and shrugged. "There are times when diplomacy doesn't work, Syd," she said. "Especially with certain personages who think themselves above the law." That was a bit of a dig. She was right, though. I'd break the rules anytime, anywhere, if it meant saving the Universe from disaster. "Having someone like you to handle those moments of need is invaluable." She stared hard, lips thin. "And I understand the implications of even asking and of you acting. So, we do our best to find balance and hope.

Instead of damage, we do good."

"Agreed." I let my shoulders sag a little, the fight with Quaid troubling me more than ever. He knew I didn't play by the norms others did. There were times I just didn't have a choice. Or did I? From Femke's mixed approval and her own previous battles with her need to act versus her need to trust the system hanging over us both, I wondered if I was only making things worse.

Femke hugged me quickly before motioning toward the door. "I know you're not officially a part of the Council," she said. "And I would never ask you to use your influence to my benefit. But I could use your help in there, Syd."

Gram's warning bubbled up while I shoved it aside. Femke was asking, not ordering. And I wanted to help. I nodded. "After you, Council Leader."

I took a seat at the edge of the room, next to Varity Rhodes when she gestured me over. I almost grinned as she unceremoniously shooed one of the other Enforcer leaders from the chair next to her, sending the tall man scrambling for another place to observe. The old witch pulled me down beside her, eyes flashing, wrinkled, long fingered hands still as strong as ever no matter the deep lines on her face or the iron gray of her now close cropped hair. I missed her bun, but the severity of her new haircut made her look fierce.

"Can't stand that twat," she said loud enough I

choked on a laugh and caught the glare from the retreating leader. The volume of her voice made me wonder if she was having hearing problems or just didn't give a crap. Probably a mix of both. "Tell me you're going to go kick Danilo's ass so we can all go home."

I squeezed her hand as Femke shot me a subtle stare to silence the old Enforcer leader, though my mother, only a few feet away, seemed amused by Varity's bluntness instead of embarrassed.

"I'm sure the Council will come to the proper conclusion," I said, just as loudly as Varity while silence fell over the group when Femke rose to her feet, "and take the necessary steps to ensure peace."

I looked up to find everyone staring at me. And though a tiny blush crept up my neck, I held my confidence in my whole body. They needed to know this was their responsibility, that no one would be coming to save them. Mom nodded ever so slightly to me while Femke addressed the Council.

"Thank you for coming," she said to the various leaders who watched her with trepidation and concern. The mix of witches, human vampire servants and even a Sidhe lord held their peace for the moment. It troubled me the only two werewolves in attendance were Charlotte and Sage. Soft footfalls and a grunt later and I had a demon cat in my lap as Femke went on. "We are faced with a difficult choice and must deliberate the consequences before making our final decision on the matter of Danilo Moreau and his leadership of the werenation."

From Quaid's attitude you had some fun in Nepal. Sassafras's voice snapped with annoyance.

Sorry to leave you behind, I sent.

He sniffed, his focus on me, clearly, as Femke continued to address the gathering in diplomacyspeak. I found my eyes glazing over and was just as happy to have him to talk to. *What did the Empress say?*

The usual, I sent. *Hate, anger, revenge, blah blah. But I think we pinned her down as the source of Piotr's attack in the first place.*

Interesting, Sass sent. *Have you talked to Sunny?*

A stab of guilt reminded me I hadn't. The former Wilhelm Queen and my uncle's wife had fallen off my radar since she and Uncle Frank were removed from the thrones of the Wilhelm Blood Clan. Shame on me, though I'd been busy. Was the fact they were no longer powerful keeping me from seeing them as important?

Stop that, Sass sent, as grumpy as I was. *They've been quiet. I'm sure Sunny and Frank have their reasons.*

Okay, panic now. *They're okay?* With the disappearance of so many vampires in the last little while thanks to the damage to the spirit magic of our plane, I worried they might one day just poof.

Of course they are, Sass sent. *I'm keeping an eye on them. I meant they have their own issues to work out. And I'm sure Sunny is putting two and two together when it comes to the Empress. It might be a good time to drag her out of her funk and enlist her aid.*

Great idea. I stroked his soft fur, sighing inwardly. *So many balls in the air.*

That's why you have me, he sent. *Now, pay attention. Femke's talking, you know.*

I snorted behind one hand as I refocused on the Council Leader.

"My attempts to speak personally to King Danilo have been rebuffed," she was saying. Finally getting to the point. "And since further pushing would have resulted in the need to assault the palace, I chose retreat in favor of this deliberation. I will take no action, nor condone it, through this Council until we have all agreed on what needs to be done."

"There are those of us who are confused why we are even talking about this." I didn't know the dark skinned man on the far side of the table, but he felt human, tinged with spirit magic. A vampire servant, then. "This clear attack on our vampire queen cannot be allowed to stand."

A few mutters greeted his words, his accent reminding me of Africa. And seeing Council Leader Ife Maalouf nod in agreement told me I had the right territory. It was odd for witches to take sides, so I guess I should have been heartened to know she wasn't sitting on the sidelines. But I didn't want this to turn into them against us and knew Femke didn't either.

"We cannot lose sight of facts, however." Everonus always gave me the creeps. The Sidhe Lord who joined the Council, with the full backing of both the Unseelie and Seelie living on our plane, stroked his long, black hair with one jeweled hand, silver eyes speculative. I wasn't a huge fan of the Sidhe in the first place, at least not the full born who called our plane home. The few I'd met along the way had rarely given me reason to trust them, their slippery natures and manipulation of normals enough to stir my anger—and that of Shaylee, despite her heritage. But Everonus had a distinctly Seelie feel to him, despite his claims to the contrary. And because I trusted Shaylee's mother, Aoilainn, about as far as I could toss her skinny fairy ass, his role on the Council was harshly suspect.

No way did he just appear out of the woodwork. His presence smacked of Aoilainn trying to gain some control or presence in our plane when she should have been minding her own damned business in the realm.

Femke nodded to him and motioned for him to speak. Everonus stood, crisp black suit hugging his tall, slim frame to perfection, the dark eyeliner rimming his plump lashes giving him a lush, over ripe look that just made me uncomfortable. But his smooth voice seemed to calm the watching Council as he spoke.

"Is it not true Queen Yana died thanks to an attack on her person by the Wilhelm blood clan?" No one protested. That was common knowledge. "And we sit here deliberating King Danilo's guilt and his attempt to exact revenge against the death of his wife at the hands of vampires?"

"No," Mom spoke up, crisp and clear as agreement began to sway his way. "That is not accurate." She stood herself, the picture of poise and calm that only my mother could shoulder. "Piotr Wilhelm was taken into custody to stand trial for the death of Yana Moreau. But he and his entire blood clan disappeared before he could be brought to justice." She met eyes as her gaze traveled around the room. "The remainder of the vampire race has nothing to do with the death of Yana and should not be held responsible in this manner." She finally faced off with Everonus, a faint, almost apologetic smile on her commanding face. "I would be the first to support Danilo Moreau in seeking justice against those who wronged him. But not in encouraging genocide by a grief stricken madman who seems bent on embroiling all of us in a race war."

I do hope Charlotte forgives me that, Mom sent.

She knows the stakes here, I sent in return.

"In my opinion," Mom said, voice dropping its commanding tone, turning deferential, "Danilo Moreau has led us to the brink, not only of a war between paranormals, but discovery of our existence by normals. Such exposure alone is reason enough to have him arrested and brought before a tribunal to explain his actions and answer for them."

Everonus opened his mouth but it was Charlotte who spoke before he had a chance.

"As the sole representative of the Moreau family present," my werefriend said, "I stand with the Council against my brother's actions. Whether justified in his attacks on the vampire blood clans or not, his blatant disregard for the safety of all paranormals must be addressed." She stepped forward, nodding to Femke, face a mask of nothing. I reached out to her with magic but she blocked me, the cold, stoic Charlotte façade keeping me at bay.

Femke nodded back. "I can only guess at how hard it is for you to speak against your brother," she said.

"Or not at all," Everonus said, though quietly. Still, I had the impression he wanted everyone to hear. Charlotte turned to glare at him and he shrugged elegantly. "You stand to take the throne if your brother is deposed."

"Charlotte Girard," I spoke up, stressing her last name, "has already turned down that throne on numerous occasions. You might want to get your facts straight before you open your mouth."

Syd. Femke's soft chastisement was just my name, but it was enough. Damn it.

Sorry, I sent in a huff. *But I'm not sorry.*

"I stand corrected." Everonus bowed to me, though

there was enough cynicism in his tiny smile I knew he was mocking me. Whatever. Asshat Sidhe, just try to stir up more trouble.

Femke addressed the full Council, her power touching each and every one of us in the room, decisions makers or not. Sassafras glowed briefly with amber fire as he shifted in my lap in response.

"What say you?" She looked around slowly, meeting every eye at the table and, to my surprise, not one person turned away or seemed inclined to shirk their duty. In fact, one at a time, the gathered witches, Sidhe and vampire servants all sent their own power into the center of her magic, Charlotte's joining in the end.

Femke bowed her head, releasing them. "Thank you," she said, sad but firm. "It is decided. We shall gather a force and return together to apprehend Danilo Moreau and bring him to justice."

TWENTY

I truly intended to have a conversation with my husband about our little confrontation in Nepal but didn't get a chance. And while I was sure he was, in fact, avoiding me when I approached him shortly after the meeting broke up, I let it happen. From the grim expression on his face and the way he blocked my power he wasn't in the mood to rehash our discussion at the moment. We really did have bigger things to worry about, so I let it go.

For the time being. But the more conflict that burned between us, the more nervous I became. I second guessed my treatment of him as I joined Mom after a quick hug for Femke and Charlotte. Sassafras in my arms, I rode Varity's flames back to Harvard while I tried to decide if I'd done more harm than good in my need to control the situation with the Empress.

The only thing that saved me from turning around and running to Quaid to beg him to forgive me was the enthusiastic pair of squealing kids who tackled me the second we emerged into Mom's front room. They were supposed to be in class but I was immensely happy to discover them here. Sass leaped from my arms as my son and daughter lunged for me, their joy washing away every worry I ever had, if only for that instant it took for me to pull them against me and absorb the pure happy that was my children.

Mom's soft smile wasn't lost on me as she and Varity retreated to her office. *I thought a day off would be a good idea*, she sent. *They've been waiting for you to come visit*. I know she didn't mean to add to my guilt, but she did. Instead of wallowing and ruining the moment, I nodded to Galleytrot as the big, black hound sank to his haunches, tongue lolling out the side of his mouth.

"Nice to see you, Syd," he said in a voice like a spring thunderstorm. The scent of earth and fresh morning wafted toward me when his magic greeted mine.

"Hey, Galleytrot." I sank into the stiff cushions of the formal sofa, for once not even caring if the paintings of the previous Council Leaders stared down at me in their judging way. Ethie snuggled her little face into my neck while Gabriel perched on my knee, gentle smile his father's through and through.

"Missed you, Mom." My son's soft voice held no

recrimination but was enough to beat me firmly with the truth—I was a terrible mother. I gathered him to me, rocking them both though they'd grown well past the size it was comfortable to do so.

"I missed you guys so much," I said, choking up from the sudden surge of sadness. I was losing giant chunks of their day-to-day thanks to my responsibilities. And though I knew they were far safer here in Mom's care, out of the path of destruction as it were, I still had doubts anywhere was safe except right beside me. So hard to know which was the truth.

The door to the main hall opened and Dad entered. He had finally begun to age now he'd given up his demon immortality to be with Mom. But time just made him more handsome, adding threads of silver to his temples, a few deeper laugh lines around his incredible blue eyes. I smiled at him as he crossed to us, bending to kiss my forehead.

"Hi, cupcake," he said in his deep voice, sinking down next to me. Gabriel giggled as his grandfather tickled him gently, falling back into Dad's lap. My father, once Demonicon's Ruler, now a professor here at Harvard's Coven Hall, seemed the most content in his simple role as grandfather.

That made me immensely happy.

"Your mother back, too?" Dad rested his cheek on the top of Gabriel's head while Ethie toyed with the end of my ponytail.

I nodded, gestured at the door. "She and Varity are in a meeting," I said, sighing my body deeper into the cushions while Sassafras perched on the back of the couch behind me, amber eyes sparking.

"I take it the Council came to a decision." Dad's good mood tempered with sadness. Though my kids were smart, and the children of power, I did my best to keep the truly awful stuff out of their lives if I could. In fact, they knew little of what happened before they were born, or even of Gabriel's role in the battle of Fates. Dad's subtle questioning was a product of his agreement the kids didn't need to know how much stress we were under.

"They did, the expected one." Dad nodded in answer before kissing Gabriel's strawberry blond hair and returning my son to my lap. I watched my father stand with absolutely no desire to rise myself, to go back to the harsh reality of what faced me sooner rather than later. All in favor of sitting there with a lap—and soul—full of love in the shape of my kids.

Ethie sat up enough to meet my eyes, her little hands stroking my cheeks as her own blue gaze, all serious, met mine. She reminded me a great deal of myself, of Gram and Mom, so much so I wasn't surprised by her next question. Protecting her and her brother or not, Ethie was a Hayle, after all.

"Is the werewolf king going to die?" She didn't seem all that upset by the prospect. That should have bothered me, maybe. Except if she was to lead the Hayle family someday it made sense she was strong enough even now to know the truth and ask for it.

I hesitated nonetheless, more so because of Gabriel. Funny how I thought him weaker than my daughter, more emotional and less capable of coping with bad news. But I knew better. He seemed as interested and detached as his sister.

I really had to stop associating my son with his father. Liam didn't have the benefit of the Hayle bloodline. And was always far stronger than anyone gave him credit for. That combination meant my son wasn't the softer of the two. Just different.

"King Danilo has broken the law," I said. "More than that, he's told people he shouldn't have about paranormals. Which means he has to be arrested and put on trial."

Ethie nodded sharply, as though that truth satisfied her young leader's need for justice. Gabriel simply sighed.

"I hope his kids are okay," he said. And for the first time I really thought of the Moreau brood. Yes, I'd thrown it in Danilo's face, but the fact was hard to swallow in that moment unfed by fury and frustration. Yana's baby girl would never know her mother and, now, likely wouldn't have the chance to know her father either.

The older kids were still tiny as well. Imagine growing up knowing your mother was murdered and your father put to death because he went mad trying to avenge her?

I hugged the pair of them tightly to me while Sassafras purred in soft counterpoint.

"You two know how much I love you, right?" Tears burned, my throat aching from the need to sob, to squeeze them so hard they absorbed back into me so I could keep them safe, forever safe. "I hate being away from you."

"It's okay, Mom," Gabriel said. "We're proud of you."

Ethie nodded against my shoulder. "Everyone needs you," she said. "Not just us." My daughter sniffled softly as something hot and wet ran down my skin. I kissed her hair before she looked up, tears trickling down her cheeks. Ethie wiped at them, face turning stern. "Sorry," she said in her piping, six-year-old voice and soul as old as the earth. "It's hard, Mom. But I know I'll have to do the same thing with my own daughter someday."

That. Broke. My. Heart.

Into a million piece. I kissed her, my own tears finally spilling over. "I hope not," I whispered to her.

The kids are fine, Galleytrot sent as my sorrow threatened to take over completely. *They miss you, but they understand. You have amazing children.*

Quaid and I are very lucky, I sent, thinking with a sudden sharpness I wasn't the only absentee parent, then chastised myself for my anger. I shunted off my emotions about him and focused on the big dog watching me. *How's Gabriel been?* Since his encounter with the Order and near loss of control of the Gateway he accidentally created to the Dark Universe, my son had been unable to use his special ability.

Sad, Galleytrot sent, more speculative than worried. *But he's resilient, Syd. Far stronger than Liam in many ways. More flexible in his feelings. Still, he's troubled by his lack of ability to access his power to create gates.*

Considering my son was the means I had to find the missing pieces of Creator, I was equally troubled. On the one hand, I wanted to protect him from everything, to keep him safe and hoped he'd never again use that power. But, on the other, I knew Gabriel was my only hope of finding what I needed to save the Universe and couldn't help but feel the need to push my son when he wasn't ready.

See? Terrible mother.

Mom's mind reached for mine. She sounded as tired as I felt. *I just heard from Femke*, she sent. *We won't be in a position to move until morning. Some of the councils are digging in their heels over status.* Mom's irritation came through loud and clear. *I'll keep you posted, but until we have everyone lined up, we're stuck.*

Thanks, I sent, not minding so much. Until Sass

prodded me gently. I was actually thinking about taking the kids home, curling up for a movie afternoon, going to bed early, maybe.

Sonja, my demon cat sent sadly, ruining everything.

Damn it.

What about her? Galleytrot's rumbling mental voice shifted from soft summer rain to the boom of a thunder's roar.

I informed the black dog quickly while the kids settled deeper into my lap. They seemed content just to sit there, poking at each other and giggling while I carried on a conversation I wished I didn't have to. By the time I was done telling the black dog about Sonja's appearance and request, his agitation had reached the kids enough they sat up and looked back and forth between him and me.

I don't know if this is a good idea, Syd, Galleytrot sent at the same time Gabriel met my eyes.

"Mom?" Ethie reached out and took his hand in hers, though from the focused look on her face I think the gesture might have been subconscious. "What's wrong?"

You must tell him, my vampire sent. She'd been quiet, all my egos had. She startled me, speaking up like that.

It's his decision to make, Shaylee sent.

No decision if the woman goes missing, my demon grumbled. Offered me a few scenarios to ensure the body was never found.

Really, Shaylee sighed. *Do you never tire of such thoughts?*

My demon cackled. *All the easier to piss you off*, she sent.

Girls. They fell silent. That was a first. I shook my head and smiled softly at my son.

"Sweets," I said. "There's someone who wants to meet you."

TWENTY-ONE

I drove the minivan up the winding hill toward the hotel, my heart hammering in my chest while I did my best to keep my composure. This was the last place I wanted to be and the last thing I wanted to be doing on no sleep and with a giant mess waiting to explode on the other side of the ocean. But when I told Gabriel who it was had asked to meet him, he was instantly insistent.

"My father's mother?" His hazel eyes lit with green sparks.

"You've met her once before," I said, not going into detail. Not admitting the one and only time Sonja saw her grandson he was a baby. That he freaked out and sobbed at the sight of her though he'd only ever been a sweet and loving infant to that point and after. "You were very little." I hesitated before going on. "We don't have to do this now. But she asked to see you and you deserve to meet her if that's what you want."

"Me, too!" Ethie's typical jealousy at not being the center of attention prodded her brother who nodded and smiled.

"I want to, Mom," he said. "Can we go today?"

That's how I ended up telling Mom where we were going with a short burst of magic, asking her to turn the other cheek if Sonja and Spaft went missing. Mom's gentle hug of power in return held a fierceness to it.

If you need help hiding the bodies, she sent, *just holler.*

See? My demon prodded Shaylee as we traveled through the veil toward Wilding Springs, Galleytrot beside us and Sass firmly held in Ethie's little arms. *I come by it honestly.*

Shaylee's heavy sigh of defeat made me laugh.

That was the last moment of good humor I had. The kids both dressed quickly, without being asked, as I talked quietly with Nicci in the kitchen.

"I have no idea how this is going to go," I told her while she handed me coffee and a sandwich. I slurped the hot liquid, grateful for the boost of caffeine, the snack going a long way to stopping my rolling stomach from rumbling.

"One word," Nicci said, eyes snapping blue fire, "just one and those two will never see the light of day again."

My demon laughed.

Five minutes later, we piled into the van, Ethie

strapped firmly into her booster seat in the back, Gabriel on his in the front. Sassafras had insisted on joining us, curled in my daughter's lap, and the giant black dog loomed beside her, making her seem so tiny and almost frail in comparison.

I caught Galleytrot's glowing red eyes in the rear view as we turned the last corner and Hilltop Hotel came into view.

They are my priority, he sent, the car shaking briefly as I pulled to a stop in front of the doors. *Have no fear.*

I'm not afraid for their physical safety. I turned and smiled at Gabriel, making myself cheerful out of sheer will, as he unbuckled his belt and looked with innocent interest at the hotel.

Between the two of us, the big dog sent, hopping out into the sunshine, paws grinding over the gravel of the driveway, *we'll ensure nothing bad happens. Nothing.* The clear, blue sky was cloudless, but the echoing thunder in the distance threatened rain under the right circumstances.

I held my children's hands when we approached the front doors, Sassafras preceding us, as always. He continued on through the opening door as it swung wide, rubbing firmly against the young woman's legs who came to greet us.

"Ms. Hayle." Emmy Parsons embraced me with her arms while her power stroked mine, the family magic woken by our embrace.

"Emmy." I smiled down at the petite brunette, released her after a quick hug. She gestured for me to enter ahead of her, silver bangles clanking around her wrist, fashionable jeans and crisp white button up making me feel over dressed in my suit. I should have changed after all. "How are you?"

"I'm well, ma'am," she said with a smile. She was new to the coven, as was her husband, Daniel, and had eagerly taken over the hotel. Vacant since the Dumont family thralled the normal owners, it was nice to have it run by family, like most of the rest of Wilding Springs these days. Refugees from destroyed covens had fled to the protection of my family and I happily embraced them. Emmy and Daniel had fit into our lives perfectly, though I knew them less than I should have. Assimilating new coven members didn't seem a priority considering all the other stuff I had to deal with. Shenka's job, now in the laps of the girls.

I really had to find time to sit and chat with everyone.

Right after you solve world hunger, save the Universe and become the perfect mother. Sass's sarcasm hit the mark over and over. *Enough self-flagellation. We have a job to do.*

Sometimes he irritated me so much.

I walked the familiar hall next to the dark wood stairs with the grand railing. They'd painted, at least, gotten rid of the almost black wood and wallpaper straight out of a seventies vampire flick and traded in for soft taupe with creamy trim. It set off the dark wood nicely and gave the formerly creepy interior a welcoming, modern feel mixed with history.

"I love what you've done with the place," I said while touching Emmy's mind. *Any trouble from your Sidhe guests?*

Not so far, she sent in return, her mental touch crisp and flavored with roses. A little cloying for my taste, but she didn't overpower. *Nicci told us who they are, but gave no instructions outside of observation. Should we be wary?*

Not at all, I sent as Sassafras disappeared into the sitting room with purpose. I could feel the two women beyond the entry, their surprise at seeing the silver Persian. I only had moments before Sonja knew we were here. *Just continue to keep an eye on them, will you?*

Of course, coven leader, she sent, fully formal. *We'll await your instructions.*

I really had to sit down with her—

Syd!

Coming.

The sitting room had once been as dark and depressing as the hall. Memories of being here, of rescuing my teen bestie, Alison, from the Dumont brothers, of meeting Odette and Andre for the first time, finding out Ameline and Quaid were betrothed… so much water long gurgled under a bridge now chopped down and burned for firewood.

Still, it was eerie to walk with my kids into that room,

now painted in lavender and pale blue, half expecting the long dead Odette to smirk at me from the settee. Instead, Sonja rose from the cushions, face hopeful, her hair perfectly styled, tight dress a bit too snug for her excessive curves. She stepped toward us as Ethie, uncharacteristically shy, stopped before I did, tucking herself behind me to peek out at the woman who only had eyes for Gabriel.

Sparkling jewelry flashing in the sunlight coming through the windows, her red painted lips parted in a smile, Sonja bent forward toward Gabriel, showing far more cleavage than was good for anyone.

"Hello, darling," she said, eyes sparkling with moisture.

"Hi," he whispered, hand tightening on mine. *Mom,* he sent, a hint of panic in his voice. *There's something wrong with her.*

Galleytrot shouldered his way past Gabriel and pushed Sonja back just with his presence. She stumbled, high heel catching on the carpet, a tiny squeal escaping her. I looked up to see Spaft watching from the sofa, spindly spider legs crossed, dark eyes narrow slits.

What was she up to? I felt no exchange of power, no attempt to thrall Sonja. Whatever was going on here it was emotional, not magical.

"Galleytrot." Sonja clutched at her chest with one hand, long, fake nails scratching her sun damaged skin.

"Sonja." He sat in front of Gabriel who half turned toward me. "Long time." There was an accusation in his voice.

Sonja shrugged, a helpless gesture, face so sad I found it hard to believe she wasn't being genuine. And yet, I felt the same thing my son did. Something wasn't right here.

"I wanted to come." She spoke around the big dog, leaning sideways to try to catch Gabriel's eyes. "I just didn't think I'd be welcome."

"An excellent assumption," Sassafras said with a flick of his tail. He leaped up beside Spaft, glaring at her until she looked down with a grimace of distaste. She flicked her fingers at him, as though he were some insect she wished to shoo. Sass ignored her, moving closer, rubbing his fur against her black skirt and leaving a wad of it behind.

On purpose. The bratski.

Spaft pinched the clump between her spindly fingers and deposited it on the floor before rising to her feet.

"Sonja deserves a moment alone with the boy," she said in her cold voice. Her parchment thin skin was so pale I could see the threads of blue veins under the surface.

But Gabriel was already backing up, pulling free of my hand. Galleytrot growled when Sonja tried to dodge past him, to reach my son. I held myself still, teeth gritted, forcing my body not to react, to ignore the instinct I had to attack her and keep her from laying one hand on Gabriel.

"I'm sorry," he whispered, hoarse. "I can't." My son turned and fled the room.

"You've poisoned him against his own grandmother." Spaft's spiteful words held zero emotion, but lost none of the impact.

"I didn't have to," I said, feeling far sorrier for Sonja than perhaps I should have. She looked broken by Gabriel's rejection. "Whatever it is you two are into, he can feel it. So can I." I pushed against Spaft and Sonja both, letting my anger out at last. "And if I find out the pair of you are planning something that could cause my child even a moment of grief?" My power settled on their bodies, pushed hard until they both sagged under the weight. "We'll be having a conversation that won't end well. At all."

I turned and strode away, my daughter marching at my side. Sassafras streaked past me into the hall, the footfalls of the big dog trailing behind. Neither Spaft nor Sonja attempted to stop us and we kept moving, past Emmy's troubled pacing until we were all outside in the sunshine again.

Gabriel was already in the van, seatbelt done up. I paused only long enough to hug Emmy and thank her before helping Ethie into her seat and climbing behind the wheel.

It was a silent ride partway down the hill, Gabriel staring out the window as though enthralled himself. When he finally spoke, his voice warbled with hurt.

"That was a mistake," he said. "I'm sorry, Mom. We shouldn't have gone."

"You had to know," I said, patting his hand. "I didn't want to make the decision for you."

"You should deal with those two," Ethie said, sounding so much like Gram I glanced back at her just to check and make sure my grandmother wasn't in the back seat, too. Her scowl was far older than her little body. "There's trouble brewing between them."

I almost shushed her, though I agreed with her. Gabriel didn't need to feel worse than he did already. But my son just nodded.

"I think she wants to care about me," he said. "I get that impression, past the darkness. But she wants something more. Craves it. It's eating her alive and that's all that she can think about."

"Any idea what?" I reached for Nicci as Gabriel spoke again. *Time to kick the two out of my town before they cause trouble.*

"No." He shrugged his thin shoulders. "I don't care, either."

Galleytrot rumbled protest. "I do," he said. "Let me find out."

I didn't comment openly, but sent him a hug. The

gloom hung over us all, our silence growing as I reached the bottom of the hill and paused at the stop sign. I couldn't let this weight of darkness sit on my kids. There had to be a way to break the spell Sonja cast over them.

And then, I had a thought. A singularly brilliant—and possibly colossally stupid—thought. "Feel like a road trip?"

Both Ethie and Gabriel perked, while Sassafras hissed from the back seat.

"What do you have in mind?" His power pushed outward and I felt how firmly he held my daughter under his protection.

"It seems like today is the day for introductions," I said. "And I know there's one more person who would love to see you again."

I just hoped seeing Ameline wouldn't add fire to the frying pan.

TWENTY-TWO

Gabriel hadn't been to the vampire mansion since I recovered him from Ameline, but from the interested look on his face—a nice change from the sad brooding that gripped him during the drive—when we pulled into the long, paved lane, he remembered. He turned his hazel eyes to me with a spark of understanding, though didn't say anything while his sister kicked the back of my seat with her sneakered toes.

"Where are we?" Sassafras leaped onto the center console between Gabriel and me, Ethie straining against her seat belt to see. I usually arrived at this place through the veil, in a hurry, on a mission. Rarely did I ever just drive up and watch it appear at the top of the hill, surrounded by green lawns and trees. It reminded me just how amazing this place was, and triggered more memories than I assumed it would. Of creeping through the darkness with Sunny and Quaid in search of my demon, held captive by the then Brotherhood controlled Demetrius. Of Mom's trial, back when Batsheva Moromond found her way to becoming Council Leader. To saving Sebastian from certain death, and altering him forever.

The gravel topped asphalt crunched under the tires of my minivan as I pulled to a stop in front of the grand stairs leading up to the entry. I'd fought a battle here with my friends and family against the Brotherhood, seeking the son that sat next to me. A black night full of anger and fear and hope, when Creator's Dark Brother almost came through to our Universe, when I was certain I'd failed and Ameline's grasp on Gabriel was near complete.

So much time had passed and yet goosebumps rose on my arms as I sat there and looked up at the stone mansion, stretching out in its stately glory on the well-manicured lawns.

"Can we go in?" Gabriel's voice was hushed and low. I realized then even Ethie had fallen silent, my son's question breaking the hold the quiet moment had over me.

I unhooked my seatbelt in answer, joining my kids outside the van. Sassafras sat in Ethie's firm embrace, paws resting on her forearm as he curled his tail around her wrist. Galleytrot padded beside Gabriel, my son's hand in his thick, black ruff. I let them go ahead of me, trailing behind them, still wondering if this was a good idea, but somehow feeling the calmest and most composed I had in a very long time.

The mansion stood empty these days, aside from a few human servants who remained behind just in case Anastasia and her blood clan returned. I knew that wouldn't happen—or, at least, assumed that was the truth—but their loyalty and worry told me at least Sebastian's family cared for one another outside the connection vampire magic drew around them.

The kids waited for me at the door. I didn't get a chance to knock. It swept open, and, to my surprise, a tall, stunning redhead who reminded me of an old fashioned Amazon, smiled and reached out to embrace me.

"Chambrelle." I hugged her back as Sunny and Uncle Frank's assistant squeezed in her eagerness.

"Syd." The statuesque woman smiled down at my children, green eyes catching the sunlight and making them glow. Not even her well-tailored dress made her appear less powerful. I always had the impression if Chambrelle Strait wanted me dead, she'd manage it somehow, immortal or not. "Hello, Ethie. Gabriel." She nodded to the hound and cat next. "Galleytrot. Sassafras." The big dog rumbled a greeting, walking past her at a steady pace before she could even step aside. Gabriel followed with one of his sweet smiles, my daughter going after him, a faint squeal echoing back from inside as the two disappeared into the large foyer.

"I didn't know you'd moved in." The sunlight was warm and comforting on my back, the darkness of the interior a little too gloomy for my taste as Chambrelle closed the heavy wooden door behind me. I caught sight of the reason for my children's laughter as a tall, handsome blond swept Ethie into his arms, Sassafras protesting with a grunt of irritation. I smiled and waved at my Uncle Frank who winked back, smooching my daughter's cheek to the tune of an enthusiastic raspberry.

"We have no claim to the castle in Austria any longer." Chambrelle didn't sound all that concerned, though she kept her voice down as the stunning, ice blonde woman with the most amazing smile I'd ever seen swept out of the side corridor and hurried toward my children. Sunny barely managed a wave in my direction before she joined Uncle Frank in mauling my kids. "Since Sunny was once a part of the DeWinter Blood Clan—"

"I'm not arguing," I said as gently as I could.

Chambrelle grimaced slightly before nodding. "Apologies," she said. "You of all people would understand."

I did. And so would Sebastian. Sunny and Frank were family, though. They could have come to me. Then again, as I crossed the marble floor with Chambrelle to hug my vampire uncle and his equally undead wife, I remembered my conflict with Sunny over the Empress. I'd thought our argument cleared up, but maybe they didn't feel welcome. If they didn't, that was my fault. And would be rectified immediately.

Sunny didn't give me a chance to open my mouth, though. All worry I'd left our relationship in a mess vanished as she set Ethie back into Frank's arms before sweeping me into a giant embrace, her cool lips pressing to my cheek before she tightened her embrace into a full body squeeze. She might have been in need of a drink to warm her up, but Sunny gave great hugs.

Before I could let her go, Uncle Frank stepped behind me, now kidless, and hugged me, too. Tears leaped to my eyes, my throat seizing a moment. Suddenly, I was sixteen, lost, confused and alone. Until these two made me part of a vampire sandwich. I sank into the hug and wished, as sometimes happened, things were simpler in my life. That my dream of normal had come true and this family I loved were all just plain old people.

Liar, my demon whispered.

That made me smile before I leaned away at last and met Sunny's eyes.

"Hey, stranger," I said. "Missed you so much."

Her own blues filled with tears, but she was smiling, too.

"Dear Syd," she said, finger tips running down my cheek. She finally let her hand fall, stepping back a pace.

"You're not here to visit?" There was no accusation in her voice, just a faint question. I took her hand as Uncle Frank hoisted Ethie and Sass again, my other linking with my son who walked with us toward the side hall. Red carpet called me, the long, arched corridor's doors closed, the space quiet.

"It's time the kids knew certain things," I said.

Sunny nodded while Uncle Frank bit his lower lip. He had to be fighting an argument but knew better. He'd practically raised me, he and Sunny and Sass, while Mom ran the coven and did her best not to screw me up too badly. I shrugged at his reticence but didn't stop until I stood outside the door to the library. And the entry to the maji cavern below.

"We'll leave you to it." Sunny tilted her head at her husband who sighed and set Ethie down with one more kiss to her cheek, a ruffle of Gabriel's hair following. I stepped in and hugged my uncle one more time.

Don't worry, I sent. *I might not know what I'm doing, but Sass and Galleytrot do.*

Uncle Frank laughed in my head. *They're Hayles*, he sent. *They'll be fine.* I met his eyes and smiled. I wasn't the only one who'd been through a trial at the hands of our family. The whole reason Uncle Frank was a vampire was thanks to his need to have power. Being born without magic to a family like mine drove him to embrace the undead. I often wondered if he ever doubted his choice.

But as he stepped back and took Sunny's hand, the smile they exchanged dashed that, as always.

Uncle Frank made the right choice for him. And, though I'd been bruised, battered and left broken a time or two, so had I. All I could do was trust my kids and hope I'd done as good a job with them as Mom, my vampire family and Sass had done with me.

We left them there, me leading the way this time. I stopped at the stone wall at the back of the room, realizing with a grin I didn't remember the damned combination of stones to press. Just for an instant, a giggle rose and threatened to push me into hysterics. So odd. And yet, as I crushed it down, hand over my mouth, my brain shuffled and sorted while the girls held me up.

These ones, my vampire sent, gently, tenderly as she showed me the wall with her choices overlaid with a pale, white glow. *Are you all right?*

I'm fine, I sent to them, all three hugging me. *I really am. This has just been one hell of a day so far.*

I pushed the stones while the kids watched, both of them silent—even Ethie, for once. My vampire had it right, as it turned out. Because when I pressed the last one, the floor beside me ground with the sound of stone on stone. Both kids gaped then grinned at each other. This was an adventure to them, after all. They had no idea what waited below. And, as their curiosity about the mystery grew, my smile grew with it.

Okay, yeah. This was kind of fun.

I led them down the stairs, Sassafras's amber eyes staring at me, the glow of his magic lighting his gaze as we left the lit room above and descended underground. Ethie walked carefully with him in her arms, cradling him as though he were some precious discovery and she was an intrepid explorer. I could just imagine the thoughts running through their heads. Were they treasure hunters, finding a secret passage to an unknown destination? Or a prince and princess uncovering the truth of their past for the first time? I allowed my own mind to wander, to permit this moment to excite me as much as it excited them. By the time we reached the bottom of the stairs and I gestured down the long, low ceilinged stone hall, I was grinning.

They grinned back, Ethie setting Sass on his feet. "Race you!" She took off before her brother could register she'd started without him, but Gabriel was close behind her as they pounded down the hall and disappeared into the side chamber.

The upper room held them captivated as I took my time, Galleytrot on one side, Sass on the other. It was amazing to me to see this place through their eyes, as though for the first time, and I took a long moment to admire the carvings, the writing etched in the walls.

It had been Liam who figured out how to enter the chamber beneath. I rarely left it open, preferring to close it behind me when I emerged, if I even used the stairs at all. And I was glad I did. Though, when I stepped up to the center pedestal, the perma light glowing from the ceiling above casting its pale, white glow over everything, I paused and turned to wave to Ethie.

She came right to my side, eyes huge, while Gabriel spun on the spot, as though trying to absorb what he was seeing all in one go.

"Mom," he said. "I know this place."

I didn't answer. Instead, I lifted my daughter into my arms and pointed at the pedestal where a five fingered shape beckoned.

"You know what to do?" I had no idea if she would be able to succeed. The opening of the chamber stairs required maji blood. But, she was my daughter and though not full maji like I was, should have enough, like Trill and the Zornov family, to allow her to activate the way.

Ethie leaned forward without hesitation, her bravery and excitement written all over her face. Sassafras sighed behind me and I met his eyes as my daughter's little hand pressed firmly to the stone.

Another one, he sent. *I'll have my hands full with her.*

You love it that way. I turned back at the sound of a whisper of power and smiled at Ethie. She beamed at me, clapping her hands together in enthusiasm while the curving staircase sighed open, sinking down into the ground below.

Gabriel went first, without pause, half trotting his way down into the dark. I let Ethie down to go after him when she wiggled. She pushed past Galleytrot on Gabriel's heels while Sass and I took our time again, my hands trailing over the writing on the stones. History, Liam had said, the history of magic. Of our family and all those of maji blood who came before. He didn't get the chance to research it as he'd wanted. But, maybe one day, Gabriel would.

I'd like that very much.

I almost ran into Galleytrot at the bottom, realizing as I stopped with his furry butt against my legs there was a logjam at the entrance. Sass slipped past me between the hound's legs and my son's feet, stepping over the threshold. His encouragement through action released the kids from their stall, though both Gabriel and Ethie seemed tentative as their shallow steps carried them into the room.

I held back, my heart aching suddenly, the song of the maji chamber singing to my children. Gabriel's face flushed before paling, to bright points of pink on his cheeks while Ethie sighed and cupped her own face in her hands, turning to meet my eyes with a gaze full of wonder.

"Mom," she said. "This is awesomesauce."

The air on the other side of the central slab

shimmered and a familiar form appeared. I held my breath for a long moment, while the dark haired beauty smiled at my stunned son, her icy blue eyes full of happiness.

"Gabriel," Ameline said. "Hello, my dear."

TWENTY-THREE

Why did her gentleness push more tears to the surface? I stood helpless, knowing I could comfort my son if he needed it, but allowing him to face the woman who stole him from me, who forced his little body to grow faster than it should have, who triggered the wakening of his incredible power. I could tell he knew right away who she was, the recognition in him not the startled, angry or frightened response I was expecting. Instead, Gabriel smiled at her.

"Ameline," he said. "I'm glad you're all right."

She laughed and my heart did, too. Though my daughter watched the soul of Ameline Benoit with suspicion borne of her natural state of being, Gabriel immediately crossed to the spirit and offered one hand. Ameline sank to her knees and for the first time I saw her own tears glitter on her cheeks as her full, lower lip trembled.

"You forgive me, then," she said, barely a whisper that carried to me in the quiet of the chamber.

"Of course," my son said. "There's nothing to forgive."

With a low cry she embraced him and Gabriel hugged her back.

I had to look away, to gather myself. I hadn't realized just how important this moment was to me. The fear she'd done some irreparable harm to his heart had lingered with me for years, though I should have known better. The toughness I'd sensed in Gabriel wasn't, in fact, scar tissue left behind by Ameline, but the part of me I passed along. Maybe that shouldn't have made me feel better. After all, his father was as gentle and kind as anyone I'd ever known. But I was well aware Gabriel would need his strength along the way, considering the power he carried. Seeing his heart was as open as ever almost did me in.

Ameline released Gabriel who held her hand as she stood. He guided her toward us while her soul unabashedly wiped tears from her cheeks. She felt real to me, the power of the maji chamber giving her form, and it was hard to remember she had once been an evil, torn, driven woman bent on hurting everyone she could. I think from the look on her face as she met my eyes there had to be times like this one she was as astonished by her transformation as I was.

"Ethie," Gabriel said. "This is Ameline. She took care of me for a little while when I was a baby." An understatement. She'd stolen him from me, made me believe he was dead by exchanging his infant form for a bespelled normal child already passed on. But I let his description stand because this was about my son, not me. I'd come to peace with how things ended a long time ago.

My daughter wasn't buying it completely, but she bobbed her head, arms crossing over her chest. "I know about you," she said in her best Hayle voice. "Gabriel told me some things."

"I see." Ameline just smiled. "There is much I regret, and yet, everything happens for a reason, Ethpeal Hayle. Please, always remember that." Again, Ameline met my eyes. "Everything."

I shivered a little, hating the feeling of premonition I had from her words. Nothing, likely. Still, I knew better than to ignore my intuition.

"Sassafras." Ameline bowed her head to the fluffy Persian. "You look well."

"As do you." He wasn't cold with her, at least. I'd told him enough he'd forgiven her, too, perhaps. "You definitely feel much better."

Ameline nodded. "I do," she said. "The pain is gone. Though there are times I wonder what I did to deserve such respite."

"What you had to do." Galleytrot's deep voice sounded dull, sad. Though his head hung low as he spoke, I felt his power pulsing with understanding, if not forgiveness. His anger with her lingered, though he did an excellent job holding it at bay. "And though I miss him still, none of us had a choice when Fate came to call."

Ameline left Gabriel a moment, going to the big dog's side. Her hesitant offer of a caress was welcomed as he lifted his big head, the crust of old hurt breaking from around his heart as his magic gave way. She bent slightly, kissing the top of his nose as he sighed out a breath of spring air that reached even me from the strength of it.

"I would undo it if I could," she whispered, just loud enough for me to hear. "And every moment my heart longs to do so." She straightened and shrugged, turning back to Gabriel. "It is he who should be here, Gabriel. Your father. Not me. And, perhaps, that is the ultimate punishment Creator intended." Ameline's wry smile held no malice as she spun to me. "Had you considered that? Cleaning my soul of my ego, so I might know forever the pain I caused and relive it in endless understanding?"

I shook my head, unwilling to believe that. "I think you have more to do," I said. "And that Liam's time was done." Why was it so hard to say those words? I choked on them a moment, had to cough away the thickening at the back of my tongue, draw a shaky breath past the pain I thought too old to make me feel this way again.

"If you don't mind," she said, "I'll instead do my best to honor him by never forgetting what I've done."

There wasn't much I could say to that.

Ameline gestured around her, attitude shifting from sad to welcoming. "Thank you for coming to see me," she said. "And what do you think of my home?"

"It's amazing," Ethie said, though she looked slightly guilty about the admission, as though she thought she should remain in suspicion of Ameline.

"Thank you," the spirit woman said. "The power in this place holds wonders I only dreamed of when I was a witch." She offered Gabriel her left hand, my daughter her right. "Would you like to explore it with me?"

Ethie seized on her like Ameline offered her a giant chocolate chip cookie, but my son retreated ever so slightly, fear showing on his face. I held still, as hard as it was to merely observe, amazed at Ameline's cleverness as my son spoke.

"I can't," he said, arms crossing over his chest as he half turned away.

She didn't move or drop her hand, just stood there with the offer open. "You worry about the talent inside you," she said. "That once you opened a way here, and fear you would do so again."

Gabriel glanced at me, a quick and guilty look. "Yes," he said.

She's good, Sass sent.

Is this wise? Galleytrot's worry wasn't surprising.

He has to accept his magic, I sent. *Of all people, I know how hard it can be to fight against what won't be ignored. But Gabriel's power is vast and, to this point, mostly unknown to us. We have no idea what he's capable of, not really.* I was far more worried about that truth than I let on to either of the pair. *He has to regain control.*

So you can find the rest of Creator's pieces. I sensed no animosity or accusation in Galleytrot's words, but the sting was there, regardless.

So my son can find balance and be at peace with his magic, I sent, a bit more firmly than I intended. *And so he can fulfill his destiny and yes, find the pieces.* I sighed in my head. *As much as I hate the idea of doing to my kids what Mom did to me, I understand there are no choices here.* Sass didn't comment, but he didn't have to, not from the smug push of his power. I let it go as I went on, while Ameline and Gabriel whispered together, Ethie looking back and forth between them with a mix of awe and jealousy. *He has a talent no one else has. He was born with it on purpose, for a purpose. And yes, he's only seven years old.* Way to break your own heart, Hayle. *He's my son. And I'll shield him from harm for as long as I can. But, if my past has taught me anything, it's that there are times when we just don't get to say no.*

Well said, Sass muttered while Galleytrot nodded.

I know, the big hound sent. *I just wish... he's so good, Syd.*

He is, I sent. *But he's not his father.*

"Mom." Gabriel glanced up at me, the whisper huddle over. "Ameline is going to help me open a Gate."

Um. What? "Here? Now?" *Is that a good idea?* My turn to worry. I sent the question directly into her spirit's mind.

I believe it is, she sent. *I have access to power you don't here, ancient power that has been waiting for Gabriel for a very long time. It will protect him from the other Universe and the Order, as it did the night I tried to bring Dark Brother across.*

It did? That stunned me. *But it failed.*

No, she sent. *Had the magic of this place not been fighting with all the power it had, Dark Brother would have emerged the moment Gabriel opened the Gateway to the other Universe.*

That was... good to know.

Let me recruit some backup first, I sent. And reached into the veil. It was only then, now I knew what I was looking for, I felt the full touch of the power of the maji chamber and my heart stopped for a single beat.

Not power, not a cohesive whole. Souls, millions of them. The core and power of every single blood maji born to this plane, embedded in the heart of the maji chamber. But not just this one. I could feel them, now, the five others spread out around the world, in far off places. One under a pyramid in Egypt, hidden under the Valley of the Kings. Another in the Orient, not far from Hong Kong. A deep recess in a remote part of England.

Amazing and beautiful, this network of magic. Perhaps I was only now able to see because I was aware, or perhaps because they were finally willing to let me. For Gabriel.

Max. I touched the drach leader's mind easily. He felt tired, but perked at the contact.

What have you found? A brief glimpse from his point of view gave me a rush of vertigo. He was flying over a green river, bright purple grass crushed by the fallen bodies of a large group of creatures while the other drach circled below, cleaning up the survivors.

More intruders? I should have been there with him—

My kids needed me—

Damn it.

Indeed, he sent. *A rather troublesome group we've only just conquered.* He couldn't have known where my mind had gone or Max would never have added fuel to my self-flagellating fire by making such a comment. I crushed my guilt at needing to be in ten places at once as he went on. *You're in the maji chamber?*

I am, I sent. *With Gabriel. He wants to try opening a Gateway with Ameline's help.*

This was the first time since my son almost allowed Dark Brother's vast, frightening army through to our side I had hope my son would succeed. He'd tried and failed in the past, though a huge part of me knew that failure came from his unwillingness to embrace his magic completely. Considering even Max was afraid of the

Order, I hardly blamed Gabriel. And yet, we needed this. If we could use his power as intended, to find the pieces of Creator and put an end to the threat of Dark Brother and the other Universe, we wouldn't have to worry about a super army coming to wipe us from creation.

I was all for that. And, from the instant reaction I had from Max, so was he.

I'm on my way, he sent. I let him go only a breath before the veil parted and the massive form of the drach leader stepped through. There was always a moment when he transformed from his dragon body to humanoid I sensed the two of them living together, as though the dragon still existed, only hiding behind a veneer of humanity. I really knew so little about the drach, it was all supposition that would have to wait for the day I actually had time to ask questions.

Max bowed to my kids, to Ameline, before doing the same to Galleytrot and Sassafras. When his diamond eyes met mine, I saw eagerness there and felt better for calling him.

"Gabriel," he said in his rumbling voice. "Do not fear your power. We are far from the Stronghold."

"I know," my son said. "I'm sorry I've been so afraid. But, I think I'll be okay now." He squeezed Ameline's hand. "I want to try."

We have no time to set a trap, Max sent to me. *Should we wait?*

I'd hate to stop him now, I sent. *We need to let him do this.*

Very well, Max sent. *And I agree. But we must prepare for the appearance of opposition, though we were sorely not in our last hunt.* Belaisle's appearance had been a massive shock, no more so than the disappearance of an entire race and their plane. I tried not to think of Trill's betrayal in that distant world as my son released his hold on Ameline and drew a breath.

We'll deal with it if he shows, I sent to Max. *I hope he does. Belaisle is mine.*

Gabriel's power had a distinctive feel to it, a swelling crescendo, subtle but filled with not only the freshness of earth and spring but with the weight of the power he gained from the Gate of the Sidhe. As the air beside him sparkled and pushed outward, an arched opening shimmering into life, I found more goosebumps crawling over my skin. I'd encountered all kinds of magic, but never felt anything quite so primal, so pure as his.

I stared, feeling a bit stupid, while the Gateway settled and the scene on the other side formed. How strange I felt a bit disappointed by the view of darkness and stars in the sky, some broken masonry on the ground the only decoration in sight.

"There, Mom." Gabriel rubbed goosebumps from his little arms. "This place has been calling to me. I just didn't want to answer." Verification his "couldn't" was "wouldn't" when it came to opening Gates.

"A piece of Creator lies there," Max said, happiness in his rumbling voice. "I can feel its presence, even through the Gate." He smiled at my son. "Well done, Gabriel."

Max didn't hesitate, his power reaching forward. And, when he turned to me with his sparkling gaze alight with his own magic, I knew it was true. Gabriel had done it again.

Confidence rising, I joined the drach leader and stepped through the Gateway.

TWENTY-FOUR

Max paused on the other side, waiting for me. I drew a breath, coughing out the dank scent of decay so different from the fresher air of the maji chamber. The atmosphere on this plane felt old, as though the oxygen was almost used up, some contamination poisoning it slowly. Death clung to every breath, though my magic kept me safe. Crumbling walls greeted us as we slowly made our way deeper into the gloom of night, a single moon overhead dull in the thickness of the gray that wasn't quite clouds. I stumbled before my demon, her power hushed and soft, leaped to my defense, her night vision bringing everything into focus. I looked down at the hunk of rusted metal jutting from the crumbling earth that had almost knocked me over, sharp edge dulled by age.

"This world is dying." Max's usually musical voice

held sadness.

"Our fault?" I didn't know how many more messes I could take responsibility for. I shivered though temperature didn't affect me these days, rubbing my arms against the chill of a thin breeze pushing more ill scent toward us.

"No," he answered, turning and striding off, though not at his typical long legged pace. He folded his big hands together inside the cuffs of his gray robe, head down, diamond eyes dim. "The death of a plane happens from time to time. The resources meant to last until the end of days are either used up by those who inhabit it or a flaw in its makeup drives it downward to its rest."

I thought of my own home plane and how quickly our people seemed to be devouring all of the available consumables. And shuddered. I could escape a fate like this one, go to another plane that didn't suffer such degradation. But what about the rest of humanity? Big picture things like that just made my brain hurt.

Max paused at the crest of a low hill, looking down over the decaying remains of what had to have been a vast city at some point. Buildings reminiscent of ones I was familiar with at home squatted low to the ground, some fallen on their sides, into their neighbors, masonry dominoes, fallen giants. The earth seemed to have risen up to claim them, though the expected encroachment of vegetation was missing. Only a few scrubby bushes and the occasional spindly tree marked places where living things still grew. I bit my lower lip to keep in my emotions. We were here for a purpose, to fetch a missing piece of Creator, not to mourn the passing of a plane. And yet, it was hard not to feel the crushing emptiness of this place, to allow its slow and inevitable end to seep into my bones, to make me ache for its loss.

"This is horrible," I whispered, lacking in eloquence if not in feeling.

"Indeed," Max said, just as softly. "The winding down of a world often is."

I heard them long before they came into view, felt their approach easily, distinguishing their pale sparks of life from the death all around us. I held my ground, Max with me, as a small group of people exited the shadows and darkness and oozed toward us. They had once looked like my own people, two arms, two legs, though they seemed to have skin the color of ash and a second pair of ears I could only assume served some evolutionary purpose they no longer required. Their clothing, as ragged and filthy as it was, wouldn't have been out of place back home. I clenched my teeth against further emotion as the small group came to a nervous halt in front of us, while still more of their number crept around to circle the place where we stood.

But I felt no threat from them, just the waking of curiosity long lost and, perhaps, the vaguest flicker of hope.

She would have been taller than me if she stood to her full height. But despair had curved the woman's shoulders forward, pushed her long skeleton down, compressed her physically as well as spiritually. And yet, her voice was clear as she spoke, my power translating her language to one I could understand.

"The last days have come, then." She only had eyes for Max. "Will it be over quickly, my god? Or will we see it trickle outward to the end?"

Max bowed his head to her, offered his hand. She moaned in what sounded like sorrow, but when she grasped his offered fingers she kissed them, pressed them to her cheek while the others sighed as one.

"I am not who you await," he said, so gentle and kind I had to look away for fear of weeping. "Your time has not yet come."

She cried out, pulled on his hand. "My god," she said, a wail in her voice. "I beg you, end it now! We can't go on this way. We must depart and our world with us."

Max's mind reached for me and, for the first time since I met him, I felt desperation and the most terrible sorrow, the sadness of an ancient soul who had seen too much. *What do I say?*

He was asking me? And yet, here was my amazing drach friend, leader of the first race, leaning on me for help. How could I not do my best?

I stepped forward, catching the woman's attention. She backed away from Max, dropping his hand, eyes huge, lower set of ears quivering.

"When the time comes," I said, "you will know it. There will be no doubt. And you will see your salvation." I don't know why I told her that. Except most religions and beliefs held some vision of heaven and it was the best I could think of on short notice. Guilt at offering false prophecy ate at me as much as the poison in the cloying air, but I was grasping at straws here.

It had the right impact. She lunged for me, hugged me. "Thank you," she whispered before turning to the others, arms raised, voice triumphant. "The Respite is coming!"

They cheered, a thin sound, but with enough hope in it I had to reach for Max. His hand was cold in mine, his skin rough as his scales emerged. *They know the drach*, I sent.

Most races do, he sent. *Including yours*. Dragons. Right.

We had the wrong idea, I sent. *Thinking you gold hoarding figments of childhood imagination*. Nice to distract with a conversation about cultural shifts.

Indeed, he sent. *Likely thanks to the Brotherhood. But I can assume this race made gods of us, at least in the end.*

Can we do anything for them? I tried to smile back at the woman as she turned to me, gestured for us to follow.

We cannot, Max sent, going after her. *Their time is almost over.*

How close is almost? I joined Max as he trod the path down toward the city, keeping my gaze on the back of her head and not on the crumbling buildings around me.

No one knows, he sent. *Likely a few years. It appears there is little vegetation and less to eat. Unless they've found some storehouse of old food, I would say they are the final generation.*

This sucks, I sent, heart hurting, mind whirling from the implications.

The worst part of being immortal, he agreed, squeezing my hand. *But a weight we must bear.*

Is it safe to go with them? I didn't want to have to fight my way out past a bunch of god worshipping and desperate survivors of a post-apocalyptic world. Too Hollywood for my taste.

We have no choice, he sent. *The piece we seek is in the direction she takes us.*

Good to know.

We didn't have far to walk. And though I hesitated to go underground, the woman and her people showed no qualms and Max's grip on me gave me little option. The gaping opening allowed little light so even my demon's vision struggled to adapt. When it finally did, I found myself in a cave system, like a maze, with endless corridors heading off right and left.

No, Syd. Not a maze. Dear elements. An underground parking garage.

Shudder.

One glimpse into the filthy windshield of what vaguely resembled a car and the grinning skull face on the other side spun my head around and kept my focus once again on the woman's bobbing head. Whispering echoes emerged in answer to my fear, but they were as thin and tattered as the rest of this world. Where ghosts normally plagued me with substance and demands, this plane was so far gone the echoes of the lost barely had a breath to release in my ear.

Still disconcerting. And creeped me the hell out. Yes, I was an all-powerful maji and stuff. But, yikes. Thank goodness Max was with me or I would have died right then and there from a giant case of the willies.

I was so focused on our guide I almost ran into her when she stopped. Max's hand held me back, shaking me out of my intense need to ignore the echoes around me. She turned and smiled at us while her people shuffled their way into the larger space. They'd moved some of the cars out of the way, made a circular area with a fire pit in the center. Stacks of old crates sat to one side, blankets and other gear scattered about. This was their home, where they lived.

From cave men to huge, powerful civilization to cave men again. So tragic.

"We knew you would come." She gestured at the edge of the circle where one of the cars stood. Something shining and white sat within the open back door. Max took a step toward it, dropping my hand and even I forgot to be afraid as I realized they'd led us right to what we sought. "We found it, knew it would bring you here." She clasped her hands under her chin in rapture. "The Respite is near."

Another cheer, this one more enthusiastic. Did they see Max's interest in the piece as proof they would soon have their salvation? If so, it was the meanest of tricks we were about to pull on them, to steal it out from under them and leave them thinking they were going to a better place, only to suffer and linger and hate us, ultimately, for lying to them.

I can't do this. I sent the words to Max in a lash of panic. He spun back to me, brow furrowed. *They think we're going to save them.*

Syd. His gentleness held firm control. *We must. And when we're done I will send my people here to ensure their end comes quickly and peacefully.*

I exhaled, lower lip trembling, unable at last to stop the tears from flowing down my face. *Thank you.*

He nodded. *We have a job to complete*, he sent. *But we are not without compassion.*

A flicker of motion over his shoulder froze me in place before driving me to act. Too late. Damn it, always too late. Distracted by this dying world, knowing better, that we might not be alone in our discovery.

The black tunnel appeared, Belaisle's grinning face nodding to me as he lunged for the chunk of white statue inside the car. Max roared in fury, turning as he, too, realized we'd been beaten to the retrieval yet again thanks to our empathy, the horror of our situation. He leaped toward the Brotherhood leader.

Belaisle was already disappearing, the arm of Creator clutched to his chest, evil grin the last thing I saw as the black of his sorcerer's tunnel engulfed him.

Max didn't wait for me, simply reacted, tearing at the veil, diving for it. I cried out, ran for him, but was too late again. By the time I reached the place they'd both been the pair were long gone.

But that was the least of my troubles.

"Mom?"

I spun around, heart pounding, to see my son watching me with horror on his little face.

TWENTY-FIVE

I gaped at Gabriel as he looked around at the gathered people, clearly nervous, but holding his place as he waited for me to respond. I drew a breath while the leader of the remains of her race stumbled and fell with a wail of despair.

"Gabriel." I skirted the others who shuffled forward toward the now empty car, coming to my son's side. My hands gripped his upper arms a little tighter than I intended and I shook him, ever so softly. "What are you doing here?"

"I wanted to see." His whisper told me he regretted his decision. "What happened here?"

I released my grip on him, turned him around, began to leave. We had to go, quickly, before the leader and her people came after us. Not that I was worried we'd be harmed, but because I could barely deal with them myself, let alone protect Gabriel from the loss of this place.

"Please, wait!" Her cry made me stop, turn slowly, painfully. She came to me, hands grasping at me. "He said he'd release us."

"He will." So dull, my words. "You must be patient."

"The god is gone." She fell again, hands pulling at my clothing. "And we are left to suffer." She looked up at me, eyes full of tears, wetness tracking through the filth on her skin. "What have we done to deserve this?"

Something silver glittered over her shoulder, a slip of sparkle lying on the ground. I pushed past her, went to it, bent to retrieve it. The ribbon that was a drach soul bound to the lost chunk of statue wound briefly across my fingers before collapsing with a sigh into my palm. Belaisle must have dropped it from the piece of Creator, abandoning it as the other ribbons had been abandoned. How many more would I carry to the Stronghold, place at the feet of the broken statue? I returned to my son, hardening my heart against the plight of these people. If I didn't find the pieces of Creator, this might be the end for all races, not just one plane that its own people ruined out of greed.

"Wait for the final sign," I said in as large a voice as I could muster, slipping the silent ribbon into my jacket pocket for safe keeping. "He will return with more of his kind and your end will come in the Respite." I could tell from her troubled face she didn't believe me, and nor did her people, because no answering cheer rose to my words. But it was the best I could do, damn it.

Gabriel had other ideas. "You're just going to leave them here like this?" He resisted me pulling on his hand, jerking his free to stare at me with shock on his face. "Mom, we can't just let them die like this."

Where the hell was Max? I needed him to explain this to Gabriel, because if I stayed here much longer my resolve to be strong would weaken. I didn't dare tell my son I agreed with him. That this broke my heart, thinking of leaving these people to suffer. But what else could we do?

We're getting out of here. I reached for the veil, felt resistance as Gabriel's power pushed outward.

Not yet, he sent. And opened a Gateway. I gasped, but not as loudly as the others. With good reason. Not only were they witnessing some pretty powerful magic, the view on the other side had to look about as close to heaven as any of them could ever have imagined. Better, even. Green, rolling hills, a crystal blue lake, clear sky, mountains in the distance. Even the breeze coming through smelled fresh, new, bright. The woman stepped forward, tentative, touching the edge of the Gateway with her fingertips, smiling in wonder at my son.

"It's time," she said.

He nodded, swallowing hard. "You'll be safe there,"

he said.

Gabriel. Even mentally, I had a hard time saying his name.

The plane is empty, he sent. *One of my favorites. I've been watching it since I was little. There's only animals, Mom. They'll be okay at least. Maybe they'll do it right this time.*

We can't play god, sweets. And yet, this seemed the perfect solution. I hesitated, long enough his green eyes, now looking up into mine with such maturity and confidence, swayed me to hold my peace.

"Go now," he said, gesturing. "Your new future awaits."

They went, leaving everything behind, eyes bright, holding hands, from the few aged to the tiny babes held in their mother's arms. Without fear, but with awe and hope. She was the last to cross, smiling at Gabriel.

"You will be remembered, my god," she said. "And we thank you for the Respite at last."

Gabriel waited for her to cross before releasing his power. The last thing we both saw of them was their elation while they celebrated their new home. Gabriel sobbed out a gasp of air as the power dissipated, falling into my arms to weep on me.

"We had to, Mom." He whispered against my shoulder. "We had to."

I didn't want to think about the ramifications of what we'd just done. Because I was equally culpable. Instead, I grasped my son firmly to me and opened the veil. The maji chamber welcomed us, the Gateway Gabriel created in the first place already gone. He must have closed it behind him when he followed us.

Galleytrot leaped at me as we appeared, power rippling with fear. Ethie clung to Sassafras, supported by Ameline. Even the soul of my old enemy looked afraid and then relieved as I released my son and let the big dog slather him in tongue kisses.

"I should have known better than to worry," she said. No comment.

We said our goodbyes, emerged to the surface, Ethie in my arms with Sass glaring like I'd done something wrong—little did he know—and Galleytrot walking so close to my son he bumped against him with every stride. The vampires were out, only Chambrelle there to greet us and I was just as glad. Another goodbye and we were in the van, heading home again, while Gabriel looked out the window in silence.

It wasn't until we were parked in our driveway, Ethie and our two furry companions out of the car, that my son turned to me. He was smiling.

"We did a good thing, Mom," he said. Didn't wait for me to answer, just got out and ran off to find his sister. I sat behind the wheel, fighting the need to cry. Worse, when I climbed out of the driver's seat and looked around at my neighborhood, now superimposed with the dead world over it.

I'd carry the echo of death with me for the rest of my life.

Dad's steady power greeted me long before I laid eyes on him, the touch of his magic helping me calm enough I didn't burst into emo tears at least. He was greeting the kids when I entered the kitchen, hugging them both and listening with interest as they shared what we'd just done.

Dad's eyebrow arched at me briefly while Ethie chattered about Ameline. *Is Gabriel okay?*

I think so. I sank into a chair, exhaustion washing over me in a solid wave. *It was horrible, Dad.*

I can only imagine. He kissed my daughter. "Upstairs and pack what you want for the night. Your grandmother and I are taking you to a movie."

She squealed and ran, her brother on her heels, though Gabriel went more slowly. Galleytrot joined them while Sassafras leaped up on the table and fixed me with his amber eyes.

"Tell me you didn't interfere with the history of a plane." Sass's biting remark triggered my own anger.

"You weren't there," I snapped. "Why the hell did you let Gabriel follow me?"

Sass shifted his position, tail thrashing, though guilt flashed in his eyes. "We didn't know he had," he said. "I was talking with Ameline and when I turned around, he was gone." So, his regret was the source of his anger, not what my son had done.

"The piece you sought?" Dad's hand settled over mine, concern as clear as Sass's self-recrimination.

"Belaisle." I snarled his name. "He's tracking me somehow." I felt my pocket where the silver thread rested. I needed to go to the Stronghold and give it to Creator's statue, but I just couldn't muster the energy at the moment.

"You need to do something about that," Sass said.

"Thank you, Captain Obvious." I stroked his fur to soften the words. "Whatever he's doing to follow me, it's giving him the edge he needs. At least Trill wasn't there this time." Did she have different means? Or maybe she was too late? "Not like it mattered. Whether she has it or Belaisle does, we're still out of luck." The gloom of the dying plane hung around me like a gray cloud. I could still smell the decay and poison and desperately needed a shower to erase the stink of it.

If not the memory.

"Let's just hope Gabriel's compassion doesn't lead to disaster." But even Sass sounded weary.

There wasn't much I could say to that.

"Max went after Belaisle," I said. "So I'm stuck waiting again." It was hard to force a smile when the kids pounded down the stairs and stood waiting for Dad. He joined them, hugging me as I said goodbye.

I'll watch over him tonight, Dad sent. *Make sure there are no ill effects.*

Thanks, I sent. *I need to go after Max at some point, so I appreciate you and Mom taking the kids.* I turned to my son, hugged him.

I'm fine, Mom, he sent, power clear and warm. *Honest.*

Love you, I sent. *My hero.*

He grinned up at me.

Ethie clung to me, but seemed none the worse for wear. "I like Ameline," she whispered before kissing my cheek.

"Me, too," I said. "Now."

I watched them go from the back yard, Dad leading the kids through the veil before it sealed behind Galleytrot's bushy tail. Though I knew there was nothing to worry about—that my children had the very best of protection in my parents and the black dog—I still shivered when they disappeared.

Turned and looked down to find Sassafras staring up at me, silver fur a stark contrast to the deep, green grass.

"As much as I'd rather crash, it's time to check in with some people," I said. "Feel like coming along? Or are you due for a nap?"

He swatted my leg. "Now who's the smartass?"

TWENTY-SIX

My grandmother waved at me from her seat next to Simon. I was surprised he let her anywhere near his computers, he was so touchy about them. But Gram perched on a chair so close she almost brushed legs with him and I wondered if she even gave him a choice.

The house above was quiet, Nona locked away in her trailer. I took the silence of her magic to mean she didn't want to be disturbed. It felt odd here without Apollo, though Owen's quiet presence at least filled in some of the void.

Sass jumped down from my arms and trotted to Gram, leaping up to her lap. Simon scowled at him, flicking flying fingers in the cat's direction before going back to his endless typing.

"Cat hair," my tech groused.

"Bite me," Sass said with enough sweetness to make

my teeth ache.

Gram's evil laugh told me she'd won a similar argument and I finally found I could smile again.

Except, of course, the whole point of this experiment with Apollo was supposed to prevent what just happened with Belaisle. I filled them in on the pertinent details, leaving out Gabriel's involvement, though from the press of Gram's power on mine she knew there was far more to the story.

Simon just shrugged. "He's in," he said, pointing at the screen. A few taps of his keys and a large monitor over his head, facing me this time, showed me Apollo's point of view from the button cam. I could only watch a moment before feeling sea sick, but there were enough black robes and young faces I had to believe Simon knew what he was talking about. "He's just not deep enough yet, I guess."

Not helpful. Crankiness returned, as hard as I tried to squash it. This could have been over and done with, Belaisle captured, the piece in my possession and safely back with Creator's statue. Instead, the experiment had proven to be a bust. We should have waited, set up a trap after all.

Should have. Could have. I was good at those.

"He's safe, at least." Owen came to stand at my side. "We know that much. The audio has been sketchy."

"I'm working on it." I wasn't the only one in a crabby

mood. Simon's forehead darkened and I could only imagine his worry for Apollo. There were times I forgot my friends cared for each other, too. Hid their fears behind their own masks.

"He's reconnected with some people, from what we can tell." Owen didn't seem concerned, so I let it go. "I wish we could tell you more."

So did I. Still, Apollo was in and safe. That was huge.

The air beside me flexed and opened, Max stepping through. I opened my mouth to ask the obvious question but he was already shaking his big head.

"Escaped," he grunted, uncharacteristically sharp. "Apologies," he said, softening to his usually calm. "I almost had him several times, but he managed to elude me in the end." His diamond eyes lit a moment. "You made it back safe from the plane?" Did he feel guilty for leaving me behind?

I nodded. "Clearly," I said with a smile. *Long story*, I sent. *I'll fill you in later.* I slipped my hand into my front pocket and retrieved the ribbon. It sank onto his palm in a silent puddle of silver as Max bowed his head over it.

She was a loving soul with enough caring for all of us, he sent.

Who was she? His sister, maybe? His cousin? They all seemed to be related to him, as though his punishment for cracking the Universe was to lose everyone he loved.

My betrothed, he sent, soft, low. *The one sworn to me, though my heart belonged elsewhere. She gave up her life to protect*

Creator and to protect me. Was there any end to the layers of grief in this tragedy? I was beginning to think not. *I will always remember her for that.*

I squeezed his fist as it closed around the ribbon. *We should go,* I sent. *Return her to the Stronghold.*

Max nodded, but I didn't get a chance to reach for the veil. Not when another mind was already pushing against mine.

Syd. Femke again, and this time she sounded desperate. *Where are you?*

Coming. I didn't need to ask. Not with the image of the werepalace firmly in her mind. It was finally time to take Danilo down, whether I was ready, or there, or not.

Because a moment's breathing room? For suckers.

Gram leaped to her feet, setting Sass on the chair before hurrying to my side. I didn't protest her silent choice, partially because I was glad she wanted to come. Max's offer of his hand surprised me, though, considering.

You don't have to get involved, I sent. *Probably shouldn't.*

I do, he sent. *You are my friend, Sydlynn Hayle. And though my direct involvement might cause issues, I can at least be present.* He wasn't kidding. It wasn't a spoken law or anything, but aside from a few minor assists, Max and the drach had held off from interfering with this plane and the laws regarding it. We'd never spoken of it openly, but after witnessing the god complex devolution of the fallen plane, I could see why such a powerful race would hold off from putting in their two cents. Though not as standoffish as the maji, willing at least to act on a large scale, poking his nose into local politics had to be risky. Still, the drach leader felt like he had no qualms about joining me and I wasn't about to look a gift dragon in the mouth. His magic embraced me, sealing the deal. *Your need is mine.*

Well then.

The veil parted before me and I stepped through, holding onto Femke even as I opened my mind to Gram and Max when I spoke to her.

Sorry I've been out, I sent. *Is everyone there?* It was hard to switch gears, my heart still gone with the dying race to the new plane, my anger with Belaisle's speedy snatch and grab, my body aching with weariness.

It's a mess. Her anger came through in sharp cuts of mental words, helping me focus whether she knew it or not. I landed on the ground outside the werepalace, the grass giving way under my feet as I dropped the few inches I'd miscalculated. When I looked up with a grimace at the mistake, I realized why. I'd used the WPC Leader's point of view as my marker. Femke hovered, blue fire wrapped around her, with her Enforcers—my husband among them, looking grim and barking orders— just a few feet away.

Nice ride, Gram sent. *Use the veil much?*

I scowled at her before crossing to Femke, shaking out the jarring landing. The WPC Leader settled on the grass beside me, Enforcers flying willy nilly, groups of witches gathering in patches in the broad yard, Sidhe and vampires in clusters, shouting at each other.

Cacophony, while hulking wereguards watched from the steps of the palace and did nothing. What fools we must have looked like, a babbling, disorganized crush of paranormals all vying for attention.

This was a joint effort? More like a mass debacle.

"I thought we were all working together?" What a crapshow. I resisted the urge to lash out and pull everyone's attention to me. This wasn't my rodeo, though.

"So did I." Femke's jaw jumped as her power surged against the magic of the other leaders struggling for control. "But the Empress decided to act ahead of schedule. Which meant a mad scramble to avoid a war." She glared at the black pavilion not far from our position. The Empress sat perched on a huge carry chair, giant men surrounding her. She was the only one who seemed calm, collected. Almost serene, if it weren't for the tightness of her expression, the way she glared at the front doors of the werepalace. The slim, dark form of Jiao hovered nearby, her eyes meeting mine a moment before she bobbed a nod to Max.

"Typical." I sighed and rubbed my tired eyes. "Plan?"

"Stalemate." Femke pointed at the palace. "Danilo has himself well shielded. Charlotte's been searching for a way in, but so far without any progress." Speaking of my werefriend, two wolves loped toward us, just as flickering shadows appeared at my shoulder in the evening air. Sunny and Frank arrived the same moment Charlotte and Sage morphed into human form. Femke snapped her fingers, a pair of black robes arriving by way of her harried assistant. Charlotte's casual nakedness always made me blush, though Sage seemed less comfortable with it, thus the robes.

"The damned fool." Charlotte rarely swore or lost her temper in a visible way, but her hands trembled as she jerked tight the knot of the sash holding her robe closed. "He's going to get everyone killed."

I turned to Max, to ask his advice, only to see him frowning at the pavilion. "What?" Again, I noted the calm of the Empress. "Something I should worry about?" Like we needed more.

"Perhaps," he sent. "But only if Moa is foolish enough—" He stopped speaking as her head turned, her beady black eyes fixed on him. His own flared with light in answer as I felt the two giant minds collide. Without another word, the veil tore in a rush of power and Max was gone.

I stared after him, shaken and more than a little worried as the Empress looked away. My attempt to reach her was blocked, but not by her magic.

By sorcery. Panic bit into my gut. "The Brotherhood," I said. "They're here."

Femke swore. "You're certain?" Quaid was already spinning to focus on her, their minds touching a moment in a flare of power before he turned away again, Enforcer fire flying as he tossed out silent orders.

"No," I said. Because I wasn't. But who else could it be? When I sought out the source, I was blocked again. Not Piers, then, or the Steam Union. It had to be Belaisle.

No way he was beating me twice in one day.

"We'll just have to watch for them," she fretted. "But it leaves me little choice. We have to act now. And I hate to do it this way." Femke's grim face turned to the palace. "We're going to have to force our way in."

Charlotte grimaced, looked away. I understood her concern. If Danilo was using the combined power of the werewolves inside to support the shields, Femke's attack would not only harm him but strip the magic of those he used to protect him. It was a huge sacrifice, a massive blow to the werenation. And yet, if the Brotherhood was involved it was possible they were siphoning that power anyway.

"There might be another way." I tested the shielding, felt the power there. But wait. There was no dark magic linked to Danilo's wards. Only the magic of the weres. I could bore a hole in it if I wanted to. Isolate Danilo. But it would probably kill him. Could I live with that? I met Charlotte's eyes. Did she know? She had to. Because she nodded to me before looking away again.

The only problem was that left me with a giant question. Why were the Brotherhood protecting the Empress? Or were they? Could she, instead, be a target? No, I didn't believe that. She would sense their presence and never allow them to harm her. She'd survived too long to fall into a trap of Belaisle's making.

In on it, then. What was Moa up to?

Sydlynn. Max's voice reached me from within the veil. *This is bigger than the werenation. Moa is after something, or she would never risk exposing Jiao's true form.*

What are you talking about? I spun on the pavilion, found the Empress staring at me again. My mind still clung to the sorcery connection, not grasping or comprehending his mention of Jiao.

I will deal with the lóng, he sent. *But you must contain her mistress.*

Oh, boy.

I almost leaped out of my skin as a rattle of bullets hit a glowing wall of blue. What the hell? Only then did I realize Danilo had brought in his mafia friends as reinforcements. A thin line of them, bully boys reminiscent of the two Charlotte had taken care of in the restaurant where we'd found Iosif, trained their ineffective yet troubling guns at us. I'd mistaken the bodies guarding the doors as just werewolves. But they were far from alone. And from what I could tell of the faces of Charlotte's people, their distaste for their allies came through as loud and clear as the rapport of gunfire.

The bullets weren't a risk as long as the shield remained intact. Still, accidents happened.

Could this mess become any more complicated?

"You're going to have to handle this," I said, striding away from Femke. "Take out the guns first. I'll be right back." I hated to leave her hanging, but Max's warning had to be my priority. Not to mention the sorcery. Femke and the others could handle Danilo for now, keep him contained. The bigger stuff was all me.

I felt someone chasing me, turned my head to find Charlotte and Sage on one side, Gram and the vampires on the other. Though it was good to know someone had my back as I glanced up and caught Quaid's dark eyes, I almost sent them back.

He looked away again a moment later, still shouting orders.

I didn't need him anyway.

Bitterness stung but I shoved it aside and rejected my first impulse to ask my friends and family to retreat. He had a job to do and so did I. Besides, I had my peeps at my back and the Empress in my sights. If she had a plan to turn this to her advantage or an ulterior motive connected to the Brotherhood I didn't know about, that was about to change.

She saw me coming, of course she did, but didn't react. Nor did the sorcery surrounding her dissipate. She just sat there on her portable throne and stared at me.

Perhaps caution. My vampire was notorious for such suggestions, but this time I didn't listen.

Screw that, I sent. *She'd better feel like talking.*

The black blossom of my own dark power opened beneath me as I prepared for battle with the opposing sorcery. While I might not be able to find the source, I could damned well do some damage to the caster.

I was halfway to the pavilion when a commotion at the palace doors drew my attention, though it took me a couple of stuttering steps to come to a halt, to switch my focus. I stopped, spun to look, shocked to find Danilo emerging onto the front steps. Femke was already moving, almost to the line of shields keeping her and the others safe, within twenty feet of him. He held up his hands for attention, the mafia men grouping around him, his own wereguards reluctantly flanking the men with guns. As though their meager, mortal weapons could protect the wereking from our power. How little they understood, even with the knowledge he'd given them.

Which made me wonder just how much the common soldiers were aware of. Not that it mattered. Anything they witnessed from this point on told them everything they needed to know about paranormals and the truth of our existence.

"You asked for parley," Danilo said. But not to Femke. His eyes were locked on the Empress. "Your compelling words have my attention. As does your compassion for my fallen queen."

I looked back and forth between them, a frown forming, heart pounding. The Empress did what now? No way did she apologize to Danilo. And, from the darkness of her expression, the calculating look on her face, she'd only maneuvered him into a position that suited her.

What have you done? I shot the question at her, boring through the sorcery shield only to find it gone.

I've done nothing, she sent. *Though I'm prepared to finish this.*

My mind dove for the now missing source of dark power, realizing my mistake. Whoever it was in charge of the sorcery shield, they had nothing to do with Moa. All the while my mind churned around Danilo's appearance. He fell for an offer to talk? Seriously? There had to be something wrong with him, past his deep seated werewolf honor, if he believed the Empress had any interest in peace. Maybe Danilo realized his mistake, because he hesitated after speaking, hands falling to his sides. Opened his mouth as though to go on.

Didn't get to say another word. Not when a black tunnel formed to his right, a writhing, red and gold form emerging from it before it snapped shut.

Inside Danilo's shields.

And lunged for him.

It was as though a fairy tale had come to life. A sinewy creature of Asian history as graceful as a breeze, as deadly as the dragon it was, flowed forward in a ripple of scales and leaped for the wereking.

He should have been dead. None of us could reach him. Even as my mind screamed in frustration, the sky above us opened up in a shimmer of light.

And the drach came flying through.

TWENTY-SEVEN

Danilo's shields collapsed, along with Femke's. And pretty much everyone on the lawn and the steps. Even I fell to my knees, the wards created by the Enforcers dissipating with a pop so loud my ears ached. The drach overhead roared, the earth under me shaking from the volume and pressure of their power.

All but the slim, red and gold Chinese dragon. She tried to run—it had to be Jiao, my struggling mind understood at last—but there was nowhere for her to go. Max dove from the sky while his fellow drach settled around the palace, a ring of giant dragon shapes surrounding everyone, their power containing us. I added mine to theirs as backup, though they really didn't need me. Femke appeared unwilling to fight them and Danilo was just rising from where he'd fallen on the steps. He appeared shaken but unharmed, his face full of sorrow, faint confusion.

Damn it. Was I right about him being thralled? The faint taint of dark power he shed as I touched his magic disappeared like a puff of smoke. But not before it laughed at me in a voice I knew.

Liander Belaisle.

Max landed hard on the grass, his transformation from dragon to human doing nothing to soften the blow of his touchdown, as though the beast in him still had shape. The Chinese dragon squealed in protest as he gestured, a band of rainbow magic encasing her. He pulled her to him with mighty jerks of his powerful arms, until she lay, panting and writhing, at his feet. She appeared smaller than I'd first thought, body slim and low profile, though still the height of a horse and as long as a house.

Jiao's squeal turned to a scream as Max's power pressed down on her, forcing her back into human form. Unlike the weres, and like Max and his people, she retained her skintight black clothing as she collapsed in a heap at his feet.

When he yelled at her, it was in the song of the drach. I felt like I witnessed a primal moment, a thunderstorm washing over rocks, destroying a landscape with the power of its attack. She shrieked back in reply, her own song sharp, painful to hear. I threw up an acoustic shield around them as I noticed the agony their argument was causing the others, the sound cut off like a switch being flipped, though the edges of the wards bowed outward, a testament to the power of their words.

Someone hit me hard in the back and I turned from my stumble with a curse on my lips to find the Empress staring up at me with baleful, beady eyes. The long cane she'd used to strike me still hovered, threatening, her thin lips twitching as her fury took over.

"How dare you interfere!" She tried to hit me again, her power in conjunction, but my vampire was faster—and so was Charlotte. The weregirl grasped the cane and jerked it from Moa's hand even as the ego inside me that created the Empress suppressed her magic and forced her to back down.

Femke was at my side, her own magic crackling. "If I discover you've had some part in this disaster, I will personally ensure you are exterminated once and for all."

The Empress just stared at me, her fury receding. Eyes narrowed, she shrugged her thin shoulders, looking even more the mummified ancient she was.

"Let it be," she said, voice soft. "I've done what I can. The game goes on."

I didn't get a chance to ask her what she was talking about, to demand she tell me about her connection to Belaisle. Why was she working with the Brotherhood? With a flicker of shadow, the Empress fled, leaving her people behind. And though I reached out to try to find her, she vanished from my touch without a trace.

I'll go after her. Sunny was already on the move, but I stopped her.

Let her go, I sent. *Whatever she's involved in, I would imagine Belaisle is at the helm and he's not very happy with her at the moment. Give her some time, she might come to me herself.*

Sunny didn't look happy, but there wasn't much alternative.

Considering we still had the were issue to deal with, I figured it was the best I could do. I'd deal with Moa later. And the sorcerer she was working with.

Would I.

Danilo had recovered enough by then he fought the drach to raise his shields. I had no idea they could just shut him down like that and was grateful they were there. I felt the power of the weres still existed, just blunted and quivering under the control of the drach.

Max finally dismissed my bubble of power and stepped free of the shields as the protections collapsed. Jiao slunk away from him, head down, before disappearing in a puff of smoke. I stared at him, shocked he let her go, but he didn't comment and I was grateful enough for his intervention with the rest of the mess I didn't scream at him.

Yet.

"Council Leader." He bowed to Femke, a towering

powerhouse over her tall, slim form. To her credit, she held her ground without a twitch in the face of his massive magic. "There are those in attendance who are not welcome here." He gestured to the steps of the palace, to Danilo and the soldiers of the mafia who stood staring, their useless guns dropping to their feet. Clearly Max's magic handled the threat of bullets as well as the shielding keeping us from the wereking. I exhaled softly in sudden fear as Max's full power showed its strength. I'd long thought myself his equal, being maji. Even let my own power out to play from time to time. But the sheer volume of energy available to the drach left me breathless and more than a little happy they were the good guys.

"I'll deal with them, if you don't mind, Lord Drach," Femke said, clear and firm.

He bowed to her, his energy retreating as the drach rose from the ground with giant beats of their vast wings and, one by one, disappeared through the veil. Max remained, but stepped behind me, his magic no longer holding Femke's—or Danilo's—back. "Forgive the intrusion," he said. "My part is dealt with. You may proceed."

Femke's mind touched mine in awe and shock, none of which showed on her face. *Oh. My. Swearword.*

She could say that again.

Femke didn't let her loss of command from Max's magic slow her down, though. Before Danilo could gain control again, she pushed her power forward, surrounding the werenation and smothering his response. Part of me wondered if he was tired of fighting or understood he'd been controlled, because he gave in with little effort. I couldn't help but feel sorry for him as Femke spoke in a booming voice boosted by magic.

"You're not welcome here." She didn't have to address the mafia members by name. They knew who they were. She made sure of that, pummeling their ordinary minds with her displeasure. "Your masters have no hold over the werenation. And if I discover even one of your kind attempts to interfere with my people again, I will personally take steps to ensure they—and all of you—do not survive our next meeting." She sent a blast of fear based magic, pure spirit energy, right through them. Some of the hardened, tattoo covered men sobbed in response. More weapons clattered to the ground as she went on. "You've seen too much today. We can't allow you to remember. But, you will remember this." Blue sparks soared overhead, cascading down over each and every one of them. "This place and these people are off limits to you." I watched their faces blank, their eyes glaze, all but fear leaving them. "Now, go. And never return."

Her magic sent them away in bursts of blue flame. I could only hope this was the last we saw of them. I just couldn't bring myself to believe it.

I joined Femke, meeting Mom's eyes in surprise as I realized she'd been there all along, as we walked the short distance to the steps to confront Danilo. He didn't fight, just stood there, shoulders bowed, head down, while his people stood behind him, their sorrow a living, breathing thing.

They knew what was coming. And not one of them had the heart to stand up for him, though as my magic examined him more closely I was convinced of the truth. As if I needed more proof.

How had I missed the control of sorcery over him?

We did look. But. My vampire whispered as my demon and Shaylee both cringed in regret. *Not closely enough. We were too busy thinking he'd done this alone. Too quick to blame, when we know better.*

Only my sorcery was happy, lapping at the edges of the darkness left in Danilo. His eyes met mine and, in that moment, his gaze told me he knew, too.

"If only you'd come to me from the beginning." Femke's voice whispered to him, barely loud enough for me to hear and in a tone that told me she already understood it was never an option.

"I couldn't," he said, equally as softly, his only explanation. I needed to show Femke what I'd seen, that he wasn't entirely culpable. But he straightened before I could and faced her, expression set, looking, for the first time since Yana died, like a true king. "You've come to arrest me?"

"By the power of the World Paranormal Council," she said, crisp, commanding. "I order you to stand down and charge you with crimes against your people and all paranormals."

Danilo nodded even as Quaid stepped past me. I watched my husband's magic encircle the wereking's wrists in a pair of glowing handcuffs, doing my best to stay calm and objective while my heart ached and my mind shrieked at me to protest. To stand up for him. Speak up.

Femke, I sent.

I already know. Her touch told me she sensed what I did. *How did we miss it?*

You were looking? I exhaled my guilt. Perhaps I hadn't failed him alone.

Piers. Quaid. All of us, Syd. Her mental voice shook. *Belaisle's skill has improved. Not one of us saw it.* Her eyes flickered to the side, met mine. *Not even you?*

I shook my head. It had to be his connection to Dark Brother giving him such subtlety. Lovely. Just lovely. I really needed to find Liander and show him just how much I cared. As slowly and painfully as possible.

Femke's shoulders dipped just a bit. "You will be removed for your trial," she said, voice softer than before. "We will be fair but justice will be done, Danilo."

"I ask one boon," he said, loud enough for everyone

to hear.

She looked surprised, but nodded. "You may ask," she said.

"That my family not be punished for my failures." He turned to Charlotte who watched with her flat, empty expression firmly in place. "I ask that Sharlotta Moreau take the throne and may she be a better queen than I ever was king."

I already knew what my friend was going to say.

"By your order, I am no longer a Moreau," Charlotte said. "And I refuse."

Damn it, Femke sent. *I knew this would happen. I hope they can live with the consequences.* "We don't have to do this now."

"We do." Danilo's jaw set. "I will not leave my people unprotected."

"Then, I have a suggestion," Femke said. "That Oleksander Moreau resume the throne."

I missed seeing the former king, standing within, watching. He seemed greatly reduced to me, an old man, not the powerful were I knew he was. He, too, shook his head, though his daughter didn't hesitate.

"I accept such a task," Olena said, proud head raised, shoulders back. "But only as regent. Until my grandson, Yanis, is of majority and able to take the throne." The oldest of the king's brood couldn't have been more than four years old. He had a long way to go to take over. And

I didn't trust Charlotte's mother, not completely. But even Danilo seemed hopeful.

"Thank you, Mother," he said.

She bowed her head at last. "I may have made mistakes with my own children," she said, glancing at Charlotte, "but I will do my very best with yours." Wow. Just. Wow. If I was Charlotte I'd be burning up with fury. My friend just stared at the ground. Fine. I'd be pissed at her mother for her. And wouldn't forget the werewoman's attitude.

"And I." Oleksander's whole demeanor changed, broad shoulders square, the old light back in his eyes. At least he I trusted. "Together we will raise the next wereking. And our nation will be stronger for it."

It should have been a victorious moment. Instead, it just felt like yet another defeat at the hands of the Brotherhood as the good man and king Danilo had been was led away.

TWENTY-EIGHT

Charlotte left with Quaid, Sage accompanying her. I considered staying behind to talk to Oleksander, but he and Olena disappeared inside with Mom and a few other of the leaders, so I let him go. I'd pop back in a few days, show my support and see if there was anything else I could do.

Charlotte's mind reached for mine as Enforcer fire engulfed their little group. *He's my brother*, she sent, without apology. *We did the right thing.*

I let her go, too, Femke at my side. When they disappeared, I turned to her with a small sigh I couldn't contain.

"I'll do everything I can for him," she said, keeping her voice low. "Now that we know he wasn't in full control."

And yet, the pressure of the thrall was so subtle we all missed it. Which made me wonder just how small a push Danilo needed to do what he'd done.

I sighed and looked out over the lawn at the milling group of paranormals remaining. Now that the impending battle was diffused and the werenation no longer the enemy, many of the council leaders were packing up their Enforcers and leaving, in slightly more organized fashion than they'd arrived. Femke really should have been talking to them, not me, but I appreciated her thoughtfulness.

"I know you will," I said. "While I finally find a way to catch the bastard who gave him the push into darkness." I could still hear Belaisle's haunting laughter in my head. Femke nodded, not commenting. Maybe I should have left that task to her Enforcers. But I had a special place in hell set aside for Belaisle and his compatriots. I'd be more than happy to add this assault to his tally.

No matter what, Danilo was still my friend, under all his hurt. He deserved justice, to know who controlled him, if he didn't already. And that meant a chat with the Empress to find out what was really going on.

As for Jiao... I suppose I shouldn't have been surprised to find she had a power like hers. I'd been wary of her from the beginning. Not threatened, really. But I sensed her difference and, from the way Max treated her from the get go, I knew there had to be something odd about her. The ability to turn into a dragon, however, hadn't really crossed my mind. A tinge of irritation woke inside me, triggered by my memory of the drach leader. He knew full well what she was and hadn't told me. Might have info about Moa that could assist. And he'd kept it all to himself. I didn't want to doubt him, not after everything we'd been through, but Max and I had a history, a past that still burned a tiny coal of worry deep inside me. Tied to Liam and betrayal. And though it was Fate who forced Max to hold me back, to keep me from saving my first husband from death, it had been the drach lord's magic and physical body that kept me from reaching Liam. I'd forgiven him long ago, but the pain of that act lingered and likely would forever.

When I turned to look for Max—and answers—I found he'd already gone. Which only made my irritation worse. Gram hadn't left me, though, coming to my side, her brows pulled together as I knew mine were. Sunny and Frank joined us as well while Gram spoke.

"While I'd love to stay and enjoy the Ukrainian evening," she said with her usual wit, "someone would very much like to talk to us."

I perked. "Apollo?"

Sunny and Frank exchanged a look. I motioned for them to join us and they did, without question. A moment later we'd left behind our brief sojourn into one disaster, my mind tickling me with the suggestion we were only heading to another.

Pessimist.

Simon was deep in conversation, Owen at his side, the pair of them talking so low I missed what they were saying. They both looked up as we entered the basement, Simon waving me forward, the light from his monitors catching on the lenses of his glasses.

I circled to his side, bending at the waist, an instant smile on my face as I saw who waved at me from the other side of the screen.

"Nice cleavage," Apollo said.

I laughed, grateful for the unexpected moment of levity. I covered myself with one hand, bending my knees so I didn't have to show him so much. "You're alive," I said. "Nice job."

He grinned, shrugged, the camera moving oddly as he held the shirt it housed in front of him, bare chest just visible below his chin. "Never underestimate a Zornov," he said, before sobering. "I'm in. More than in." He glanced to his right before going on, voice lower. "One of my old recruit buddies is Belaisle's new second in command. Kayden's all chummy again and wants me to join his elite team."

I didn't know if I should be nervous or happy. "You said yes?"

Apollo rolled his eyes. "No, I told him to offer the

perfect chance to someone who wasn't spying on him."

Sigh.

"I'm about to head out," he said, the view shifting as he began to put his shirt back on. I turned away, listening as he talked. "Si said the audio's been an issue, but don't worry, okay? I have it handled." He was up and moving toward a wooden door. It looked like he was somewhere underground.

"Say the word and we'll come get you." That was really the smartest, safest course of action. "And Belaisle."

"Let me keep working this." He paused at the door, hand on the knob. "Just trust me, Syd. When I have Belaisle in my pocket, I'll call you. And you can take his ass down."

The door opened and he emerged from the room he'd been in. I squeaked as he almost ran into someone, the camera just high enough to catch the face of a young man with blond hair. The audio chose exactly then to cut out, of course, the static making Simon wince and turn the sound down. But the video was perfect, catching the smile of the blond, the way he clapped Apollo on the shoulder, shaking the feed. Showing me everything, including who stood behind him when the man I assumed was Kayden stepped out of the way.

Belaisle. And he wasn't alone. Eva Southway stood at his side. She was talking, I could see her lips moving, and for a moment, the sound popped back in.

"—track her anywhere, thanks to Piers—"

That was all I heard. Because a moment later, Liander Belaisle looked up and into Apollo's face.

And the feed went silent and dark.

I tried not to panic. To freak the hell out. Instead, I turned to Simon whose face went rigid in shock.

"Tell me it's a glitch," I said, surprised by how calm I felt.

He didn't meet my eyes. "I have no idea," he said. "But I'll find out."

I stepped away from Simon, turning to Owen. He looked distressed, but not enough for me to think Apollo was dead. "Anything?"

He just shook his head, mute.

Okay then.

When I turned to face Gram and the vampires, I drew a shaky breath. From the looks on their faces, my grandmother had filled Sunny and Frank in on our plan. All three seemed anxious, almost apologetic, worried. Considering I'd just put someone into harm's way and left him there to deal with it on his own, they should have been furious.

I know I was.

"Well," I said, forcing casual past my self-recrimination, "at least now we have proof Eva is working with Belaisle. Piers will be thrilled."

Gram crossed her arms over her chest, giving me the stink eye. "Don't go changing the subject," she said. "I know where your head is. This is not your fault."

"Did he tell us where he was?" I turned to Simon who shook his head.

"I have GPS, though, remember?" He tapped on his keyboard "I know exactly where he is."

"No, don't." Owen grabbed my arm, turned me toward him. "Please, Syd, trust Apollo. No one can talk himself out of a corner like he can. He'll be okay." If there had even been a hint of doubt in the younger Zornov I would have pulled the plug, torn the world apart at the coordinates Simon gave me. But, instead of fear, there was only surety, confidence in his brother.

Still, Belaisle was where Apollo stood just a moment ago. The temptation was so powerful I could taste it.

"If you barge in now," Owen said, voice low, for my ears only, "you might get him killed."

Sobering thought. "I want Belaisle." So badly. So. Freaking. Much. The look on Danilo's face would not leave me alone, nor would the whisper of Belaisle's mocking laughter left behind with the magic he'd used to control the wereking.

Think about that a moment, my vampire sent. *He wanted you to know.*

Taunting us, my demon snarled.

No. Shaylee hesitated before going on. *A lure.*

A trap? Did he want me to chase him? If what Eva said was true, he knew where I was right now. At this second. A cold sweat broke out all over me, plastering the silk shell of my blouse to my body. Everyone in the room with me was in danger.

Don't be silly, my vampire sent. *If he wanted to attack Wilding Springs, he'd have done so.*

Tried that, my demon sent. *Lost the farm.*

Right. Deep breaths, Syd.

There is always the possibility of sending in or recruiting a spy in our midst. Leave it to Shaylee to think of that. Her mother, Aoilainn, was, after all, the Seelie queen and mistress of deception.

Happy thought, that, my demon growled.

I find that unlikely, but I suppose we can't ignore any options at this juncture. My vampire's voice, normally calm and cold, sounded almost eager. She did love a good puzzle. *What worries me more is the fact he tried to make you chase him in the first place. That's new.* My vampire paused before going on. *And makes me worry he thinks he has a way to stop you this time.*

We'd just see about that.

We need to set that trap, my vampire sent. *Use this against him. It's the only way we'll win.*

"Twenty-four hours," I said, swallowing my anxiety, giving in to my vampire and to the look on Owen's face. "If we don't have contact with Apollo before then, we go looking. Agreed?"

Owen nodded quickly, turned back to Simon.

Agreed, my egos said in chorus.

I uncoiled as best I could, stomach churning unhappily, before letting it go.

"I'll find Piers." Gram hugged me. "Tell him the bad news."

"Thanks." I just didn't have the heart to break it to one of my closest friends his mother was as big a traitor as I thought she was.

"Anything we can do?" Sunny and Frank both seemed forlorn, lost, holding hands like a young, beautiful couple who'd somehow lost their way.

"Yes," I said, slipping between them as Gram disappeared in a tunnel of black. "You can come home with me and watch a movie. Maybe make cookies. And pretend like nothing is wrong for a little while."

They draped their arms over my shoulders we walked back to the house, me hugging them around their waists. It was a warm dusk for late September, the kind of day that felt like summer might be coming back for a visit, if just for a little while. Crickets sang their early evening happy songs from the grass, a pond ringing with the joy of a group of eager frogs. The hum of electrical wires filled the backspace of the song of nature and, truly, for that stroll on the warm pavement down the block under the just waking light of the streetlamps with the vampires

278

at my side, I believed anything was possible.

Sydlynn. Max's voice reached me, broke the spell of beauty, pulled me to a halt.

Max. I was still annoyed with him, I realized. He must have sensed it, because his power gently hugged me before he spoke again.

You have questions.

Duh. I rubbed my forehead while waving off the concerned looks of Sunny and Frank. *I do*, I sent. *But you're calling for a reason.*

The Fates need to see us, he sent.

Right now? I looked up at the stars, drawing a deep breath. *It's been a long couple of days, Max.*

I understand, he sent, urgency in his voice. *But they insist. And they've asked for you to bring Gabriel.*

TWENTY-NINE

They wanted me to what? I shook my head, a frown forming. *Forget it*, I sent. *Leave my son out of this.*

My choice as well, he sent. *But they are most persistent. And say if you don't bring him they will have him brought.*

Like bloody freaking hell. I steamed as I paced a small circle on the street. Sunny and Frank watched, silent and steady, there for me though they had no idea what was going on. I loved them for that, stopped and hugged them both.

"The Fates want to see Gabriel." I stepped back from the vampires who both radiated concern.

"Is it safe?" Sunny's question was less fearful and more calmly curious.

"I think so." I shivered, rubbing at the fresh goosebumps on my arms. I was so tired of this suit, seriously. How long had I been wearing it? I needed a shower and some junk food and sleep. Maybe coffee. Not another trip through the veil with my son.

The vampires exchanged a look before Uncle Frank spoke.

"His power is beyond the rest of us," he said, blue eyes sad. "And I know he's just a boy, but Syd... if they're asking."

"I have to go." I nodded to them. "Thanks for coming, you guys."

"We'll go to the house," Sunny said, taking Frank's hand. "Check in with the girls." So they knew about that, did they? "And Sass will want to be updated. We'll hold down the fort until you get home."

So much love. Did I even deserve it? I embraced them again before turning and opening the veil. I couldn't say thank you. I'd cry. I just hoped they knew how grateful I was.

I arrived at Harvard in the growing dark, though Mom's light was on in her office. I didn't want a conversation about this trip, so I shielded my power as I tiptoed to the hall and the kid's doors. Gabriel's was across from Ethie's. Guilt I was leaving her behind warred with fear at bringing him along. Galleytrot lifted his big head as I eased the door open and pressed my finger to my lips to keep him quiet.

What's wrong? He was on his feet, big mane shaking as the hound sensed my concern.

Nothing, I sent, sitting next to my son. Gabriel's eyes opened and he sat up, appearing to be wide awake.

"We're going, aren't we, Mom?" He turned and slid out of bed, reaching for his jeans lying on the chair next to him. "They asked me to come visit." He knew already?

The Fates. "We are," I said, glancing at Galleytrot.

"Not without me," he rumbled.

Before I could tell him otherwise, Gabriel finished buttoning his pants and laid his hands on the big dog's head. "Not this time," he said, with kindness but firmly. "There are things I think I need to do alone."

Galleytrot's low whine broke my heart but he bowed his big head to Gabriel.

"Be safe," the dog whispered.

"Always." My son looked up at me with a smile. "Can we go now?"

So eager. I just hoped our trip to Center was everything he imagined.

I wasn't messing around with this visit, hell no. When I opened the veil it was directly in the Fate's chamber, refusing to risk setting down in the courtyard below. Zeon and his maji could bite my ass for the break in protocol. No way was I giving that zealot a chance to lay one eyeball on my son.

The leader of the maji hated me, that much was obvious, and thought Gabriel a mistake. I'd do everything I could to protect Gabriel from him and his vitriol.

Anything.

Max was already there, waiting for us and, despite the fact I usually had to alter my size to fit the space, Gabriel and I had no problems, nor did we need to grow to come face-to-face with the two blind Fates. The brother and sister team didn't seem concerned we'd ignored the usual method of arrival, instead smiling at me as though knowing I was there.

But no, not me. Their greeting was aimed beside me.

"Gabriel." Sister Fate hurried forward as best she could, still blind. Her senses seemed to have improved, because she found him without stumbling. Either that or they had a connection to him that made it easier for her.

That thought would keep me up nights.

After she was done hugging him, her brother took his turn.

"We're so happy to meet you at last," she said while her brother nodded.

"You, too," Gabriel said. He was normally a little shy, reserved, but the smile he beamed at the two of them was friendly and open, as if he knew them but was only just seeing them in person.

Which gave me a sick feeling in my stomach. "You've been talking to my son." Accusation at the ready? You betcha.

"We have." Sister Fate seemed unfazed by my anger. Her white eyes turned to meet mine, gentle smile on her face. "He is as tied to us as you are, Sydlynn. And deserves to understand who and what he is."

"It's okay, Mom." Gabriel waved me off, followed the two Fates to the edge of her fountain. "I'm not scared."

Well, that made one of us. I glared at Max who shrugged.

I had no idea, he sent.

Whatever.

"We wanted you to be here," Sister Fate said to my son, "because we have news." Her arm draped over his shoulders as he sat next to her, though she tilted her face up toward me. "We had another vision, more powerful even than when we had full access to our foresight." Interesting. "We can only assume Gabriel opened a new Gateway?"

Max quickly told them what we knew, though neither my son nor I shared what Gabriel did after Max was gone. They didn't need to know. And I doubt it would have mattered. Because even though the drach informed the pair the latest piece of Creator was in the hands of Belaisle, neither seemed concerned.

"All we can say," she told me with excitement, "is your plan for a trap will work. But, be wary of what you believe when you question your captives."

So cryptic. My favorite. "Would you like to elaborate?"

Brother Fate shook his head, finally showing

frustration. "That was the last piece of information we were able to glean," he said. "Which is why Gabriel's presence was so necessary."

Tell me they weren't about to suggest what I thought they were going to suggest.

Yeah, no hope there.

"We want Gabriel to open a Gateway here, in our presence," Sister Fate said. "So we can try to reactivate our foresight permanently."

Oh, *hell* to the *no freaking way*.

I wasn't the only one who wanted to protest, it turned out, but for totally different reasons.

"ENOUGH!" I spun to find Zeon and a few of his closest psycho maji friends crowding the entrance to the Fate's fountain room. "You will hand over that creature and allow it to be destroyed before it ruins everything."

My power crackled in response as I threw up a barrier between him and my son. Max joined me, his drach magic slipping behind mine, the song of his race vibrating at such a high frequency my teeth ached. Still, I appreciated the backup.

Zeon didn't back off, but he stopped making demands. Instead, he spun sideways and cut open the veil. I scowled at him, wondering what his plan was. If he tried to toss my son through to another plane he wasn't thinking straight. It took me a moment to understand what was happening and, by the time I did, it was far too late to stop.

I knew that world on the other side of the tear. The blue sky, the crystal water of the lake, the green grass with mountains in the distance. And the small, huddled group of people with filthy clothing and an extra pair of ears. At first, I thought they were sleeping, all piled together. Until I saw their faces.

Their open, staring eyes.

And I gasped a breath.

Oh, no.

My son pushed to my side and my hands scrabbled to catch him, to keep him safe, but he escaped me. He crossed my shields unharmed, my power allowing him through, until he stood next to the towering, glaring Zeon. But Gabriel only had eyes for what lay beyond the veil.

"What happened to them?" His tiny voice ached with hurt. "Are they dead?" My son looked up at Zeon whose judging face didn't seem to register with Gabriel. "Why are they dead?"

"Because," Zeon boomed, "you tried to play god. You sent these people from the plane that was their home and you offered them paradise. But this place was not meant for them. And it killed them, poisoned them with every breath." He looked up at me and, for a moment, there was real fear and compassion in the maji leader's eyes. "Listen to me," he said. "The veil barrier exists for a reason. To keep races away from planes that aren't intended for them. There are those of us who can cross and not suffer harm. But the rules are the rules, and Creator herself set them down." His empathy faded as he looked down at my son, lip twisting. "This spawn you've brought into the Universe has changed that. No more does the veil barrier mean anything. When he creates a Gateway, anyone and anything can pass through it. No matter the race. Do you understand how dangerous that is?"

"But the creatures from the other Universe." I stumbled over an excuse, an answer, anything but to accuse my son of murdering these people he tried to save. "They've had no barriers, have been able to pass to any plane."

"They are different," Zeon said. "They are not of our Universe, they know no boundaries. And," he jabbed one thick finger at Gabriel, "he is the reason they are here, in case you've forgotten."

I choked on a reply that would have sizzled the air.

"Meddling in creation isn't for the likes of you and your dark child," Zeon said. "This abomination you've brought into our Universe in your cursed womb will be the destruction of us all." He reached out, his power heading for Gabriel, but met with three pronged resistance. Mine, instant. Max's, just as fast.

And the veil's. The hole in the fabric between worlds

snapped with power, slamming into Zeon's chest and shoving him backward. It sealed shut when it was done, leaving the solemn and terrible scene etched in my head, if no longer physically visible.

Zeon staggered, his hand on his chest where the magic had struck him. Real fear showed on his face, shaking finger once more pointing at my son.

"You've turned the very veil against its true purpose," he said, voice trembling, his maji followers muttering their own fear behind him. "Our fate is sealed." He turned away, but not before meeting my eyes. "Those deaths are on his head. As are all those who came before and will come after. Mark me, Sydlynn Hayle. Your son will be the end of us all."

He spun then and marched off, maji following behind him. I couldn't have cared less about his retreat routine, not when I was faced with the massive tragedy before me.

With a voiceless cry, Gabriel crumpled to the ground and burst into silent sobs.

THIRTY

War broke out inside me, the need to go after Zeon and tear him to pieces fighting with my mother's instinct to protect my son, to comfort and cradle him against what the maji leader just did to hurt my precious baby.

Mommy won, partly because of Max.

"It is irrelevant what Zeon thinks," he said, voice low and subdued. "Only Gabriel matters now."

I really was a horrible parent. My son spun, his back to me, arms over his head, little spine hunched as he tried to hide between his own knees. His entire body shook with silent grief and the moment I bent to touch him he jerked away from me, pulling himself into an even tighter knot.

It didn't help when I looked up both Fates were turned toward me, sadness on their matching faces.

"Forgive us our selfishness," Sister Fate said. "Gabriel

should never have been exposed to any of this. Perhaps we were wrong and he is simply too young."

"No," Max said, hands clenched at his sides. Did he feel the same guilt I did? No way. No one else could understand the searing, tearing agony of regret I felt in that moment, the stabbing attack I wielded against myself over and over while the egos inside me groaned their sympathy. I'd betrayed my own son's heart. I'd left him open to be hurt, possibly irrevocably. I was a monster, not him.

How could I have done this to Gabriel?

"We need him." Brother Fate's sorrow turned to grim sternness. "It's too late now to reverse what we've done with Gabriel, you must see that. Perhaps we should have waited. But he has led our enemies to two of the pieces of Creator. Plans have been set in motion. There's no turning back now."

Like hell there wasn't. Both Fates took a step closer, their empty gazes turned down toward Gabriel still huddled on the ground. I moved between them, my own agony spinning into a tornado of fury so powerful I could barely breathe, speak. But I had my magic to communicate for me.

They staggered away as I pushed them back from him, breath panting from my lips. I may have been a horrible mother, but I had no problem tapping into my protective instinct. My demon howled her fury, Shaylee pushing her power down into the ground, shaking us just enough the water in the fountain splashed over the edge. Only my vampire remained quiet, thoughtful.

To hell with her. And them. I was done using my son. And so were they.

I spun and lifted him into my arms, holding him against me. Gabriel sagged in my embrace, boneless, still weeping in silence. I couldn't look down into his face and remain upright, in control. Something I only needed to do a few minutes longer.

Max let me go, coming between me and the Fates, his sad face the last thing I saw before I jerked open the veil and took Gabriel home.

But no, not home. I have no idea why, instead of Wilding Springs, my aching heart carried us to Harvard, to Mom's sitting room. To where she stood with my husband at her side.

Both looked shocked at our arrival, Mom's concern only a fraction of the fear that flashed over Quaid's face. I stumbled forward, heartbroken for my child, only to have Gabriel throw himself from my arms and at his father.

Quaid embraced my boy, hugging him tight as, with a choking, gasping sound, Gabriel finally began to cry out loud, releasing the terrible hurt in great, coughing sobs. I crumpled a little, my soul dying with each sound, Shaylee retreating from me to weep herself, my demon's power burning low and full of sorrow. Only my vampire remained with me, cool and calm, holding me up when I was certain my son's hurt would be the thing that finally killed me.

"Syd." Mom came to my side as Galleytrot burst from the hall leading to the bedrooms, rushing to Quaid. His big nose pressed into Gabriel's leg just as my son released his hold on his father and fell onto the back of the big hound. He clung there like a wounded animal a moment before sliding to the floor. Galleytrot engulfed him with his massive body, hiding my son from me in a cave of black fur between his front legs. I wanted to go to Gabriel, to comfort him, but guilt held me back, kept me in place, Mom's hand on my arm. "What happened?"

Quaid's furious chocolate eyes flared with magic. "What did you do?"

I choked on my answer, wanting to protest, but there was nothing I could say in defense. Not one blessed thing. I shook my head instead, mouth moving but nothing coming out. Galleytrot rumbled a growl as Gabriel's sobs finally softened and ended. For all I knew he'd fallen asleep, worn out by the grief, or he was simply retreating further from us.

Too gentle. I should have known better.

"Where did you go?" Mom's soft, practical question, her steadiness, helped me push out an answer, my eyes locked on hers.

"Center," I whispered.

"Why did you take Gabriel to the maji?" Quaid's anger hit me like blows, every word a weapon, his power behind them. I'd never seen him so angry. But, instead of fueling my self-recrimination, his attack triggered my own temper. I jerked free of Mom and yelled back.

"Because I had to!" Didn't I? Gabriel's fate was decided a long time ago, in the maji chamber, when Ameline forced him to open his first Gateway. I had no choice. And yet—

"Don't hand me that crap," Quaid snarled, body quivering, hands clenched at his sides. "You always have a choice, Syd. And you know it." He swallowed hard. "What happened?"

I shook my head, trying to deny it, knowing I had to come clean. Stuttered through the admission of what happened on the dying plane, of Gabriel's attempt to save the people his compassion drove him to assist, how they died. And how he found out.

Mom's white face seemed all the paler as her blue eyes darkened, one hand rising to cover her mouth. "Oh, Syd," she whispered.

Quaid's reaction was much more explosive. "What the hell were you thinking?" He took two steps toward me, tanned cheeks deep red from the pressure of his fury, blue flames crackling around him as both fists came up, almost in my face.

I stood there, mute and tired and hurting, my anger

the only thing I had left.

"You've lost your mind." He lowered his voice and his hands, shaking with the effort it took to hold himself together. I felt through the connection of our magic just how close he was to flying apart. "You've gone so far into this fantasy you have of being the only one who can fix the Universe you've put everyone you love in danger, and you don't give a crap about it, do you?"

He might as well have slapped me. What anger I had left trickled away as my guilt returned, devouring me from the inside out. So much spite and rage I couldn't take. Not from him. Especially because I was so afraid he was right.

"I don't know you anymore," he said, his shaking easing, anger retreating. "I don't think I ever did." The core of his bitterness didn't go away. It lived between us, a fire ready to reawaken at any moment. When did he start to hate me? Where did this come from, this darkness keeping us apart?

How did I miss that my husband didn't love me anymore?

With a groan, the first sound he emitted since falling silent, Gabriel pushed free of Galleytrot and ran for his room. I instinctively lunged for him, only to have Quaid step in my path.

Anger came back. Hell yeah.

"Get out of my way." My power surged, demon

reacting against him like she'd never done before. She was ready to tear out his throat and I was right there with her.

"You think I'm going to let you anywhere near him ever again?" Quaid pushed against me, his power hitting me in the center of my chest. Just a soft blow, but a challenge none the less.

Oh, no he did *not*.

"Children." Mom's voice snapped between us, a blade cutting the fury that held us together. "Enough. This is about Gabriel, not the two of you."

Quaid's power retreated but he remained where he was, standing over me, arms crossing over his broad chest. As if, for a second, I'd ever feel intimidated by him.

"I'm going to Hong Kong," Quaid said, voice full of command and judgment. "And I'm taking the kids with me."

Even Mom gasped at that.

"Over my dead body," I said. "Just try it."

"They're not safe here," he said, before glancing to Mom. "No offense, Miriam. But I think we know now they're not."

"Safe from what?" Ice shards jabbed into my heart. "Safe from me?"

Quaid didn't answer. He didn't have to.

I hit him as hard as I could, my fist smacking the tight muscle of his shoulder. He rocked a little but barely registered the blow. I knew violence wasn't the answer.

But I had to do something, and bruising my knuckles on his tough hide was better than slamming him into the wall with the full force of my magic. Frustration and fury and guilt all wound together and tightened a noose around my neck.

"What the hell is wrong with you?" I was shaking now, my turn. When had things gone so wrong with us? We loved each other. Had a great life, amazing kids, a happy existence. Why did strife drive us apart when it should pull us together? He'd turned his back on me long before this moment. He was just proving to me now he didn't care.

He never did.

"What's wrong with me?" Quaid's eyebrows shot up, arms dropping to his sides, genuine shock on his face. All anger was gone, raw emotion showing through our magic connection. He was hurt, deeply, lost and afraid. "Syd, you put our son in direct danger twice, for your own gain. And then exposed him to a race that wants to have him killed." He waited for that to sink in while I writhed inside and hated myself enough for the both of us. "What's wrong with *you*?"

A ball of fire erupted in my gut. Spite, bitterness, rage, uncontrollable and full of bile. And I used it against him instead of myself.

"Gabriel isn't your son," I said.

The moment those words left my lips, I died inside.

The ball of fire crumbled to ash and I raised one hand, gasping a breath, to take it back, to apologize. Did I really just use that against Quaid, the very thing I swore I never would?

His face tightened and he backed away a step, stumbling over the edge of the carpet. Quaid's whole body shook once, the power between us going silent as he cut me off from feeling him. But I could still sense enough and knew I'd done the unthinkable, the unforgivable.

"I've known, you know." He didn't meet my eyes, deep voice cracking as his power rose around him. "Our whole married life, I've known." When he finally looked up, his eyes were flat, empty. "You loved Liam more than you ever loved me."

Not true! I threw myself forward, but, as was my fate these days, I was too late to catch him. With a flare of blue flames that singed my skin as I tried to hold him, Quaid was gone.

THIRTY-ONE

I stood there, staring at the place where my husband had been, hands still grasping the empty air, heart collapsed in my chest. It wasn't until something nudged my hip I looked down, breaking the spell I'd created around myself, a moment in which I could believe what happened hadn't just.

Galleytrot's dark eyes burned with red fire as he growled softly. "Syd," he said. "How could you?" And padded away toward the kid's rooms, leaving me to crumple, at last, under the weight of all of my grief.

But Mom was there to catch me. Her arms around me, guiding me to the sofa, her hands stroking my hair, rubbing my back, voice whispering kindly, the scent of lilacs taking me back in time to when I was a girl and everything was easier, simpler.

Before I ruined the lives of those I loved.

I finally pulled myself together, wiping tears from my face. "Mom," I said, voice cracking. "How could I have messed this up so badly?"

Mom stroked my hair back from my face. "I used to ask your father the same question about you. I thought I'd done damage I could never repair. But we figured it out, Syd."

I shook my head, leaning forward, face in my hands, elbows on my knees. "I have to make this right." Poor Quaid. How could he think such a thing? Fear fluttered, the old worry about him, about me. So many times we'd lost each other. I'd thought we'd finally have our happily ever after. But now...

Dear elements. What now?

"Quaid will cool off," Mom said. "And Gabriel will be fine. He's suffered a trauma, Syd. But he has a vast and complex power, one we both know he's been given for a reason." She sighed, settled back into the cushions. "Now you understand just how difficult it is to raise children of magic. And how hard it is to make the choices that will not only keep them safe, but in Gabriel's case, the very Universe. Quaid was wrong, sweetheart. I, of all people, understand. You have no choice." She pulled me toward her again, kissing my forehead as she hugged me. "You had no choice."

I rose from the couch without answering her. I just didn't have anything to say. Hadn't I been telling myself the same thing all along? How was I supposed to balance being a mom with being the Light One, especially when one of my kids seemed to have all the answers to the threat facing our Universe? It wasn't fair. My son wasn't a tool. But Gabriel was the Gateway.

Confused and hurting, I went to his door. Found Galleytrot on the bed, my son curled up against him, asleep. And Ethie on the other side, arm flung over her brother's shoulder. It took me a long moment before I could convince my feet to move, to go to my children. Galleytrot glared at me, but I ignored him. Bent and kissed my daughter's sleeping face. Then my son's. Gabriel twitched, cheeks still wet from his tears. I pressed both hands over my mouth to hold back the sob building in my chest as my own tears fell on his face and trickled down into his pale hair.

I'll take care of him, Galleytrot sent, cold and sharp. *But it's best you go, Syd. He needs time to mend.*

The hound's words should have made me angry. Instead, they just added to my pain. Shoulders bowed, head low, I opened the veil and went home.

The kitchen was quiet, but not empty. And, for an instant of shock, when I realized I had a visitor, my breath caught in my chest. Not because seeing Charlotte was such a strange thing, but because I hadn't expected to have to admit my guilt to anyone so soon. I planned to have a hot shower to wash away the horror of the last few hours and then hide under the covers, probably cry for a while, and maybe sleep.

She took one look at me and her face altered from her normal stoic blankness to fear. "Syd?" Charlotte stood, the chair under her scraping over the tiles and she came to me, embracing me, even as I once again crumbled like a broken doll.

Charlotte guided me to a chair, held my hand as I told her everything. It was easier this time, actually, less painful. It helped I knew she didn't judge me, simply sat and listened, nodded on occasion. The padding of paws and the tremor of the table told me Sass had come to join us. I didn't look up, couldn't meet his amber eyes, knowing he would hate me for what I'd done to my son. But, when I finally finished, wiping at my nose with the cuff of my jacket, I did raise my head, and found the silver Persian's empathy in the sideways droop of his ears and the downward curve of his whiskers.

"Oh, Syd," he said. "I'm so sorry."

A cry escaped me as I reached for him, pulled him into my arms. Sass and I rocked a moment as his purr rose, crackling around his own grief, his energy doing its best to support me while his hurt mingled with mine. I finally set him down in my lap, stroking his fur, letting out a long, vocal sigh as I shook my head.

"And that was my day," I said. "You two?"

We all laughed, a little shaky. But I was feeling better

now. Less overwhelmed. Still guilty, but free of the crushing weight of all that emotion. I would think this through, work it out, with my son and my husband. And we'd talk, cry, love each other again. My fears about Quaid were unfounded. He was as afraid as I was, I felt that in him. We just needed to find the time to be together and communicate, resolve it all.

"Actually," Charlotte said, a flicker of her own guilt showing, "I'm here for a reason."

Of course she was. I squeezed her hand, showing her it was all right.

"It doesn't matter." Charlotte looked away, lips tight, face grim. "Screw him. You have enough to worry about and he doesn't deserve pity from anyone."

I exchanged a look with Sassafras. "Who?"

Charlotte's fingers tapped a beat on the table top before she tsked. "Andre Dumont."

"What's going on?" Oddly, this was exactly what I needed. A distraction. I grasped onto the mystery and prodded her further. "What does Andre want?"

"He asked to see us both," she said. "He's dying."

"He's been dying for a while now," Sass said with his usual snark back in place.

Charlotte flashed her teeth in a fierce grin. "For real this time."

I climbed to my feet, brushing dust from my rumpled suit. "Let's go get this over with," I said. "He may be a rat bastard, but if Andre is asking for us I'm actually curious to know what he has to say."

Charlotte hesitated before nodding and standing beside me. I shook my head at Sass as he pawed my arm.

"You stay home," I said. "Please. We won't be long."

Sass sighed, nodded. "Frank and Sunny are asleep upstairs," he said. "I'll tell them where you went. And if you're not home in an hour, I'm coming after you."

As if Andre and his coven could do anything to harm me. Still, I appreciated the support.

Taking Charlotte's hand in mine felt right. So did leaving behind my suffering to watch one more deserving get what was coming to him. I worried that made me a bad person, but accepted it as truth anyway.

The broad front steps of the Dumont mansion were dark, the sun long gone to bed by now. Tall shadows stretched out from the full moon hanging low in the starry, cloudless sky. Kristophe waited for us, sitting on the top stair in the light of the single lamp over the door, his long hair messy, face anxious. He'd always seemed so put together. Again I was struck by how badly he'd let himself go, aged beyond his years in the yellow illumination over his head. To hide what? I didn't know his full story, or that of his brother, though I could guess at the pressure of growing up Dumont. All I'd really gleaned came from Charlotte. Her grim face at that moment told me she knew more than she wanted to.

Why did I care? I mused over that as Kristophe stood and turned without a word, leading us inside. The house was quiet, the air stale as though no windows had been open in centuries. The tang of decay was stronger than I remembered and as we crossed the foyer and passed behind the stairs, it only grew stronger.

From what I remembered, the master bedchamber lay up a floor, down an ornate hall. It had been Mia's once. But the room Kristophe led us to was buried down a narrow corridor, behind a plain wooden door. I met Charlotte's eyes as Kristophe opened it and stood aside, head down, waiting for us to enter.

I almost didn't, gagging on the stench of death wafting from the room. But Charlotte was on the move and I couldn't leave her to do this alone.

"Stop!" I turned to find Jean Marc striding toward us. Charlotte kept going, disappearing inside. A quick glance at Kristophe, his shoulders twitching with guilt, told me this wasn't a sanctioned visit. That Jean Marc thought he was in charge, despite his father's hard cling to life.

It was immensely satisfying to flash the older Dumont a middle finger salute before crossing the threshold and sealing the door behind me. He might not want us here, but it was Andre who summoned us. And I found even more now I wanted to know what he had to tell me.

You are not welcome here. Jean Marc's power oozed through my shield enough to reach me.

Your father is still leader, I sent. *I can sense it. And it's his will that called to us. So, mind your betters, boy. And wait outside.*

It was obvious from the resentment in Jean Marc he was only waiting for Andre to die. And fair enough. But I had a feeling Mom was right about the Dumont power and the elder Dumont brother was in for a shock when daddy dearest finally gave up the echo.

None of my business. I shoved aside all thought of Jean Marc and his ambition, stepping forward to Charlotte's side to face the monster she'd doomed to die.

THIRTY-TWO

The gloom in the chamber did little to hide the wreck of a man lying under the covers of the large four poster bed. Andre must have chosen this bedroom for its lack of windows. Perhaps he had no desire to see outside any longer, to feel the breath of fresh air on his decaying cheeks.

I thought I was prepared for this, after the day I'd had. After knowing he was literally disintegrating from the curse Charlotte placed on him. But I honestly had no idea how far a body could decompose and remain alive.

No. Idea.

Andre's breath whistled in and out from between his cracked lips, the only part of him that didn't seem to ooze some fluid. I held my ground—and the contents of my stomach—only out of sheer will. He looked like a special effects zombie from some B-list movie, overdone for major creep factor. But, when he opened his eyes, the single one remaining him shone with awareness, the icy blue rimmed in red.

Charlotte stared, silent and solemn, though without an ounce of pity to be seen or felt. I was finding it increasingly difficult to share her detachment as each moment passed, forced as I was to use magic to filter the stench of his decay from my nostrils so I wouldn't pass out from the smell.

No one should have to suffer like this. When his hand rose from the covers, a small piece of flesh fell with a wet plop from the side of his thumb.

Okay, now I was going to puke for real.

But Charlotte simply crossed to him, though she didn't touch him, taking a seat in the simple chair at his bedside as though there to comfort a friend. I joined her only through absolute control of my churning guts, thankful the second seat was a little further away and I could use her to block part of my view.

Andre turned his head, infinitely slowly, leaving clumps of hair behind as the few wisps of his blond locks clung bravely to the oozing remains of his scalp. His chest barely rose and fell, the covers slightly disturbed at the movement of his inhale and exhale. Thankfully the majority of his wasted body was covered in silk pajamas long soaked through by the oozing of his flesh and a heavy comforter. I didn't see toes or anything resembling feet-like lumps and wondered if he had them anymore.

Gag. This was too much.

"Charlotte." Oh. My. Swearword. He could still talk. If that was talking. Wet, bubbling, a dark tongue edged in black snaking out between his dry lips as he struggled to speak. He'd crumbled so much further than when I'd seen him.

Was that really just yesterday?

"Andre." She nodded to him, all casual. How? How was she managing when I could barely breathe?

He coughed softly, almost in apology, the single hand in view on the comforter twitching in response. When he spoke again, his voice was clearer, kind of normal, frightening coming from the disgusting remains of his wasting body. "I didn't think," wet breath, "you'd come." His single eye swiveled in the sunken socket, a patch of white bone showing. I bit hard on the inside of my cheek as he looked at me. "And Sydlynn. So kind of you," if he breathed in like he was sucking on water one more time I was going to heave over the side of the chair, "to accept my invitation."

No comment.

"What do you want, Andre?" Charlotte's tone was light, playful. Was she taunting him? I suppose I hardly blamed her. He'd tortured her most of her young life, abused her physically, mentally, sexually. She'd only told me the barest fraction of what he'd done, including her most recent encounter with him that led us here, to this place, with him dying from her power inside him.

"I know I don't deserve your pity." His voice dropped in volume, fingers clenching at the covers. I looked away as one of his thin, blackened fingernails lifted free and feathered to the floor. I quickly jerked my foot back so it wouldn't land on the toe of my shoe. "But your revenge is complete. I've asked you here to beg you to release me from this torment."

She didn't say anything, just sat there, head cocked to one side. I almost reached for her, to ask her to just do as he wanted, when she finally spoke.

"You've learned your lesson, is that it?" I wondered if he heard the threat in her mild tone, if he really knew Charlotte at all. I felt it, sensed it, knew it for what it was. She would let him rot like this forever.

Andre shuddered before speaking. "I swear," he whispered, as though he'd lost the brief burst of energy that he'd greeted us with. "If you would only reverse this curse, I will be your slave. To torture and kill, revive and destroy, over and over again. Only free me from the agony of this endless death."

Charlotte's laughter tinkled like a soft bell, sweet, cheerful. I winced, though held still. This was hers to see through to the end and I was just an observer.

"Andre," she said, still smiling. "How darling of you."

He didn't speak, simply watched her with his single

blue eye, desperation in the power that hovered over him, around us.

Charlotte. I gently touched her mind. *It might be time*.

I know. Her own was far sadder than her outward expression led me to believe. I was surprised by her softness, the regret in her. *But, Syd. I wouldn't know where to start. I didn't intend for this to happen. Only for him to die. This decay... I'm ashamed of what I've done*. Fierce pride hit me hard. *And I'm not*.

Completely understandable, I sent. *What do you want to do?*

"I could care less about your fate," Charlotte said, feigning a yawn behind one hand. "But, if Syd is willing to try to save you, I won't stop her." She met my eyes. *I'm sorry to drop this on you*, she sent. *But I just can't, Syd*.

I nodded, hugging her with energy. *Thank you for trusting me with this*, I sent as gently as I could. *I know how much he hurt you. But if you let him die without trying to redeem yourself, I fear he'll win even after he's gone*.

She just stared at me a long moment before looking away.

My power was reluctant to touch Andre, and I didn't blame it. The family magic hated him for the same reasons I did. My demon's huffing told me she wouldn't be much help and even Shaylee turned her back. But my vampire sighed and came with me, exploring the damage that had been done.

Not just on the surface. To every molecule and cell in

Andre's body. It was like sinking into a cesspool of rot and bile, while the core of Charlotte's curse clung with wolf like tenacity to his soul and echo, trapping him within, forcing him to live his death.

I pulled free without trying to reverse the damage. There was just nothing there to repair. I considered briefly calling the Kennecott twins to see if their healing abilities could accomplish this thing, but changed my mind. He was too far gone and I wouldn't subject them to this.

The ball was back with Charlotte. It was up to her to foul out or slam dunk.

Andre must have sensed my failure because he sighed, a burbling sound, his body settling further beneath the sheets as though it had given up entirely on him and was collapsing at the skeletal level.

"So be it," he said, voice stronger again. "Jean Marc will be pleased."

"Your son waits for your death," I said.

"Parasite." Andre turned his head, the last of his earlobe on the pillow beside him, blood oozing over bone. I gulped and tried to distract myself, focusing on a tiny hole I'd acquired in the knee of my dress pants. "Little does he know there will be no inheritance for him to exploit." Andre's cackling laughter was the sound of heart pounding nightmares. I'd be carrying that around with me for a long time.

"Andre, I have questions." Would he answer? Did it matter? Maybe not. But this man wasn't the antagonistic asshat I was used to. Perhaps near death he would be willing to speak with candor.

"I know you do." His eye met mine again. "It's part of the reason I asked you to join us."

"You're willing to tell me what you know?"

Andre's smile exposed bone and retreating, blood red gums. "My son has been working with the Brotherhood," he said, strength somehow surging through him, clearing his voice, giving him vigor I was amazed to witness. It was as though the ghostly image of who Andre had been settled around him, and all I saw as he went on was the man he used to be. "Like father, like son. And mother. Yes," he nodded, "Odette was in bed with the Brotherhood. As has been the case with the Dumont family for generations." His French accent deepened as he went on and I wondered if he was remembering a time long past, when he was young. "I gave him everything. Belaisle was supposed to protect me." His energy sagged all at once and Andre's glamor vanished. It was almost more horrible this time, because I'd allowed the false vision to blind me to the truth. "But he betrayed me in the end. And for that I will tell you everything."

Charlotte stirred. "If you do," she said, "I will consider letting you go."

Andre sighed again, this time with hope. "There," he

said, finger pointing, barely able to move. I followed the gesture, standing and going to the end of the bed. "Lift the mattress." I really didn't want to touch it, using magic to hoist the end of the heavy king size. Gagged even through my scent protection at the stench, the sight of the giant stain soaking through the bottom of the mattress, dripping with Andre. I quickly grasped at the small black box tucked in the space between and dropped the offensive weight, backing away to sink into the chair with the box in my hand.

The most disgusting thing ever. And yet, the box itself was clean, at least. I don't think I could have handled having to wipe Andre off it. Still, it helped to focus on it and not on what I'd just seen. The tiny silver latch in the shape of a dragon's wing released as I pressed against it, lifting the lid while Andre spoke.

"I don't know why it is so precious to Belaisle," he said. "But it is, and I stole it from him just to make him angry. I know my son seeks it, but I've kept it hidden. And now I give it to you." He cackled again, stopped when a cough took him.

The inside was crimson, velvet and soft. At the bottom lay a black ribbon, coiled and silent. But when I reached in to touch it, a tiny seed of power reached back and I gasped as I understood what I held.

"A drach soul," I said.

Andre's one eye widened. "Ah," he said. "But for

what purpose?"

"You don't know?" Damn it. What was so important about it Belaisle wanted it back? I'd have to take it to Max and find out. The ribbon caressed my finger before climbing out of the box to wind around my wrist where it locked like a bracelet.

"I do not," Andre said. "Nor, I hate to admit, do I have any information that will help you. I am far outside Belaisle's present plans. And the past will not assist." His blue eye fixed on Charlotte. "I've told you what I know," he said. "Is it enough, wolf child?"

Syd, she sent. *You're right. It's time.*

I hugged her with power and let her go to do what she needed to heal her own heart.

Charlotte stood, hovering over Andre, her power pushing outward toward him. "Andre," she whispered into the thick air. "I've hated you for most of my life. And that hate has left a gaping wound I've never been able to heal. It's the worst thing you've done to me—and that I've done to myself. I won't have it any longer." She drew a breath, magic settling around him. "I release you," she said. "And I forgive you."

He wept, choking on his own grief or regret or whatever it was Andre's black soul felt in that final moment.

I shouldn't have been surprised Jean Marc chose that exact instant to push through the door, to break my shields when I was distracted by his father's passing. Not that it mattered. There was nothing either Dumont brother could do as Charlotte's hands gestured over Andre and released his soul at last.

The body collapsed into a wet ooze as his ego rose, black and furious, a wolf clinging to him with fury in her eyes. The two battled over the bed while the Dumont family magic wailed a banshee cry around the room, swooping and screeching so loudly I had to cover my ears. My own family power surged in response, protecting me and Charlotte, but she didn't need it, ignored the Dumont coven magic when it swooped at her, though Kristophe ducked with a girly shriek of fear when it came at him.

Andre's echo didn't stand a chance against the wolf. It shredded as Charlotte's power shook it, the black bits disappearing into puffs of smoke. When it was over, the blonde wolf stood watch as the shining remains of Andre's soul rose, smiled at me from a young man's face, and vanished in a flash of pure, white light.

Jean Marc didn't hesitate, his power reaching out to the still screaming family power. I felt him grasp at it, try to hold it, pull it to him. Only to feel it dissipate with a sigh of sorrow, the crumbling, fading remains of the Dumont family magic popping like a decayed balloon.

I watched his face turn from shock to anger to despair as he understood his father's final revenge. And though pity tried to raise its head and prod me to care, I couldn't bring myself to do so.

Worse, my mouth moved before I could stop it.

"Sucks for you," I said.

THIRTY-THREE

Mom wasn't long arriving, Varity and Enforcers with her. By then, Charlotte and I were on the front lawn, Kristophe with us. We'd left the screaming and defeated Jean Marc behind while the former Dumont family slowly gathered at the foot of the stairs, looking dazed and lost.

I'd never liked Kristophe, but the man who turned to me with a faint smile on his face was nothing like the jerk I thought I knew.

"Thank you," he said, softly, with real feeling. "For letting Father go."

"Thank Charlotte," I said while the air above us filled with blue fire at Mom's arrival. The former Dumont family watched in hopeless silence as my mother and her Enforcers immediately approached, soothing with magic, to pick up the pieces.

Kristophe offered his hand to my werefriend and, to

317

my shock, she accepted it.

"You're welcome," she said.

Mom came to my side, setting a gentle hand on Kristophe's shoulder. I waved to her as I led Charlotte away, not wanting to be involved in this mess any longer. Mom let us go, leading Kristophe toward the knot of his former family while I opened the veil and guided the now silent Charlotte through.

We emerged in my back yard, though I don't know why I let us out there. Nostalgia, perhaps. The night was warm, hugging us with humidity left over from the day, reminding me though I was now, even more so, in desperate need of a shower and some sleep. My fingers traced over the clinging heat of the black drach soul as Charlotte turned to me with tears in her blue eyes.

"You carry so much," she said, voice trembling. "And it's not fair to ask. But I need you to carry this for me."

For her? Anything.

We sat on the bench at the back of the house, our feet bare and toes in the grass where we shed our shoes, while Charlotte told me everything. From the first moment she realized as a young girl Andre and his family weren't the adventure she hoped, to the torture and rape she endured at his hand. I wept silently for her, listening to the seemingly endless litany of hurts, all of her experience running together into one mass of pain I couldn't believe she'd endured alone for this long.

When she was done, I wiped my face with both hands before gripping her fingers in mine. I turned to meet her eyes, found her smiling at me, face radiant.

"Thank you," she said. "I love you, Syd. And my heart is finally whole."

We embraced and she left me there, waving as she went, to be with her brother, to offer him what comfort she could. I wanted her to go, knew she would have stayed for me if I asked. But she'd done enough, been through enough.

Still, perhaps she was right. It wasn't fair of her to ask me to carry her burden, too, though I was grateful for her trust.

It brought a lot of things into perspective. I sat there in the dark, alone and thoughtful, ache of agony leaving me as the evening breeze washed away my pain and hers. By the time I drew a deep breath and sighed out the last of the tension in my body, I was ready to face Quaid and my son and make this right again.

The moment I passed the threshold to the house I felt the press of power in the basement and knew I had more to do before my day was over. It took only a few steps to reach the door, to walk down into the darkness. To find Sassafras, his thick tail beating in irritation, standing guard over the slim, dark haired young woman waiting for me there.

"She insisted," Sass said.

"It's all right," I said, nodding to Jiao. "I'll take it from here."

Sassafras hissed at her, spiteful, with his fur standing on end. "I'm not leaving," he said.

I'd have been surprised if he did.

"I've been waiting for you," Jiao said, her soft voice tinted with a faint Asian accent mingling with crisp British. Her dark eyes didn't blink, black clad body silent, still.

"I'm here," I said. Where did this calm come from? I suppose I'd been through so much her appearance wasn't enough to shake me. Did that mean I was in shock? Could have been. Or just beyond giving a crap.

"We await another," she said, just as the air shimmered and parted and Max appeared.

He didn't seem surprised to find Jiao there. In fact, he nodded to her before meeting my eyes with his diamond gaze.

"All is well?" I was almost irritated by his question. No, all was not freaking well, damn it. But I just shrugged, too tired to talk about it.

Jiao turned to him, bowed at the waist. I had no idea what they'd said to each other in the yard in front of the werepalace, but whatever it was, Max had won. In more ways than just to shut her down, it turned out.

"Master," she said. "I have thought long about your proposal." Not that long. Grumble, mumble. "And I would be honored to serve as your apprentice."

His what? Brain explosion.

"Are you out of your idiot drach mind?" I didn't mean to lash at him, but holy freaking what the hell?

Max smiled at me but didn't answer my challenge. Instead, he bowed his head to Jiao.

"Done," he said. Before she could respond, before I could argue, his magic leaped forward and engulfed her.

Jiao cried out, stiffening under the compress of power. I watched it sink into her, fill her up, her dark eyes glowing a moment before turning to diamonds. Black, faceted gemstones replaced her normal irises as his power claimed her.

From the despair flickering over her face she'd not expected this outcome. Which just told me once and for all this was a ruse, a game of the Empress. That Jiao was a spy after all. Not that it mattered now. I laughed out loud as I realized the truth.

"Tell Moa," I said, "she's lost her pet. You're his now, sweet cheeks."

Jiao just stared at me with horror on her face.

Max seemed unperturbed by her reaction. "You have much to learn, youngling," he said. "And when you are through, you will lead your people to a grand future. I assure you of that."

Her expression altered finally, to resignation and at last into the schooled, blank look that reminded me of

Charlotte.

"Yes, Master," she said.

You realize she's still loyal to Moa. I crossed my arms over my chest, glaring at Max.

Her heart will change, he sent. *She will never again be able to act against me, and that is all I need to ensure she keeps her race's best interest at heart instead of that of the Empress.*

Whatever. I snorted my disbelief, but let it go. *I need to talk to you about something.* The black ribbon tightened around my wrist, prodding recollection.

"You may speak freely," he said. "Jiao is now part of my power and can be trusted."

He had to be freaking kidding me. Sassafras whined a warning, but I shrugged. If Max wanted to be a giant idiot I wasn't going to stop him. I was so far past the last point of caring I practically threw my arm up and into his face.

"Recognize this?" His eyes widened at the sight of the drach soul wrapped around my wrist.

"Where did you find that?" His fingertips barely brushed the ribbon. It sighed against me but didn't go to him, still firmly bonded to my skin.

"Long story," I said.

Max's deepening frown told me something was wrong.

"Sydlynn," he said. "That shouldn't exist here."

"Sorry?" I looked down at the ribbon, watched it flex and settle. "It's a drach soul, Max."

He shook his head, clearly troubled. "Not of this Universe," he said.

Not of this...

Oh. My. Swearword.

"Are you saying this soul came from the other side?" I flinched this time as the ribbon wriggled against me. All of a sudden it felt dangerous, like a threat. But I quickly calmed as it rubbed against my skin, like a little kitten looking for love. I felt nothing dangerous from it.

"I believe so." Max's diamond eyes swirled with power.

"Well, Belaisle is after it," I said, covering the soul with my free hand, hiding it from sight. "Which means I'll protect it with my life."

Max nodded, frown deepening by the moment. "I must consult with my people," he said, tearing open the veil. Jiao whimpered softly as his power pulled her with him. "Keep it safe, Sydlynn Hayle. I will return." And then, he and his new apprentice were gone.

THIRTY-FOUR

Sass followed me in silence as I ascended the stairs back to the kitchen, not sure what to think about the black ribbon clinging so happily to my wrist. The silver Persian leaped up on the table with a soft grunt while I headed for the coffee pot, not so ready to go to bed as I thought.

"Tell me that thing isn't going to attack you at the least opportune moment." His voice sounded as tired as I felt.

I managed a shrug as I dolloped two giant teaspoons of sugar into a mug, the metal rattling on ceramic. "Maybe," I said. "My luck would say yes, of course, any second now." I listened to the drip of the coffee maker, one hip against the counter, mesmerized by the steady flow of dark nectar in the equally dark kitchen.

Syd. Owen's voice sounded excited. I inhaled and

bowed my head. What now?

Evening. Coffee sloshed over the rim of my mug as I haphazardly dumped as much into it as I possibly could. Why did I get the feeling this endless day was far from over and that I would be needing the caffeine?

Great news. His mind opened to me, showed me, from his point of view, Simon next to him, Demetrius on the other side, and then the screen of Simon's computer. Apollo's feed was up and running again, it appeared, though the double point of view shift was almost too much for me. I wobbled before shutting Owen out.

That is great news. It took a lot to muster even that much enthusiasm. *I'm glad he's okay.*

You're not okay. Owen's empathy wasn't surprising. He'd always been a softy, since I met him.

I'm fine. I shut that down, taking a big gulp of steaming java to steady myself. *Any news?*

You're going to love this. He tentatively pushed images at me again and, rather than take the effort to stop him or even go to the house for a firsthand account, I crossed to the table, linked Sass into the magic feed and closed my eyes as Owen went on. *Not only is Apollo okay, he's made some pretty serious friends.* I watched the older Zornov's movements, saw a clear image of not only Liander Belaisle, but Eva Southway, too. And Kayden, Belaisle's second. *The audio isn't working, but the vid feed is awesome.* Owen's excitement made me smile, despite everything.

We know where he is. We can track him and follow him everywhere. Set that trap you wanted. On our terms.

That's great. It really was. And I should have been more wound up, but the longer I sat, coffee or no coffee, the more tired I became. *Keep an eye on him.* I might not have needed the kind of sleep most people did, but even I had my limits. No way could I act right now. And Belaisle could wait.

I'll let you rest. Owen's sorcery embraced me. *We'll let you know if anything else happens.*

I'm really glad Apollo's okay. It was the best I could do and, bless him, Owen took it for such.

Thanks, Syd. We won't let you down.

He let me go with another quick embrace while I sighed over his words. Was I that demanding?

Um. Yeah. Duh.

Sassafras grunted softly as I opened my eyes and met his amber gaze.

"You need to tell Femke," he said.

Groan. "You're kidding me, right?" But, as usual, the fuzzy butt nailed it. After everything we'd been through, she deserved to be in on this victory. And it really was a victory. We'd finally turned the tables on Liander Belaisle and the Brotherhood. It could mean a giant boost for morale, especially if we could somehow link the win to the WPC.

For some reason, telling her with magic didn't seem

good enough, either.

Sigh.

"While you're in Hong Kong," Sass said without venom or judgment, "you might want to use the excuse to talk to your husband."

Mom must have told him about the fight. Damn it.

"I hate it when you're right all the time," I said. Maybe I was tired enough and worn down enough I wouldn't argue with Quaid. That we'd find a peaceful place to work this out. That thought gave me a tiny jolt of energy, enough to push me to my feet, to open the veil.

"Naturally." Sass hesitated before speaking again as I left him there. "I love you, Syd."

I love you, too. A lot of people were saying that to me lately. Why did I feel like they knew something I didn't?

There was one other person I wanted to talk to before I spoke to Femke. I had to know just how much influence Belaisle had over Danilo. I wasn't sure why it felt so important, except maybe the closeness I felt with Charlotte drove me to understand her brother and his motives.

Besides, if I could figure out what Liander did, I might have another positive to hand to Femke.

Instead of landing in the foyer outside her office, I touched down at the feeling of a werewolf and found myself inside his cell. Danilo looked up, his face unsurprised as he nodded to me.

"I've been waiting for you," he said.

I sat down next to him at the plain table, feeling the binding of Enforcer power keeping his magic suppressed. Not that I was worried he might overpower me or anything. But if Belaisle had a hold on him once I wanted to be ready to fight back.

"You want to know," Danilo said, voice soft and deep. "If he made me do it."

I nodded, head heavy. Too tired for this, frankly.

"No," Danilo said. "Belaisle was just along for the ride."

My face fell into my hands as I groaned out a sigh. "Danilo," I said. "Why?"

The former wereking sat back in his chair, face dark and closed. "The beast in me, maybe?" He shook his head. "I'll offer no excuses. Yana was everything to me, Sydlynn. And I let my fury and hate rule me. I welcomed Liander Belaisle and the Brotherhood. I accepted every offer of help. Including the mafia."

"I'm pretty sure I already know what you gave the normals in exchange for their help."

His face twisted as he looked away. "My people are safe," he whispered.

Because Femke saw to it. "What about Belaisle?"

Danilo shook his head. "He only wanted to observe. To watch the Empress. To be part of my revenge."

I didn't believe that. But it made my tired mind

wonder about the reaction Moa had to my interference. Was she hunting Belaisle herself? Using Danilo as the means to find him? She'd be pissed to find out I was going to beat her to the punch.

Let her be. If she'd offered to work together, maybe I wouldn't be sitting here like this. With him.

Danilo met my eyes again, acceptance in his gaze. "I know you don't owe me anything," he said. "But I beg you, watch over my people."

"As if you have to ask." His request actually made me angry. "One of us has to."

I left him before he could respond. Because, frankly, I didn't give a crap what he had to say. Danilo had betrayed all of us, and for what?

For nothing.

I was so done. But I still had Femke to see. She'd want to know the truth.

The veil parted, welcomed me. Usually when I went to Hong Kong I appeared outside Femke's office. But I wasn't in the mood to deal with her assistant, Xue. So, I took the chance, pushed a bit of power ahead of me to warn her I was coming, and stepped out the other side next to Femke's desk. I was actually acutely disappointed to discover she wasn't there. Since when wasn't she?

A glance outside at the dead of night answered my question. Still, Femke seemed to be as tireless as me and, I realized with a bit of a jolt, I'd never really seen her at home, in her quarters. Only in her office, on official ground. I had no idea what her personal space even looked like. And I professed to know her.

Wow.

Then again, she'd never been to my house, either. Funny, the little details that knock you over when you're exhausted, emotionally and physically.

I reached out for her, trying to find her with power, but no luck. Maybe she wasn't even here. She could be anywhere. Seriously, how silly of me not to check ahead. But when I opened fully to her, I met with nothing. Emptiness.

Where was she?

I was so tired, it didn't register I should have felt something. Even if she was asleep, on the other side of the plane. Anything. Instead, my head swimming with fatigue, I headed for the door to her office, to talk to her assistant if she was around. To track down Femke's living quarters, maybe, hoping to find her there.

The moment my hand touched the door, I felt a warble of power. Kneejerk reaction pushed me forward, and the glass door with me. I stepped out into the lobby, heart pounding painfully in my chest as the surge of blackness coming toward me woke me up at last with a fresh burst of awareness.

Too late. The story of my life. Darkness took me and I knew no more.

Strong hands supported me, chocolaty energy washing through me. I sighed and reached for Quaid's magic, embracing it, stroking it with my own. His jerked away, his reaction pulling me into full alertness.

I looked up at him from where I had fallen, my head in his lap. His dark eyes were full of anxiety, fingers pushing hair back from my forehead. I groaned as I tried to sit up, his arms supporting me. My stomach rolled over a moment, headache appearing suddenly and with sharp daggers driving behind my eyeballs.

"What happened?" My tongue scraped against the roof of my mouth, dry and thick.

"I hoped you had the answer to that question." His voice shook just a little, hands tightening on me. "Syd, where's Femke?"

I shook my head, groaned when the headache spiked at the movement. I sagged against him. "I don't know," I said. "I came to talk to her but I couldn't find her." The memory of the hit of dark power drove a gasp from my lips, pushed me up and to my feet where I wavered, unsteady and afraid. "Sorcery," I said.

Quaid's grim nod just made things worse. I turned my head to look where he was staring, mouth open in a soft cry of shock at the sight of Xue, empty eyes staring back at me. Dead, gone, skin pale and cold. "Femke's missing," he said. "I can't find her anywhere."

THIRTY-FIVE

And I thought the last twenty four hours were hell.

Everyone was searching for the missing WPC leader, myself included, without any result. Femke was long gone and I knew if sorcery was hiding her we'd never find her. Not without knowing specifically who had her.

Everyone assumed it was Belaisle. I naturally contacted Simon and Owen, but from what they could tell Femke wasn't being held by the Brotherhood. In fact, they told me and the anxious Quaid as we stood in the Zornov's basement Liander seemed agitated about something. There still wasn't any audio, so there was no way of knowing if it was Femke's disappearance that had him worked up. It took a lot of convincing to keep Quaid from going after the Brotherhood leader immediately, and by the time he stormed off I worried we'd only broadened the distance between us.

The Empress was nowhere to be found, but I didn't think she was involved, either. Not when sorcery had a hand in things. I did consider Eva Southway, though I couldn't understand why she would want to kidnap Femke. Piers was on it, his frustration at his mother's now proven betrayal keeping a wedge of his own making between us.

It was Charlotte who suggested the mafia might be wrapped up in it, especially when her former employer, Iosif, went mysteriously missing from wherever she'd stashed him. Quaid's Enforcers, backed by every paranormal race on the plane, scoured the world for her while I stood by, feeling lost and ineffectual.

Why hadn't I left my talk with Danilo and gotten to her sooner?

It took less than twelve hours for the other Council leaders to demand someone sit at the helm of the WPC for the interim. And I was hardly shocked when Mom was nominated. She accepted with giant reluctance, though I was happy it was her, knowing she'd gladly step aside—and leave no stone unturned in finding Femke. At least with Mom, there wasn't a hint of power struggle. Which made me doubt the other leaders, if only in passing.

What if one of them was involved?

Paranoia did not become me.

All of my attempts to talk to my husband failed. He

was so torn up about Femke's disappearance, Quaid threw himself into his work and ignored all of my attempts to comfort or talk to him. I let him have his distance, finally, knowing how he felt. Guilt was a powerful motivator and a terrible master. I just hoped we'd find her safe and sound so he could eventually forgive himself for something that wasn't his fault.

Pot calling the kettle burnt.

My request that Max assist was instantly met with his appearance, though seeing Jiao at his side gave me the creeps. His little black clad shadow ignored me, cold and uncaring, even as Max sadly informed me he, too, was at a loss in locating Femke. His refusal to talk further about Jiao and her people, to help me find the Empress, triggered irritation so powerful I finally told him to leave. Sad but resolute, he did and I avoided talking to him since.

At least I had someone to focus on besides Femke's loss. No more screwing around. If Eva Southway had a way to track me—my interpretation of her short snippet of conversation with Belaisle all I had to go on—I wanted to find a way to use that to my advantage. Of course, it just added to Piers's anger and distance when I told him so. He, of course, blamed himself for allowing her to continue to use him long after he'd cast her out of the Steam Union.

Speaking of mothers and sons, better to focus on

trapping and capturing Belaisle than the whole situation with my own child. Gabriel refused to speak to me, to anyone, spending his days in his room with Galleytrot, silent and staring when he wasn't crying. Even my daughter couldn't get through to him and the stress was wearing on her to the point she couldn't look at me without bursting into tears.

I really was the worst mother ever.

I considered taking Gabriel back to Ameline, but Galleytrot refused to allow it. With the disappearance of Spaft and Sonja, who left on their own before Emmy could kick them out, he worried they might be lurking. My assurances I would take my son directly to the maji chamber were ignored. The big hound's need to protect Gabriel—as he couldn't, ultimately, protect his father— cut me off and I wasn't prepared at the time to fight him on it.

My son's healing was a priority. The rest could wait.

Mom's first act was to hold Danilo's trial. Thanks to her careful manipulation, she was able to at least spare him, though I wondered what life in prison would seem like to a werewolf. His guilt probably ate at him so powerfully he wished he could say goodbye. Part of me was glad he lived, a bitter and furious part that knew the whole truth about his involvement. Mom's choice to hide it in favor of protecting the werenation from that utter betrayal was the right one. And meant Danilo would suffer.

And suffer.

Good enough.

Oleksander was certainly stepping up, though I expected nothing less from him. I didn't know why I mistrusted Charlotte's mother, only that her coldness and the way she hovered over the shoulder of her young grandson made me nervous. Charlotte seemed to be spending more time at the werepalace, though, so I trusted her to watch over her nephew and make sure everything was all right.

Simon now had a direct line both to Mom and to Piers, passing everything he learned from Apollo on to the need to knowers.

I still had no idea what importance the black ribbon of drach soul carried, though knowing it came from the other Universe still freaked me out. Drach on the Dark side? This soul felt clean to me, fresh and almost young, ancient at the same time. Not evil, at least. Did that mean the drach in Dark Brother's Universe were good, too?

There was no way of knowing. All I could do was keep it safe from Belaisle. And worry he might be lurking around every corner, thanks to Eva's supposed link to me.

The shock I received when I first saw Payten at Mom's side in Hong Kong lingered. Especially when Quaid appeared to talk with his new leader. But, I quashed all fears when he hurried away again before I could talk to him. He was too focused on Femke to even notice Payten was there. And I refused to allow jealousy—unfounded and unwanted—to add to my marital strife.

Not for the first time, or the last, I thanked the Universe for Nicci, Tippy, Donalda and Josie. Without them, I know my entire life would have fallen to pieces around me. When I finally returned home to a hot shower and the need to burn the damned suit I'd worn for so long, the feeling of their magic supporting the family gave me the peace I needed to catch some sleep. It wasn't until the next day I understood how necessary they were. Especially when the news of the Dumont collapse reached us. Instead of being forced to put out nervous fires, I was greeted by a calm and comforting coven who lockstepped with me as I sent my condolences along with the other covens.

If only the rest of my life was so organized.

Which made me think of Shenka. I didn't force the second issue, partially because, in my heart, I hoped she'd come home like the girls said she would. But Tallah had a firm hold on her, I could tell already. And the fact Shenka refused to talk to me at all wasn't helping.

I might not have agreed with the Hensley leader's methods in certain areas, but there was one thing I did see as a step in the right direction. It was time to break with convention and start inviting the non-witch people in my life to join my family for real. Sunny and Frank, Charlotte and Sage, the Zornovs. United we stood. I was tired of divided.

No matter how hard I tried, though, to stay calm, to focus on tasks at hand, my thoughts always, always went to my friend, lost out there. In the hands of enemies who would suffer for her kidnapping.

Wherever Femke was. Whoever had her. I was coming for her. And the elements help them when I did.

Like what you read? Find out more at
pattilarsen.com

Here's a look at the first chapter of
Book Four of the Hayle Coven Destinies

LORD OF THE DRACH

ONE

I sat to one side, in shadow, out of the way. The last thing Mom needed was my interference, especially since we both knew how this particular fiasco was going to end.

The representative witches of the North American Council sat on the podium behind a blue draped velvet cloth, elevated above the crowd below. I always hated how pompous that made the Council look. Eight witches lording over the rest of us. Made my skin crawl.

Maybe, with a little luck and not too much bloodshed, we'd see an end to the old system today.

Mom, as the Leader of the Council, sat in the center of the line, her normal calm and composed expression about ninety percent professional and ten percent compassion, the perfect mix, in my opinion. Still a stunning woman with black curls and eyes so blue they captivated, Miriam Hayle really was the best person to lead this particular Council—and the one to come.

Last night's warning was all the head start I received, but hopefully it was enough. The hurried meeting of the Shadow Council of which I was leader—a conglomerate of all coven heads working behind the scenes of the regular Council—told me they were done watching and wanted a bigger piece of the action.

"You have to agree we need a better system, Syd," Karyn Barrett, the young leader of the Barrett coven, said, dark ponytail bobbing along with her words for emphasis. She'd dyed over her patch of blonde bangs, giving her a more grown up appearance. "After all the confusion and misinformation that led to the downfall of so many families."

I did agree. The Brotherhood had taken our complacency and old way of doing things and used it against us, killing off one third of all witches in North America and nearly destroying our way of life. Something had to change. The secretive and arrogant means in which our people were governed were no longer satisfactory or, in my opinion, working the way they should.

I was completely for change and the massive upheaval it usually brought about. Disastrous messes were my specialty. But I wasn't behind the kamikaze way they planned to dive bomb Mom at the quarterly Council meeting. Over two hundred covens, big and small, planned to be there in one capacity or another. It would be chaos and insanity but, as far as I was concerned, the best thing to happen to witchdom in centuries.

As long as Mom knew about it. Which I made sure she did over a late night glass of wine in her kitchen at Harvard. She was back from her update meeting in Hong Kong, her temporary position as leader of the World Paranormal Council weighing on her, in the faint lines around her eyes and the weariness to her smile.

I hated to dump more pressure on her. But when I filled her in on the intent of the coven leaders, she just shrugged.

"It's not like I haven't been anticipating something like this," she said. Reached out and squeezed my hand with a faint smile/grimace. "But thank you for telling me, sweetheart."

"What are you going to do?" I refilled her glass as she sat back with a sigh.

"What should have been done a long time ago." Her blue eyes sparkled suddenly, mischievous grin on her face. "You really are very clever to suggest the coming mayhem, my beautiful daughter."

"Does that mean we're going to set a precedent that will have the rest of the world Councils screaming for your blood?" I grinned back at her, saluting with my wine glass.

"Oh, I do hope so." Mom laughed.

And now, here we were, about to find out. I shifted in my seat, avoiding the gazes of the other coven leaders, keeping to myself for now. My usual place with the major families I left vacant, on purpose. As a show of solidarity to Mom and the choice she was about to present to the Council.

But not before she was asked to make it. I felt the gathering stir, surprised at the butterflies of excitement waking in my stomach, the tug of a grin wanting to explode over my face. Had I grown so used to conflict it actually made me happy to be in the middle of it?

You have to ask that question? My demon snorted while Shaylee sighed, the Sidhe princess's prim tone at counterpoint.

We're merely here to ensure the orderly follow through of Miriam's commands. She sounded like she was having a good time, though.

As if, my demon shot back, flames rippling beneath her words like a giant, burning grin. *This is freaking fun and you know it, fairy girl.*

You two, my vampire sent in her quiet, calm voice, *have no idea. This is the* bomb.

I snorted a laugh into my hand. *What did you just say?*

You're watching too much TV lately, the vampire essence sniffed. *I pick things up.*

"Thank you for your patience while we complete old business." I glanced up as Mom's voice ended the first half of the meeting.

Here we go, my demon sent, vibrating with anticipation. If she had a tail, it would have been twitching.

"Now, for new issues." Mom settled back with a kind, if firm, smile for the gathering, and calm as you please. I admired her so much for her poise. Here I was practically giggling like a hysterical child. *You rock, Mom.*

Why, thank you, sweetheart. Only then did I feel the thrill of anticipation in her and realized, now more than ever, I was my mother's daughter after all. *All set?*

Ready when you are. I hugged her with power. *This is awesome, you know.*

I hope so. But yes, I think you're right. She sighed in my head as a tiny woman on the end of the front row surged to her feet and made her way to the middle of the room. *Let's find out, shall we?*

"Council Leader." The woman's soft, brown curls bounced as she bowed her head to Mom. "Coven Leader Valerie Bell. North Eastern Canada."

Interesting. The Canadian covens were usually more laid back, less inclined to speak up, at least in my experience. The fact one of theirs was the first on the line impressed me.

"Coven Leader Bell," Mom said. "You have new business?"

"I do," she said, huge, blue eyes sparking with power. A deep breath and she plowed on while a queue of witches formed behind her. "The Brotherhood attack saw the destruction of prominent families, all of whom are missed and mourned by each and every one of us." Mom nodded for her to go on. "But, since then, other covens have risen in power. A fact that has, as yet, to be reflected on the Council that represents us as a race on this continent."

Murmurs of, "well said," and "here, here," rippled through the gathered coven leaders. The crowded room felt heated suddenly, as though they let out a fraction of their energy for Mom to taste. She reacted with her usual confidence even as the sitting Council members exchanged nervous and angry looks.

She didn't prepare them? Oh, Mom.

"Your suggestion, Coven Leader Bell?" Mom's question silenced the room. Were they expecting her to fight back? Likely. I met Karyn's eyes and nodded slowly to her. Shocked hazels turned to understanding to respect and grudging gratitude, all in an instant. She knew what I'd done. And why.

"That a new Council be selected from the strongest of the covens," she said. "A rebalancing of power to reflect the new structure of the North American witches."

A cheer rose, soft and hesitant, but present. They hummed as a group, vibrated. Those in line behind Leader Bell stood waiting, ready with their own arguments, I could only imagine.

If only they knew they didn't need to prepare a speech, my demon sent.

I'm sure they were lovely and all, Shaylee sent with absolute glee.

Enough, children, my vampire murmured. *I'm trying to listen.*

Snort.

"I see." Mom nodded wisely, glancing left and right as she seemed to ponder. The present Council stared back at her, nervous but, I could only guess, certain she would defend them and the way we'd been governed for so long. "Might I ask the line of you waiting to speak—are you all bringing forward a similar request?"

Nods, shuffled feet, grim expressions on the lot of them. The entire room seemed to hold time at a standstill while Mom leaned forward, fingers steepled, elbows resting on the arms of her chair.

"Might I suggest an alternative?" They weren't expecting that from her, though from the stubborn antagonism that rose, they misunderstood. All but Karen who spoke up before an unnecessary fight started.

"I'd like to hear your alternative, Council Leader." She glanced my way, a tiny smile on her lips while her two closest cronies, Paula Santos and Dagney Rhodes, glared bloody murder at me.

I'm trusting you, Syd, Karyn sent.

Trust Mom, I sent back. *She has only the best interests of all at heart. You must know that by now.*

I do, she sent. *But, if you don't mind, I'll add you to the mix anyway.*

There was nothing I could do about that.

The other coven leaders seemed to deflate at Karyn's agreement, though tension remained, thickening the air of the chamber in degrees as the seconds ticked by. Interesting how she'd emerged as the clear leader of this odd group. I'd expected it to be Tallah Hensley.

Speak of the devil. Where was she? It was the first time I realized the Hensley coven leader was missing. And hadn't, from what I could tell, sent a representative in her place.

Now that was odd. Considering Tallah's rigid need for control these days. Why did her absence make me so nervous?

Mom dropped her hands to her lap, smiling faintly. "We've been through so much as a race over the centuries," she said. "Persecuted, pursued, burned at the stake. And, in response to that history, we've become closeted, closed minded, secretive. To the detriment of all. In our attempt to protect ourselves, to guide and shape our race, we've created a collective fed by old hurt and the unwillingness to act together for fear of doing the wrong thing. When we needed each other most, we have failed each other." She swept the room with her blue gaze, voice rising in volume, power behind it. "I say, no more." Mom's magic, tied to the fresh, young Council energy, swept around the chamber as she went on. "It is time for a new way of being. For witches to come together in joy of who we are, not in fear of what might happen if we work as one." Another soft cheer, this one spontaneous. Tears burned the corners of my eyes, my chest tightening as I choked up.

Wasn't expecting that. Not even a little.

Leader Bell's thickened voice responded, evidence I wasn't the only one Mom's words touched. "What would you have us do, Council Leader?" And, just like that, they were behind my mother 100%, waiting on her words, ready, willing and able to jump on the wagon.

You are magnificent. I hugged her again, not wanting to distract her.

Syd, she whispered back. *Don't make me cry in public. Please. I'm barely holding on as it is.* "My people," Mom said, rich voice vibrating with emotion, "as your chosen Council Leader, I propose a vast and sweeping change to the way we care for each other. That we embrace all covens, all voices. That we rule, not by the dictates of a few, but with the voices of many."

They gaped at her before a few started to applaud. But, the clapping stopped as they waited for her to say it already.

Mom rose to her feet, arms wide as though to embrace everyone in the room. I felt the soft, kind touch of her power and fed it with my own, the light, sweet caress of each and every witch in the room joining mine until Mom glowed like a vibrant, blue star.

"From this day forward," she said, "this Council is comprised of all coven leaders of all duly registered covens in this territory. And every coven, small or large, shall have an equal vote. So mote it be."

I'm not ashamed to say I was on my feet with everyone else, crying and cheering while Mom bowed her head and wept in joy.

ABOUT THE AUTHOR

Everything you need to know about me is in this one statement: I've wanted to be a writer since I was a little girl, and now I'm doing it. How cool is that, being able to follow your dream and make it reality? I've tried everything from university to college, graduating the second with a journalism diploma (I sucked at telling real stories), am part of an all-girl improv troupe (if you've never tried it, I highly recommend making things up as you go along as often as possible). I've even been in a Celtic girl band (some of our stuff is on YouTube!) and was an independent film maker. My life has been one creative thing after another—all leading me here, to writing books for a living.

Now with multiple series in happy publication, I live on beautiful and magical Prince Edward Island (I know you've heard of Anne of Green Gables) with my very patient husband and multitude of pets.

I love-love-love hearing from you! You can reach me (and I promise I'll message back) at patti@pattilarsen.com. And if you're eager for your next dose of Patti Larsen books (usually about one release a month) come join my mailing list! All the best up and coming, giveaways, contests and, of course, my observations on the world (aren't you just dying to know what I think about everything?) all in one place: http://smarturl.it/PattiLarsenEmail.

Last—but not least!—I hope you enjoyed what you read! Your happiness is my happiness. And I'd love to hear just what you thought. A review where you found this book would mean the world to me—reviews feed writers more than you will ever know. So, loved it (or not so much), **your honest review would make my day**. Thank you!